FAIR PLAY

CATHRYN FOX

Discover other titles by Cathryn Fox at www.cathrynfox.com. Please sign up for Cathryn's Newsletter for freebies, ebooks, news and contests: https://app.mailerlite.com/webforms/landing/c1f8n1
ISBN 978-1-989374-31-3
ISBN Print 978-1-989374-30-6

ELLA

"What does this button do?"

I smack my best friend's hand away from the football's team brand new camcorder, and give her the evil eye. She knows better than to play with it, which makes the shocked looked on her face all the more amusing. But the fact is, I've been entrusted with the very expensive device to record the Falcons' first home game. Since I can't afford to replace it, I can't let my friend go around poking at every shiny knob and possibly breaking something.

"What?" Peyton says, blinking dark lashes over big innocent eyes. "I'm just asking a question."

"No. You're pushing buttons you shouldn't be pushing. Now sit there before I send you to the bleachers with everyone else." I point to the bench to the left of us and raise a warning brow.

She gives a light laugh, brushing off my threat. "You'd never do that. You love me too much." She's right. I wouldn't. Peyton and I have been best friends since kindergarten, and for the last three years we've been college roommates choosing apartment-style living over a sorority house. She's here for a degree in social work, and I'm here because I want to be a filmmaker. Yeah, working in Hollywood, behind the scenes, has been my dream since childhood.

Beside me, Peyton gives a very big, very happy sigh and takes in the football field from our perch—only the best, first class seating for the camera woman. "I do love the perks of being your best friend," she says as she admires the football players warming up. A few are so close we could practically reach out and touch them if we wanted to. I don't.

"I really can't understand the fascination," I murmur. "A bunch of guys in tight pants chasing a ball."

She crosses her arms, and waggles her brows at me. "What's it called again when a player passes the goal line with the ball in his hand?"

"Winning," I say, giving her a look that suggests she might be dense, but when she breaks out laughing, I crack a smile. Yeah, I get it. I'm the one who's dense. It's true, I know nothing about football, but I need this fourth-year credit to complete my cinematic arts degree and really, do I need to understand the game to record it for the team to analyze later? That would be a big fat no. I hope.

"Well, at least you know how this thing works," Peyton says, once again scoping out the buttons on my camcorder. "How about this knob? What does it do?"

"Peyton, cut it out." I slap her hand again and laugh at her childish antics. How we remained friends all these years when we're so different is a mystery. But we love each other like sisters. Sisters? Wait, that's not right at all. I'm an identical twin and my sister Ivy and I go together like hotdogs and

Ferris wheels. Peyton and I, however, no matter how different, we just work.

I stare at her. "Don't you have football players to drool over?" Unlike me, she knows every player, and doesn't hold the same kind of grudge against them as I do.

I adjust my ballcap to shade the sun from my eyes as I glance out at the football field. I catch sight of my sister Ivy as she kicks one leg out and flirts with one of the players, trailing her finger over his chest. Blonde and bubbly. That's Ivy. We were raised by the same two parents, yet we're so different, and I wouldn't be caught dead in a cheerleading outfit that barely covered my ass. That's her business though, and I don't judge or interfere in her life, just like she doesn't interfere in mine.

I'd like to think when push comes to shove, she'd be there for me, just like I'd be there for her. At least, I think she'd be there for me. We might not hang out, but we love one another and have each other's best interests at heart. Of that I'm certain. It's funny really. Ever since we were young, we fell into certain roles. The extrovert and the introvert, the outgoing one and the quiet one. I always stood in the shadows and let her have the limelight. Pretty Ivy, the theater student who lights up a room with her smile and flamboyance when she enters. Which of course, makes me the introverted smart, quiet one. We both easily fell into those roles and have yet to stray.

Peyton gives a low, slow whistle. "I don't know what you have against tight pants. Look at all those cute butts and luscious muscles. Talk about slurpalicious." She rakes her teeth over her bottom lip. "Don't you want one little nibble, one taste?"

I give her a playful shove to move her away from the camcorder. "No. No nibbles. No tastes." I'm a virgin with no plans to change that anytime soon, and as my best friend, she damn well knows it. I take up position behind the camera, and look at the world through my beloved lens. I exhale a contented breath. This is where I belong. This is where I feel most at home.

Okay, yeah, so it's true. I'm the world's biggest nerd. Do I care? Nope. Not one little bit. I'm happy to stand in the shadow and view the world through my camcorder lens. As I do, I catch sight of Ivy again as she shakes her ass for the boys on the field. Truth be told, I actually hate football players. Back in high school, they bullied my friend Jacob until he ended up taking his own life. Terrible hazing went on at our school. The bullying was torturous and cruel, and no matter how hard Peyton and I tried to help Jacob, get him help, the bullying continued, and actually increased the more we tried to stop it. A stab of pain sears my heart at the painful memory, and I suck in air to breathe through it. I know I shouldn't lump all jocks into one category, shouldn't label them all as egotistical bullies, but a single player has yet to prove me wrong. Arrogant assholes. What more can I say?

I check my watch, as my stomach growls. "Hungry much?" Peyton says. "Maybe you'd like a nibble after all?"

"Really, Peyton. Did you just meet me?" I tease and reach into my backpack and grab a granola bar, all the while trying to cleanse my brain of football players and their tight asses—one player in particular. Peyton holds her hand out, and I place a bar in her palm. Granola bars and juice boxes on the go. The life of a busy fourth year student—or that of a toddler.

She tears into her wrapper and looks me in the eye. Her brow is furrowed as she examines me like I'm a bug under a microscope—a new kind of species no one can figure out. "You really don't find any of those guys attractive?"

"Nope, not a single one of them." A little white lie never hurt anything, right? "I prefer brains over brawn."

"That's a pretty blanket statement don't you think? I bet a lot of them are smart." Peyton doesn't hold the same grudge as I do. She figured it was a few bad apples on our high school football team who persecuted Jacob until his suicide, not every jock in the world. I don't forgive as easily. Maybe it's the social worker in her. She sees the world through a different lens, and that's her right.

"Yeah, probably." I shrug. She's right, but it doesn't matter. I'm not going to hold it against her if she wants to date a player.

She grins. "What about Landon Brooks?"

A chunk of granola lodges in my throat and I try not to react, try not to let my eyes bulge out of my brain as I choke. Reacting will only fuel her ridiculous fantasy that Landon and I would be good together. She's wrong, a million times over. A trillion, even.

I snatch a juice box from my backpack, rip the straw open and jab the foil opening. After a big sip, I roll my eyes. "Oh, Please, Landon's ego is as big as—"

"His cock?"

Ohmigod.

My granola bar jumps back into my throat and I take another huge sip. In my calmest voice, I stare at her and say, "That is not what I was going to say. I mean, come on. I have no idea how big his...his thing is, and I don't want to know."

"His *thing*." She laughs. "Oh, come on, Ella. You can say cock. I know you've watched porn before. We've watched it together, for God's sake. We all have fantasies, and that's normal."

Flustered, I say, "Okay, fine. His cock. That's the last time you're going to hear that word on my lips, and the last time I'm going to think about it." It's possible that's a lie. I might actually think of it tonight—when I watch porn.

"His cock is going nowhere near your lips then?"

I plant one hand on my hip and glare at her as she teases and twists my words. "How many ways do you need me to say it, Peyton?"

She braces her hands on the bench behind her and leans back, lifting her face to the sun. "I can tell you like him."

"I do not like him."

"What do you have against him anyway?"

Oh, other than the fact that he's living rent free in my head, nothing. "He's an asshole, and wait, why did you say his ego was as big as his cock. How do you know that?"

She gives me a slow grin that says she knows me too well. "Ah, look at that, you are thinking about his *thing* again." She wags her dark brows. "You know, they just don't call him Torpedo because he's lightning fast, on the field. It's because he has a big—"

"Stop," I say. I take a fast breath. *Do not think about Landon's torpedo.* I'm two seconds from demoting her to the bleachers, when she sits up straight, her mouth gaping. "What?" I ask, my blood draining to my toes even though I have no idea what's going on. I only know that look on her face and it's bad. So very, very bad. She looks past my shoulder and points her finger.

"Uh..."

Ohmigod. I mouth the words, "He's behind me, isn't he?"

As she gives a slow nod, I spin around. Landon is adjusting his helmet as his gaze moves over my face. He's not smirking, or showing any sign that he overheard us. Thank God!

"Hey," he says and my stupid ovaries quiver as my gaze lands on his brutally handsome face. He's not typically handsome, with a square jaw, perfect skin, perfect features. No. He's a bit harder, his face scarred from fights, and football. It only makes him hotter.

"Hey," I squeak out.

He smiles at me, then looks past my shoulder to Peyton when she clears her throat. "Hey, Peyton."

"Landon," Peyton says. "Looking good out there."

He turns his attention back to me. "Coach wants to know if you've got this thing all figured out." He gestures with a nod to the camcorder and I try not to react to his sexy Texas accent. "You know how to work all these buttons?"

"Yes, I do," I say, and while I get that he has no idea how to use the camcorder, there are plenty of buttons this guy knows how to press. Yes, I'm talking about the buttons between a girl's legs and the ones on the end of each breast. I've heard the rumors, and have zero intentions of ever finding out if they're true. I'd have a better chance of landing an assistant director position with Spielberg right out of college than this guy has of landing a position between my sheets. Not that he wants that, but chances of either of them happening: zero.

His gaze rakes over me, and my goddamn legs nearly give out as those dark eyes ignite my blood from simmer to inferno. What the hell is wrong with me? I do not like football players. I do not like Landon.

Yeah, you just keep telling yourself that, Ella.

"Wait, am I seeing double," he asks, and looks from me to Ivy and back to me again.

"Ivy is my twin," I say with an exaggerated sigh, and steal a fast glance at her across the field. As if feeling my eyes on her, her head lifts, and she stares at me. I can't see her expression from where I'm standing. I can only imagine she's in shock to see me talking with Landon. Not because I don't associate with football players, but because a nerd like me would never be worthy of his attention. She has nothing to worry about. He's all hers.

Have at him, sis.

"How come I've never seen you around before?" He shifts from one foot to the other, and I become acutely aware of his height, and of the way his muscles fill out his uniform. Does he even need all that padding? The fresh scent of soap, fabric softener, and something uniquely Landon fills my senses. It's not a bad scent. Nope, not bad at all. Which really sucks.

"I hang in different circles," I tell him and like the nerd I am, I snort, and tap the camcorder. "Cinematography."

"Oh yeah?" Dark eyes leave mine to steal a quick glance at the camcorder, and for a second he almost seems truly interested. "You're one of those audio/visual students?"

I nod and resist the urge to roll my eyes, because honestly, the fact that he doesn't know what my major is called isn't his fault. I don't know a thing about football, and I kind of get the sense he's trying to be nice, although for the life of me I can't figure out why. I'm pretty sure he's not trying to lure me to the locker room so the team can beat the crap out of me, like those boys in high school did to Jacob.

"You mean nerds?" I ask, with a raised brow, and Peyton kicks my ankle. I whimper, but don't take my eyes off Landon. God, he's so alluring, his face brutally interesting, I'm not sure I can.

Something passes over his dark eyes. A hint of sadness? I'm not sure why I suddenly feel like I've bruised him somehow. Jeez, I'd never purposely hurt anyone, whether I liked them or not.

"I never said that. I just mean..." He shrugs one of those broad shoulders and it's all I can do to keep my gaze from dropping...from admiring all his muscles. "You, uh, you like movies, huh?"

"Yes. I like movies," I respond, and resist the urge to walk through the door he just opened. Once someone brings up movies, I could go on and on about films, rambling about what I like, what I don't like, but I don't want to bore him to death. He has a game to play, women to impress.

He rubs a scar beneath his eye, and it flares red. "Seen anything good lately?"

How did he get that? Football, or something else? "Yes," I say again, and he smiles.

"Any recommendations?"

Porn.

What. The. Hell.

Get yourself together, girl!!

"Depends on what you like." I say, trying for casual when my stupid brain is conjuring up all kinds of unwanted images. Landon on top of me, underneath me...

"You should come to the party tonight." He gestures to the field with a nod. "I'll show you what I like."

Holy shit, no. He is definitely barking up the wrong tree here. I am not one of his groupies, bunnies, cleat chasers, or whatever the hell they call women who sleep with footballers. Wait! My brain takes a moment to catch up, alerting me that the guy everyone calls torpedo—and not just because he's lightning fast—invited me to a party. Did I just enter the twilight zone or something? I think I might have heard him wrong.

"I'm busy," I say.

This time his smile is cocky, full of brazen confidence, and I get it. I really do. I get why women hand their panties over. "Come on, you can't be too busy to celebrate our win?"

"Pretty sure of yourself," I say in a bored voice, even though there's a storm going on inside me.

He cocks his head. "Attitude is half the battle, don't you think?"

"You don't want to know what I think," I mumble.

He grins, and despite myself, my stupid lips twitch. God, why am I acting like a dim-witted moth around him? Yes, he's a shining star and has his own gravitational pull, but I am not into egotistical football players. My only goal is to keep my head down, finish my degree and get a job in Hollywood. Why I'm suddenly on this guy's radar is beyond me. Did he lose a bet or something? Have to talk to the nerdy girl? If not, and if there's something about me that appeals to him, he should go after Ivy. We look alike, except she dyes her hair blonde, and he could have her with a snap of his fingers.

"Her name is Ella," Peyton says. "She'll be at that party."

I spin, and give my former best friend the death glare. She studies her nails, like she doesn't have a care in the world. From across the field, a whistle blows, and I nearly jump ten feet in the air when a big, strong hand lands on my arm. I spin to face Landon, and he snatches his hand back.

"Sorry, didn't mean to touch without permission." He holds both hands up, palms out. "I just ah, I gotta go. Coach is calling." He pauses for a brief second.

"What?" I ask as I reposition myself at the camcorder and reach for the record button. Wait, why is it on? Rattled, and pretending not to be, as Landon continues to stand there, six feet of sex in a football outfit, looming over my small frame, I flick the record button off, and close my eyes, hoping when I open them again, he'll be gone.

"Aren't you going to say good luck?"

Nope not gone, and goddamn that cocky grin of his. I'm going to give my traitorous body—one spot in particular—a good hard lecture when we get home. With my vibrator.

"Good luck," I murmur, sounding uninterested.

He backs up an inch and I can almost fully refill my lungs again. "See you tonight, Ella."

"Not going to be there," I say.

He pauses and I sigh as I look at him. Why won't he leave already?

"How about this? If I score a touchdown, you come, if I don't...then it's my loss. In more ways than one."

His loss? Okay, I really am in some alternate universe. Football players do not flirt with me, and that's the way I like it.

"Why would I bargain with you? What could possibly be in it for me?"

"Come tonight." He flashes perfect white teeth. "Find out."

"We'll be there," Peyton says, finality in her tone, letting us both know it's going to happen and the conversation is over.

"We will not be there," I clarify through clenched teeth. We have a better chance of getting snow in Southern California this late September evening. Not. Going. To. Happen.

"See you tonight, Peyton," Landon says. "See you too, Ella." He points to the camera. "Now you'd better press record. You don't want to miss my touchdown."

My God, could the guy be any hotter...I mean, cockier. Yeah, cockier, that's what I meant. The guy is *not* hot. Nope not hot at all.

Much.

2

LANDON

With a homefield win in the bag, my teammates and I all slap one another on the back, and nod to the cheering crowd as we tug off our helmets, and raise them over our heads, before file off the field and head toward the locker room. The crowd cheers louder when Sam, our wide receiver, attempts a flip and lands on his head. I'm not worried, the guy is as tough as leather, and it'll take more than a concussion to bench him.

Grinning, I shake my head at his undignified flop and steal a fast glance over my shoulder to flash a smile Ella's way, but she's not looking at me. Did I really expect to be the object of her attention? Not really. Just hopeful thinking, I guess. I grin. Does that touchdown mean she'll come to the party tonight or is that just more hopeful thinking?

Ella Holmes.

Christ, when Coach said he'd hired someone new, after the last one couldn't handle being on the road with us, who knew he'd hire someone so damn sweet and interesting, or that she'd be Ivy's twin, for Christ's sake. How did I not know Ivy had a twin sister? Truthfully, it's been a long time, freshman year actually, since a girl intrigued me. She might not want anything to do with me, but that simply fascinates me more. I kind of like it, really. I like that she's different from the girls I usually talk to.

I was a little thrown off my game when I first set eyes on her, thinking I was seeing double, and while she looks like Ivy, the two are nothing alike. Ivy would never be caught dead in overalls, and a ballcap covering her long curls. I mean, I like Ivy and all. We're friends and we've partied together, and she's slept with many of my buddies. She's just never been into me.

I guess I just don't have the pretty boy face she's attracted to. I've let that roll off my shoulders, because I'm not hard up for women. Nope. None of us have to date the palm twins anymore. Outside of football, you could say fucking is pretty much the team's pastime. Getting my grade up in English had better soon be my pastime, or Coach is going to bench my sorry ass. Fuck, I hated English class last year, and here I am putting myself through this torture again. Why couldn't Shakespeare just speak English? Well, I mean he spoke English, but what the fuck ever. Didn't we all outgrow riddles with Dr. Seuss?

I turn back around, my thoughts returning to Ella as someone jumps on my back. Judging by the person's light weight, and the long sleek legs wrapped around my waist, it's not a teammate. Nope, furthest thing from a teammate, in fact. Soft hands wrap around my body, and nimble fingers link together on my chest. I angle my head to see who it is, and my head rears back when I see Ivy's brilliant smile, her long loose hair framing her pretty face. Look at that, she has freckles like her sister. Nevertheless, giving a piggyback ride to the cheerleaders after a winning game is nothing new, it's just that Ivy has never jumped on my back before. She's never jumped on my *anything*.

Why now?

"Great job out there, Landon," she says, her mouth near my ear, her voice a low seductive whisper. "You were *torpedo* fast."

Why the emphasis on torpedo? It's not like she was ever interested in riding my torpedo before. I put my hand over hers and hold her steady as we head toward the doors. But something gnaws at my gut, something uncomfortable and foreign. Drawn by a force I don't understand, I slowly turn, and even though she's at a distance, I can almost feel Ella's camera pointed my way, capturing my every movement. But that's ridiculous, right? I'm nothing to her. Sure, we all have big egos, but I'd be giving myself credit if I thought I was on Ella's mind the way she's on mine. I've never met anyone more disinterested, which totally fucking sucks. She's the kind of girl I could have real conversations with.

Ivy slides down my back and spins me to face her. She goes up on her toes, puts her palm on my cheek and forces me to look at her. "Hey, what's the matter with you? We just won the game. We should be celebrating."

"Yeah, celebrating. Tonight." She gives me a wide smile and wets her bottom lip. She looks like she has something to say but I speak first. "How come you never told me you had a sister?"

Her eyes narrow, turn venomous, then, as if catching herself, she gives a dismissive wave and chuckles. "Ella. Oh, come on. She's head movie nerd and has nothing in common with us. Why on earth would I mention her?"

"I don't know. I just thought you might have..." And Ella and I both like movies, so we do have something in common. Not that Ivy would know or care about what I liked. I'm a footballer, and I'm not naïve. I know people see me as a dumb jock. My goal is to make it to the NFL, but it's good to have a backup plan just in case, and when I retire, I'd like to write a screenplay about a horrific incident that happened to Brady and me when we were fourteen. Putting that incident down on paper might sound ridiculous to some—especially since I'm having a hard time passing English—which is why I've never told anyone I wanted to document that day. Not even my best friend.

"Well, she's hardly your type," she says, and sidles up to me. Her hands go to my chest and her fingers spread. "No sense in bringing her up."

"Landon, come on for Fuck sake," Caleb says. "Let's get this meeting over and get a cold one."

I put my hands on Ivy's and remove them from my chest. "Gotta go. Team meeting. See you later."

Disappointment moves over her face. "Sure, and you can count on seeing me later."

I pause for a brief second. What is all this attention suddenly about? Sure, she's gorgeous, but she goes for the pretty boys. Why the sudden change? I have no time to think about that when our infamous quarterback, Brady—my best friend and roommate—grabs me by the collar and hauls me backward.

"Dude," I say and he lets me go and throws his arm around me. He punches me in the gut.

"Hey, Ivy, huh?"

I look over my shoulder in time to see Ivy turn, her gaze zeroed in on her sister, who is packing up her equipment. I can't see Ivy's face, but her stance is tight, her palms fisted at her sides. Something tells me the twin sisters don't get along. Here I thought twins were tight.

"That girl is tight."

"Yeah...tight. I was just thinking about that."

"That's my boy," Brady says, and squeezes his arm around my neck. Of course we're both talking about something entirely different. I laugh it off, and he says, "You getting with her tonight?"

"Is that all you think about?" I ask.

"Of course not." He plasters on a mostly serious face. "You know I think about football too."

I laugh at that. "If I don't start thinking about English..." I stop and make a slicing motion across my neck. "Benched."

Brady goes completely serious, and that's one of the things I love most about him. He's a baller and a man whore, but he cares about me and my future. Ever since that day we skipped school and got caught in a lockdown at the theater... my brain freezes, and a shiver goes through me as I take a trip down memory lane. Well, we were always best buds, but after that horrific day, we bonded in a deeply meaningful way. Apparently, trauma can really bring two people together.

"You need a tutor, man."

"Yeah, I was thinking the same thing."

He goes quiet like he's deep in thought. "Why don't you check in with student services?"

"Yeah, I guess."

In the locker room, we're all in a good mood, everyone ribbing each other and talking about our plays. A few palms land on my back, congratulating me on my touchdown. We all shower, and thirty minutes later we're in the classroom. Whether we win or not, Coach likes to go over the rival team's plays right after the game, when they're fresh in our mind.

I'm still keyed up as I grab a seat and pull out my notepad as Coach stares at a file on his desk. His head lifts and a knot tightens in my gut as his gaze cuts to me. Fuck. Why do I get a feeling that worried look on his face has something to do with my English grade? I stifle a laugh. I'm the guy who wants to write a screenplay. Who the hell do I think I am? If the NFL doesn't pan out, my dad has a nice little corner office in his car dealership.

The door yawns open and my thoughts switch gears when I catch a glimpse of sweet little Ella with her hair stuffed under a ballcap, shuffling a camcorder, tripod, and backpack. I zero in on the freckles around her nose, and a surge of energy has me sitting up a bit straighter as adrenaline rushes through my blood.

She steps inside, and lets out a loud oomph when she almost trips on the bag one of the guys left on the floor. I'm two seconds from jumping up and grabbing her when she finds her balance, and tries not to look embarrassed. Brady's gaze goes from Ella to me, and he angles his head with a pensive look on his face as I try to relax my shoulders and present casual.

There is no way for him to know she's Ivy's sister from where we sit, and okay, yeah, it's true, she's not the kind of girl I gravitate toward, which is why Brady is giving me a curious look. I'm not sure what it is about her, I only know that something about the audio/visual girl interests me. Could it be the chase? Or could it be something more? I don't know and maybe I shouldn't give that any deeper consideration. I have a career to focus on and an English class to pass. Fucking is a team pastime. Relationships, not so much, and Ella has long term written all over her, and definitely not with a baller.

Coach calls Ella up to his desk, and a few minutes later, the game she recorded fills the large white movie screen at the front of the class. I spot myself in the background warming up before the game. Guess she must have hit the play button early. Ella backs away, and heads toward the door, and I stare at her backside, drawn to the curves she hides behind baggy overalls.

"Great job today, guys, and there's one play I definitely want to go over," Coach says, pulling our attention forward as he hits his screen with his long pointer. He circles his desk, and stands before us. He directs the pointer at Blake. "Blake, when you ran—"

"Peyton, cut it out."

Coach shuts his mouth and his brow furrows when a voice fills the room—Ella's voice. Holy shit. My gaze jerks to Ella. Her hand goes perfectly still, inches from the knob, and her entire body stiffens. Jesus, is she even breathing?

"Don't you have football players to drool over?"

"I don't know what you have against tight pants. Look at all those cute butts and luscious muscles. Talk about slurpalicious. Don't you want one little nibble, one taste?"

"No. No nibbles. No tastes."

"What the fuck?" Jared says, as desks scrape the floor, every player leaning forward to better listen to the private exchange between Ella and Peyton.

Ella spins, her mouth agape. Wide eyes meet Coach's. "Turn it off," she shrieks her voice bordering on hysteria.

"You really don't find any of those guys attractive?"

"Nope, not a single one of them. I prefer brains over brawn."

Coach stands there for a second, like he's trying to put the pieces of a puzzle together.

"Please, turn it off," Ella whines, and my heart jumps into my throat when the guys start laughing, clueing in that it's Ella's voice they're hearing.

"This shit just got real," Trey yells, and bangs his fists on his desk. I take a fast glance around the room. This is bad. So damn bad.

"Turn it off," I shout, and all eyes turn to me, including Ella's. I focus solely on her, take in the pleading, almost desperate look on her face as Peyton's next words ring out and rattle around in my brain.

"What about Landon Brooks?"

My entire body goes stiff. Goddammit, I need Coach to turn it off as much as I need him to leave it playing. A part of me wants to know what she thinks of me. A part of me doesn't.

"Oh, Please, Landon's ego is as big as—"

"His cock?"

"That is not what I was going to say. I mean, come on. I have no idea how big his...his thing is, and I don't want to know."

"His thing. Oh, come on, Ella. You can say cock. I know you've watched porn before. We've watched it together for God's sake. It's okay to have fantasies, and that's normal."

"Okay fine. His cock. That's the last time you're going to hear that word on my lips, and the last time I'm going to think about it."

"His cock is going nowhere near your lips then?"

Every guy in the room starts hollering, and joking, and shouting out profanities—everyone except me, that is. I glare at them, but they're too busy having fun with this at Ella's expense. Goddammit, I need to do something, and I need to do it now. I plant my feet on the floor and stand.

"Turn it off," Ella pleads again, her voice a small whisper, as her cheeks redden to the color of a ripened cherry. Her hands go to her face, and she lets out a horrified groan. I'm about to throw myself at the laptop when her pleas prompt Coach into action. He hurries to his desk and waves his hand over his laptop like he's trying to figure out what the hell to do. He stabs a few buttons and the video ends.

I sink back into my seat as the room falls silent. Ella backs up, hits the door with a thump. I'm a second from jumping back up and running to her rescue when Coach slams his laptop shut and takes a fast breath.

"Can I see you outside?" he says to Ella, and when she nods quickly, the two disappear into the hall.

"What the fuck, dude? What did you ever do to her?" Caleb says, and the guys start messing with me, everyone except Brady, who is eyeing me. I give the boys a cocky grin and shrug.

"What can I say." I point to my scars. "Some like this face, some don't. My cock, however, all girls like that. She just doesn't know it yet." The guys break out in laughter and I sort of feel like a total prick for saying that about Ella. In this environment, we all have a role to play, and we all play it well. We're a team, a brotherhood, and the last thing I want is for these guys to think I'm soft.

"That's my man," Beck says, and gives me a fist pump. I stare at the door, look through the small glass panel, but all I can see is Coach's back. Shit, man. I really hope he isn't firing Ella. She seemed like she needed this job, but it was more than that. There was something about her as she looked at the camera, like it was her lifeline or something. Then again, I'm a jock, all brawn and no brains, so what the hell would I know right? I snort. Yeah, I should just cut and run, now that I know what she really thinks about guys like us. Here she thought I was judging her when she called me out, asking if I was labeling her a nerd. I wasn't. But she sure as hell was packing us all into one nice and tidy package, wasn't she?

The guys simmer down when Coach walks back into the room, and I get a glimpse of Ella adjusting her backpack over her shoulder before she darts down the hall.

Forget about her, dude. You do not need the drama.

Deciding to do just that, I turn my attention to the front of the class again, and Coach, looking a little flustered, says, "Let's just call this a day, okay. Go, get out of here," he says and the guys all jump up, ready for our aftergame party. He points to me as I slowly stand. "Landon, I'll need a word with you."

My stomach tightens. I'm not sure why he wants me to stay behind, but can't help think it has something to do with my English, or Ella. Either way, my lungs are tight, like I'd just been sacked by a linebacker.

"Want me to wait?" Brady says.

"No, go. I'll catch up with you guys later. Save a keg for me."

Brady grins. "Later."

I stop at Coach's desk, and before he can get a word out, I say. "Don't worry, Coach. I have no plans to get involved with Ella, or even talking to her again. She's trouble and who needs that kind of bullshit, right?"

Intense eyes—eyes that never lose sight of the win—meet mine and hold. "You do."

What the fuck is that supposed to mean?

3

ELLA

I pace around the living room of our small apartment, the knot in my stomach tightening until I'm doubling over in pain. With my mind spinning a million miles an hour and shaky hands folded over my abdomen, I let loose a groan so loud and painful I'm certain my parents can hear it all the way to our orchard in San Francisco Bay. I expect the phone to ring any second now, my mom checking to see if I'm okay.

"I can't ever face any of them again," I tell Peyton. "Ohmigod, I've spent the better part of my life working at staying under the radar, and now, well now I've gotten noticed, all right. In the worst possible way."

"Oh, come on," Peyton says as she stretches her long legs out on the sofa. "It's not that bad."

I jerk upright, my mouth open as I stare at her like she might have just grown a second head. "Not that bad? Not that bad! How can you say that, Peyton? They heard our entire conversation, and...Ohmigod," I say again and tug a fistful of hair as

I resume my pacing. "I might as well just pack up and leave campus right now."

"Come on. What did they really hear, Ella?" She gives a casual roll of her shoulder, and I want to grip her and give her a good hard shake.

I throw my hands out. "Oh, just that I think they're all brawn and no brain, and...and...oh God, they heard us talking about Landon's cock." Ohmigod, I'm mentioning his cock again when I swore I wouldn't. My head drops, and a tortured animal sound rises in my throat as I put my hands over my face.

"You mean his torpedo?" I glare at her through the cracks in my fingers and she jumps to her feet, and takes my hands from my face. "Right, right. This is not funny, and it's all sort of my fault since I accidently hit the record button."

"Sort of your fault. It's entirely your fault," I say. Okay, it's my fault, too. What was recorded on the camcorder was my responsibility since I was in charge of the damn thing, and I engaged in conversation about the players when I know better than to talk about someone behind their back.

Stupid. Stupid. Stupid.

She blinks at me, and that wild look in her blue eyes tells me she has a plan, one I'm not going to like. "I know how to fix this."

"Yeah, me too. Grab the first bus to Canada. You don't happen to have a winter coat and hat I can borrow, do you?"

"Don't be so dramatic." I open my mouth to tell her I'm being less than dramatic, but she continues with, "It's not as bad as you think. In fact, this could be good." I glare at her so hard I'm beginning to give myself a headache. "Look," she begins, her expression changing as she goes all therapist on me. "There isn't a guy on that team who doesn't like to talk about, or hear about, his cock. You gave Landon hero status, Ella."

"Oh please, like he needed me to say anything to give him hero status. The guy is already like a god on campus." Peyton offers me that all-knowing smirk again and I snarl at her. "For the millionth time, I do not like him."

Liar, liar, pants on fire.

She puts her hands on my shoulders, aware that I'm about to stomp off to my bedroom like a petulant child. "Fine, you don't like him, and you can't quit this gig because you need the money, the credit, and—"

"And now I'm stuck having to face him one on one." I slap my forehead. "Could this day get any worse?"

"Coach could have asked you to tutor Caleb." She pulls a face like she'd just eaten something distasteful. "That could have been worse."

"I'm not so certain," I say under my breath. Peyton might have had a thing with Caleb that went bad fast, but he's nothing to me. Tutoring him in English would be easier, because every time I looked at him, or sat close to him, I wouldn't have some ridiculous fantasy running around inside my brain.

You hate football players, Ella.

Why on Earth do I have to keep reminding myself of that?

I take a calming breath and glance toward the window when a car goes by, honking the horn. Freshmen, likely. "I could go to the Dean." It's an option, but I already feel the fight going out of me.

"What will that accomplish?" Peyton puckers her lips as I consider it. She's right, it won't accomplish anything. In fact, it might make matters worse for me. If I don't get this credit...

Despite that, I say, "It's blackmail, Peyton. Coach Meyer is blackmailing me into tutoring a student."

"He could have fired you."

"I wish he would have," I grumble.

"No, you don't. You can't take a chance on losing your scholarship." Her hands fall from my shoulders and she walks to the kitchen to grab two water bottles.

"You're right," I mutter, defeat clear in my voice. "I don't and I can't. But to ask me to tutor Landon..." She hands me a bottle and I take a big sip and wipe my mouth with the back of my hand. "That's going too far." I give a shake of my head. "After overhearing our conversation, he knew he had me right where he wanted me." With a snort, I lift my water bottle and click it with Peyton's. "Well done, Coach. Well done."

"Yeah, after hearing you talk about Landon's cock, I don't know why—"

"Can we just not say that anymore." I take another fast sip to wet my parched throat. "Can we just not say Landon's cock."

She taps her chin, and frowns. "Come to think of it, I guess I can understand why he asked you. He knows your grades since he interviewed you for the position, and you made it clear you weren't interested, and Landon has a way of charming the girls out of their pants. I guess Coach figured you weren't susceptible to his charm, and could get the job at hand done."

Don't think about hand jobs, don't think about hand jobs.

Great, now I'm thinking of hand jobs.

I wipe my damp brow, and push my hair back. "Yeah, well he doesn't have to worry there, but it's still blackmail, and he could have hired a guy to tutor him. I'm not the only option on campus."

Her mouth turns up at the corner. "Landon can probably charm a guy out of his pants too."

"You are not helping."

"It's a win/win." She lifts her hand and holds out one finger. "One, Landon needs his grade up." She holds up a second finger. "Two, Coach needs Landon to play." A third finger joins the mix. "And three, you need the credit and don't forget the extra cash that comes with tutoring will definitely go a long way in getting that new camera you want."

I pause as visions of the Panasonic Lumix flashes in my mind. I've been drooling over that piece of equipment since it hit the market. My birthday is coming up and I wouldn't dream of asking my parents for it. No, all their disposable income goes to keeping Ivy in school, in her very expensive sorority, at that. How lucky that I received an academic scholarship, considering they couldn't afford to send us both away to Kingston College here in South California. The droughts the last few years have really hit our farm hard, and forking out the money for two of us was out of the question. Thanks to my hard work, Ivy now gets an elite education, without ever having worked for it. I just wish she'd put a little more energy into her Arts degree and less into getting her MRS. Yeah, she's basically here to find herself a rich husband. I don't begrudge her, though. I want only what's best for her. I always have. Just like she wants what's best for me.

"Okay, what do you have in mind for fixing this?" I finally ask.

"You need to come to the party tonight."

I back up, and give a hard shake of my head. "No way. That is not going to fix anything."

"Sure it is. All the guys will be there, and you can apologize to them. You can't hide from this, and coming forth, owning what you did is the best approach."

I groan. She's right. I know it, but how the hell can I face those guys? "Can't I just do it tomorrow after practice or something?"

"Nope." She grabs my hand and starts hauling me into my bedroom. "It has to be tonight. You won't get any sleep if you don't get this done and over with right away. You can apologize and say you were wrong when you called them all brawn and no brains."

I crinkle my nose, upset with myself. "That really wasn't very nice of me."

"It wasn't and you're a nice person, Ella." She stops and turns to me. Her face is soft, her eyes wide and sympathetic. "I know why you did it, though. But none of these guys were responsible for what happened to Jacob."

Hearing Jacob's name on her tongue floods my veins with ice. Jacob was a good guy, the best guy I knew. His future was ripped right out from underneath him, thanks to a bunch of jocks flexing their muscle and proving their worth by constantly hurting and belittling others. It's been four long years since it happened, and it's still so fresh. Peyton, Jacob and I had always been the three musketeers.

Peyton, who is way better at forgiveness than I am, takes my hands in hers. "Breathe, hun."

I nod and take a deep, fueling breath. "I'm okay, and you know what, maybe you're right. Maybe I should march into that party tonight and apologize. I mean, Landon did invite me, right?"

"He got a touchdown just for you."

My thoughts come to a screeching halt. "After hearing what I said, he probably hates me."

"Then you better make it right, because you have to tutor him. A straight up apology is best, Ella. You know that."

"I do."

"Okay." She lets my hand go. "Now we need to find something hot for you to wear. You need to show off your great tits."

I glance down at my overalls and T-shirt, not fashionable by any means, but I don't care, at least they cover my...great tits. "If I'm only going there to apologize, why do I need something hot to wear?" I eye my friend. "Peyton..." I begin. "Oh hell no. If this is about hooking me up with Landon."

"This has nothing to do with Landon."

I snort. Honestly, I'd trust a lion luring a gazelle in for a play-date before I'd believe that.

"Look, all I'm saying is it's your fourth year here. Do you want to go out into the big bad world with your cherry still intact?"

"My cherry—"

"All I'm saying is maybe it's time you got rid of your pesky virginity, and—"

I eye her. "Pesky? That's what we're calling it?"

She pulls out a dress and holds it up to me. "Sex is so much fun, girlfriend. You are missing out big time, and when you get out into the real world, wouldn't you rather have some experience behind you..." She winks and adds, "Or on top of you. It won't just be footballers at the party. Lots of guys will be there."

Oh, but there is only one guy I'm interested in giving my pesky virginity to, and Peyton must know it, which is why she's pushing so hard.

Wait, what!

Okay, there must have been too much testosterone on the field today. I'm not thinking with clarity here. I'm not interested in giving anyone my virginity. I don't think.

"This won't do." Peyton tosses the dress onto my bed, and hauls me across the hall to her room. I stand there as she roots through her closet, tossing clothes everywhere, until her room is a mess. She's seriously on a mission, because she's the tidy one in this duo. "Got it." She comes out breathless, like she'd just run a damn marathon. "This one will look amazing on you. It's tight on me now, and you're smaller, so it's yours if you want it."

She frowns and I know she's bummed that she's put on weight. "You know you're gorgeous, right? All the guys are crazy about you."

"Not all of them," she mumbles, and before I can ask she says, "This is about you, not me."

Sensing she doesn't want to talk about her bit of weight gain, I take the fabric into my hand. "It is pretty." At least she didn't come out with something that showed off my cooch-cooch, as Peyton calls it.

"Put it on."

I unbuckle my overalls and let them fall to the floor. Unceremoniously, I kick them off. "One of these days, I'm going to have to teach you how to remove your clothes seductively. That drop and kick move isn't going to cut it."

"It's not a performance."

"Not right now, but someday it will be." She's so serious it makes me laugh.

"Ivy is the actress, not me." I pull on the dress and her eyes light.

"I knew it. Look at those tits."

I turn to the mirror and adjust the wrap dress over my breasts, covering them up just a bit more. I have to admit, I normally don't gravitate toward tight dresses that show off my curves—I'm venturing into Ivy's department here—but I kind of like it.

"Do you think I look too much like my sister?"

"You look like you, Ella. Beautiful, sexy and tonight, tongues are going to hang."

A strange little thrill goes through me. I'm not one for attention, and have never needed validation from the opposite sex, yet I can't help but wonder what Landon will do when he sees me in this. I turn around, and look at my ass. I give a little twerk to shake my booty and Peyton claps her hands.

"Sexy Ella is in the house. Although I must say, on the field today, Landon liked what he saw."

Another stupid thrill goes through me. "Do you think?" I ask quickly, too quickly, judging by the smirk on Peyton's face.

"He invited you tonight, didn't he?"

I crinkle my nose. "Do you think he lost a bet or something?"

She laughs. "Hell no, girlfriend. You just don't see what the rest of the world sees." She stands behind me and takes my hair into her hands as we both look into the mirror. "How about a little blonde highlights right here in the front, to frame your face? I have a kit." She brushes a few strands over my shoulders.

"Then I'll really look like Ivy."

"No, you'll look like you. I love your brown hair, but this will really brighten your face."

I shrug. "I dunno."

"Trust me?" Our eyes meet in the mirror.

"There isn't anyone in the world I trust more."

"Good, then get out of this dress and into something old so we can dye your hair."

I change quickly and she drags me to the bathroom, and less than an hour later, I have blonde highlights framing my face. I grin at myself in the mirror as Peyton finishes blow drying my curls.

"So, what do you think?" she asks.

I turn my head left then right, let my hair bounce over my shoulders. "I actually like it," I tell her, but from the big smile on my face, she can already tell.

Squealing with excitement, she sets the blow dryer down and turns me to face her. She runs the strands of my hair through her fingers. "This blonde really makes your blue eyes pop. Landon isn't going to know what to do with you."

"Peyton," I scold. "None of this is for Landon."

She blinks dark lashes over not-so-innocent eyes. "I only mean he was the one who invited you and you're just so damn gorgeous, Ella. You're the only one who doesn't realize it."

"Thank you. I appreciate the compliment, but the thing is, I don't want a guy to like me because I look a certain way. I want them to like me for who I am." I put my hand on my chest. "In here, you know. If they want this..." I pause and circle my finger around my face. "They can get with Ivy."

"I know, and that guy you're talking about will come along, trust me. Until then, let's just go have some fun."

A little bubble of excitement wells up in my stomach as I give myself one last glance in the mirror. Honestly, I can't believe in the three years I've been on campus I've yet to go to a frat party. We dress in our party outfits, and Peyton groans when I slide into my flats, but I don't care. Comfort is a big deal for me.

"I'll let that go," she grumbles and slides her arm into mine. We head outside and the night air is warm, and humid, which will likely make a mess of my new hair. Since Landon's house is just a few blocks away, we walk over. Peyton has a car, but no sense in bringing it, especially if she's drinking. I could always drive. I plan to stay sober, as I have apologies to make.

As we approach the house, music blares from the open windows. It's a good thing most of the houses in the area are rented by college students. No family would put up with the football team's antics. Cars are parked all over the place, and I wouldn't be surprised if the cops get called. Then again, the police give a lot of leeway to the players, as long as no one is underage or drinking and driving.

"Excited?"

"I'm the laughingstock of the football team, Peyton, and I'm here to apologize. I'd hardly call what I'm feeling excited." My steps slow. "I know you come to these things all the time, but I don't know, maybe it's not the right place for me to apologize. The guys are probably all drunk by now."

She grabs my arm. "You need to get it done and over with tonight. The longer you wait, the worse it will be. Trust me, and I promise, if you're not comfortable, we leave. Girl code. I promise. Also, you'll need a safe word."

I stiffen. "A safe word." I falter. "Why the hell would I need a safe word?"

"It's what friends do, that's all. If you're going to go off with a guy—"

I hold my hand up. "Not going to happen."

"Let's just say the planets all align or something and you find yourself with a guy. Technically the upstairs bedrooms are off limits, but that's never stopped anyone before. So if you go to a bedroom with someone, and I can't find you, I'll worry. Just shoot me one word to let me know you're okay."

"What word?"

She frowns and glances around, then a slow grin spreads across her face. "Hmm, how about torpedo."

"You're not very funny."

"Torpedo it is, and if you're uncomfortable and need to leave, send another word."

I fold my arms. "Can't wait to hear this one." Just then some jock with spiky red hair sticking out from a ball cap comes stumbling out of the door, and stops on the steps and stares at me. "Okay, I think I've had too much. I'm seeing double." He leans over the railing and proceeds to throw up into the bushes.

"Lovely."

"That's Jonny, star catcher on Kingston's baseball team. His nickname is Red, obviously from his hair. Just ignore him. How about..." She taps her chin, like some guy isn't puking right beside us. For two girls who are best friends, we sure see the world differently. Then again, this is her scene, not mine. "What is something you say a lot, so no guy would notice?"

"None of these guys know me as it is."

She crinkles her nose, and I'm not even sure she heard me. "You're a film student, so if you said action, it might just go right over their heads."

"Or they could take it that I'm looking for action."

"Well, that's true. All right, what do you suggest?"

"I don't know." I consider it for a moment. "My God, is it always this hard?"

"That's what she said," Peyton blurts out and starts laughing hysterically.

My lip quivers at the corner and as much as I don't want to laugh, I do. "You're your own biggest fan, aren't you?" I shake my head. "Okay fine, if we're going to be immature about this let's make it V-Card. That way if I say it, you'll know I'm protecting mine."

"Deal. V-Card it is."

"Who has a V-Card?" Jonny asks as he wipes his mouth and turns our way.

Ignoring him, Peyton grabs my hand and hauls me inside, and within minutes, red Solo cups are being thrust into our hands. I grip mine and search the room, my gaze scanning over the scantily dressed girls, the couples with their tongues down each other's throats, and the boys doing keg stands. The second my eyes land on Landon, my heart jumps into my throat, and while I might not know a lot about these kinds of parties there is one thing I know for sure.

This was a big freaking mistake.

I can't stay mad at her. Hell, I want to, but seeing her standing there, a little lost, a whole lot vulnerable, fucks me over in the weirdest ways. The air seems to be stuck in my lungs, heavy in my chest as I take her in, admire her in that clinging dress that hugs her curvy body. She might be Ivy's sister, might be dressed the same as her tonight, but it's easy to tell they're polar opposites.

I can't fight the smile pulling at my mouth, despite the fact that the guys have been busting my balls ever since the team meeting. While I can take their bullshit, I don't want any of them messing with Ella, or calling her out for saying we're all stupid—or for watching porn. There isn't a guy in this room who doesn't watch it, and I don't want her to think there is anything wrong with it.

I take note of the Solo cup in her hand, and while I know my teammates are good guys, there are plenty of guys here I don't trust. Mainly that asshole Cameron Reid, star pitcher for the baseball team, and wouldn't you know it, that fucker is headed straight her way. Fresh meat. That's totally his style. I heard he still plays that ridiculous freshman initiation game of baiting and nailing the virgin.

Ella's eyes go wide as he steps up to her, and Peyton leans into her, whispers something in her ear. Ella nods, and Peyton waits a second longer, like she wants to make sure Ella is sure about something, and I'm glad she has a good friend with her. Ella nods again, and Peyton crosses the room, giving Caleb, who is staring at her, a wide berth as she sidles up to my buddy Liam.

Someone bumps me from behind, and my beer spills all over my shirt. "Jesus." I turn to find Jared stomping around, and slurring his words. "Slow it down, bud. You won't make it another hour."

He holds his cup up, and I take it from him and set it on the table. He shrugs, gives me the finger, and heads to the kitchen for a refill. I look back to where Ella was standing, but she's gone. Panic wells up inside me. Where the fuck did she go so fast? Maybe she bolted. Cameron is nowhere to be found either. She better not have gone anywhere with him. I tamp down the anger rising up in me, shocked at the speed it appeared. The truth is, Ella can be with any guy she wants. I have no say, but if she's going to mess around with Cameron, she should know what kind of guy she's getting involved with. Then again, who am I to talk. We're ballers, and around campus we're the known man whores—guys who have a different girl every weekend.

"Need a tampon?" Brady asks as he comes up to me and slaps me on the back to pull me from my stupor.

"What the fuck, dude."

"You're standing here staring off into space." He pokes my forehead. "You got a cramp or something?"

"Fuck off," I say and he leans forward as I fake punch him in the gut. He hands me a Solo cup and I take a drink of his beer and hand it back.

"Ivy is looking hot tonight, don't you think? Or maybe you've got a thing for her sister."

I shouldn't want to bring sweet Ella into our world where fucking is nothing but a pastime, but dammit, selfish bastard that I am, I do. I really wasn't prepared to see her in a tight dress, her hair and makeup done.

"What do you know about her, anyway?" I ask.

"Just that she really doesn't like you." His grin is cocky when he adds, "And does not want your cock anywhere near her lips."

The sudden image of Ella on her knees before me, her big blue eyes wide as she opens her mouth to take me in fills my brain and thickens my damn dick. Fuck, what is it about her innocence that gets to me? She's like a goddamn angel sent from heaven. Innocent and untouched. But she can't be a virgin, right? She's a fourth-year college student, for Christ's sake. Then again, Cameron wouldn't be chasing her if she wasn't. Although how he would know for certain is beyond me.

"And..." Brady says, pulling my thoughts back. He pokes me. "She's your new tutor."

"Yeah," I say, halfheartedly as I run my fingers through my mess of hair. "That's all kind of fucked up." Under my breath, I add, "I can't believe she came tonight."

"Me neither. Why do you think she's here?"

"Don't know."

"Why don't you go find out."

I turn to Brady, and our eyes lock. "You think so?" Why the hell am I asking my best friend's thoughts on this. Who I'm with is not his business and I don't need his permission. The fact that I am asking, though, that means even I know I should leave well enough alone. I just wish I wasn't so goddamn drawn to her. If it was just her body I was after—fuck, I could have her sister, judging by the way she was acting earlier.

"Go." Brady gives me a shove to set me into motion, and I head toward the door just as she steps back in, alone. At least she was smart enough to ditch douche bag Cameron. Her eyes drift to mine and need slams into me, pounds hard against my chest. What the hell is wrong with me? No girl has ever pulled this kind of reaction from me before. It's a bit unnerving, really. I take one step, but before I can get to her, I hear someone call my name. Ivy comes running up to me, jumping into my arms, and laughingly wraps her arms around me, burying her face in my neck.

"There you are," she says and shakes her head to roll her hair to her back. "I've been looking everywhere for you."

"Been right here the whole time, Ivy." I try to shake her loose but she tightens her hold on me.

"I guess I haven't been looking in the right places." With her dress—one very similar to Ella's—high on her thighs, she wiggles her body against mine, and I groan as her pussy presses against my stomach. Is she even wearing panties, and what the fuck does she think she's doing? I'm not her type, never have been, so why all the attention, suddenly?

"Did you know your sister is here?" I ask.

Her eyes go wide, shock registering on her face. "What the hell? This is so not her thing." She glances around like she's searching for her sister, and while she's acting all surprised, I get the strangest feeling she knew Ella was here.

"I was just about to go say hello to her." I look past Ivy's shoulder, and my eyes lock with Ella's. She stands there perfectly still, and a moment later something passes over her eyes, and I watch her transform in front of me. She hugs herself, and takes a small step back, like she's trying to disappear into the woodwork. I grip Ivy's arms to release her hold on me, but can't shake her off. Cameron is back, and he puts his hand on Ella's back to set her into motion. She stumbles a bit, like she's unsure, then casts me a quick glance before letting him lead her into the kitchen.

"Fuck," I grumble.

Ivy blinks at me. "What?"

"Your sister. She shouldn't be with Cameron. I know him and he's only after one thing."

"What guy here isn't?" she challenges with a laugh.

Okay, so what can I say? She's right about that. I shrug, and Ivy slides from my body, and goes all kitten like, rubbing herself against me.

"So what are we waiting for?" she asks and when I don't bite, I catch a hint of anger simmering just below her smile. "Can you tell me why you're wasting time worrying about my sister? She's a big girl."

"Yeah, maybe, but I don't think she knows what she's getting herself into." Christ, I grew up with four sisters, and a mother who is a minister. If I don't do the right thing here and see to her safety, they'd all kill me. But this isn't just for them. Something about Ella brings out the protector in me.

She scoffs. "After what she said about you, I'd think you'd want to kick her out of here."

"You heard about that, huh?" I ask, and take in the sour look on her face.

"Everyone heard about that. She's the laughingstock on the campus, Landon. Even I'm embarrassed to call her my sister."

Something tightens inside of me. "Then it must have been very hard for her to come here tonight."

"Right?" She rolls her big blue eyes. "Why put herself through the embarrassment?"

"Maybe I should go find out what's going on."

She runs one finger up and down my chest. "Can't you go later?" She glances at the stairs. "I kind of want to go up there right now."

"Upstairs is off limits." Not that that has ever stopped any of the guys from going up there and fucking in my bedroom.

"This is your house, your rules." Her whiny voice grates on my nerves. "You can change them for me, Landon."

She's not wrong. "I'm going to go check on Ella." Ivy pouts and tries to pull at me as I move around her. Just then Ivy's friend Jessica walks past me, and I glance over my shoulder to see Ivy reach for her friend's cup and take a big drink. Ivy starts bitching to her friend as I enter the kitchen.

Ella's back is to me, yet everything about her tells me she knows I'm right behind her. Her body tightens as she watches the guys do a keg stand. I step up to her, and I'm about to put my hand on her shoulder when I remember what happened the last time I touched without permission. Instead, I bend and place my mouth near her ear. "You came."

She slowly turns, and my fucking heart jumps when big blue eyes full of shame, and embarrassment, meet mine. Her smile is wobbly, everything about her on edge when she says, "Can't fool you."

I take a long breath as her sweet vanilla scent fills my nostrils. "Nope." I tap my head. "I suck in English, but I'm not all brawn."

Color crawls up her neck and into her cheeks as she glances down, and folds her arms, once again retreating into herself. "That's why I'm here. I…I…"

"Follow me," I say and lead her out of the kitchen to a corner in the living room that is somewhat quieter. I lean against the wall and she stands there shifting from one foot to the other. "I'm glad you came."

A garbled sound crawls out of her throat. "Why, after what you heard me say?" She buries her face in her hands.

I make a move to pull her hands away and stop myself. "Uh, can I touch you?"

Her head jerks up, her hands still in front of her. "What?"

"Your hands. Can I touch them?"

She examines her hands, frowning like she doesn't get why I asked, then her gaze slides back to mine. "Um, yeah, okay." I take her hands, and I'm instantly bombarded with want as I close callused fingers over her very soft skin. I put her hands by her sides.

"I'm not upset. Not anymore, anyway. I guess I just want to know why you said those things."

"I was just being stupid. I don't really think you guys are all brawn. I'm here tonight to apologize to every single guy on the team. I've been the victim of name calling and bullying..." She swallows like she's remembering something hurtful, and without even realizing it, my fingers curl into fists wanting to hunt down and beat everyone who hurt her. "I know how that feels, and what I did was no better. I'm sorry, Landon."

"Apology accepted."

"What..." she begins in a quiet voice. "What I said about your...your..."

I take her hand in mine and give it an encouraging squeeze. A breathy little sound catches in her throat as her fingers curl in mine.

"Your..." she tries again.

"My cock."

"Oh, God, Landon," she blurts out and sags against the wall, our fingers still entwined, like neither of us are in a hurry to let go. "I am so embarrassed, and I shouldn't have said I didn't like you when I don't really know you."

I inch a bit closer, and heat arcs between us. I'm sure she feels this pull every bit as much as I do. "You want to get to know me, then?"

"Yes, no...I mean. I just..." She picks at an imaginary piece of lint on her dress. Does she have any idea how gorgeous she looks in it? Then again, I liked everything about her in overalls, too.

I put my finger beneath her chin and lift it until our eyes meet. "Out with it."

She puckers up her lips and I count the freckles on her nose. Does she have freckles in other hidden places? Damned if I don't want to find out, but she's so fucking innocent and I really should just back the fuck off. I didn't like the hazing game played in freshman year, didn't want to participate in it. Stealing someone's innocence for sport, or any other reason, is not my thing.

"Why...why did you want me to come tonight?"

"I wanted to show you something."

Her entire body goes stiff, a fire back in her eyes "Landon—" Before I can stop her and tell her I'm not interested in showing her my cock—that's not entirely true—and that it's my movie collection I wanted her to look at, the guys come barreling at me, lifting me onto their shoulders to celebrate my winning touchdown.

Just then Ivy comes up to me, a bottle of champagne in her hands. She shakes it, pops the cork and the sweet syrupy contents sprays all over me. Everyone is laughing and carrying on and opening their mouths to take a drink. I quickly lose sight of Ella as the guys take me outside and toss me onto the trampoline someone set up on the front lawn. Ivy and a few other girls jump on with me, upsetting my balance, and no matter how hard I try, I can't seem to climb off.

Ivy clings to me, jumping up and down, rubbing her tits on my wet shirt until her dress is wet and her hard nipples are poking my flesh.

I catch sight of Ella at the front door, watching the action. Peyton comes up behind her and pulls her inside. I lose sight of her, and after numerous tries, I finally manage to drop to my hands and knees and shimmy off the damn trampoline. Ivy calls out to me, but I ignore her and push through the crowd to get back inside.

I make my way through the rooms, but Ella is nowhere to be found. Did she exit through the back door, and bail? I can't find Peyton either. I head out back and search the crowd. Fuck. She must have left. I go back inside, and no longer in the mood to party, I head upstairs. No one had better be in my room, fucking on my bed.

I practically kick open my door, and when I take in the girl standing there, examining my things with her flashlight app, my blood surges and my heart jumps into my throat.

"Find what you were looking for?"

5

___

ELLA

___

"I ...Oh, shit."

I lift my phone, and shine the light directly into Landon's eyes as he stands in the doorway, waiting for me to answer his question. He winces and holds both hands up as I damn near blind him, and while he's distracted, I take that moment to admire all six feet of him. A burst of white-hot heat flashes inside me, partly because he just caught me snooping, and partly because he's tall, hard, and so goddamn hot a girl would have to be insane not to be affected.

"Can you turn that off?" he grumbles, as the scent of his skin washes over me. His pillow smelled the same, and I'm pathetic, because yes, I smelled his bedding. What the hell is wrong with me?

"Oh, sorry." I turn the app off, draping us in darkness, the only light in the room now coming from the streetlamp shining in the bedroom window.

"Well did you find what you were looking for?"

I found a lot of things, mainly his impressive collection of old DVDs. It's insane that we have the same taste in movies. "I ah, was looking for the bathroom." It's not a lie. I was looking for the bathroom, when I stumbled upon his room. Temptation proved to be too much, and now...busted.

FML.

Seriously though, I was surprised that he loves movies as much as I do, even the classics. Maybe that's why he asked me to come tonight. Maybe he wanted a movie partner. I'm smart, quiet, a wallflower. Definitely not the kind of girl a hot football player sleeps with. I told him I was a film student and liked movies, so yeah, I guess he wanted me here to help him find the next cult classic. Ohmigod!! Maybe he wants me to watch porn with him. Maybe he thinks I'm a big old horny college student.

He wouldn't be wrong.

Then again, he invited me before he knew I watched erotic movies.

"I got lost," I say and he stares at me, with what I think is disbelief all over his face. It's hard to tell in the dark.

He jerks his thumb over his shoulder. "Across the hall," he says, and I swallow as his voice, husky and deep now, curls around me, sending shivers down my spine. My nipples tighten, as he pulls in a labored breath, like he can't quite fill his lungs. What is going on with him?

Wait, does he think I'm Ivy? I mean the two were pretty wrapped up in each other tonight, and with my new blonde hair—although he likely can't see it in the dark—there's a good chance he could think I'm Ivy. I mean, he did shut the door, locking the world out and us in and let's face it, a girl only goes to a guy's room for one reason at a frat party—and it's not to snoop. Plus, he's been drinking. I'm not sure how much, but there's a good chance he's too drunk to know the difference between us.

"I should go." My God is that my voice? Since when did I ever sound husky? I guess that's what arousal does to a person's voice. I force my quivering legs to work, but as I get closer to him, catching his scent, my entire body vibrates in a way it never has before, clearly reacting to the hot-blooded male standing before me.

So what are you going to do about that?

He extends his arm, and captures me around my waist. "Or you could stay," he says, easily positioning me in front of him, manipulating my body like I weigh no more than a football. Why the hell do I like that so much? Am I really one of those girls who likes when a guy goes all alpha? Oh good God, I might be. His head dips, and his mouth is right there, inches from mine.

Torpedo.

Oh, man, why did that stupid word have to jump into my brain. Oh, probably because I need to make a fast decision —a decision that could very well change me. So what's it going to be? Am I going to text torpedo to Peyton? Or V-card?

"You want me to stay?" I ask, needing to hear him say it, even though I'm like ninety-nine percent sure he thinks I'm Ivy.

He hesitates for a brief second, and my blood instantly runs cold. Oh, crap, maybe he suddenly realized it's me, and knows he made a mistake.

"Yes, I want you to stay," he finally says, his voice a low, husky murmur that slides over my skin and settles deep between my legs. "Tell me you want the same."

Is this it? The moment I hand over my V-card?

"I want the same," I say, and lean into him.

Ohmigod, I'm doing this. I'm really doing this.

His hand slides around my neck, and a low tortured moan vibrates around me as he fists my hair and presses his lips to mine. He inches back and asks, "Is that what you were really looking for?"

My mind whirls, races, searches for the truth. On some level was I hoping he'd find me in here and kiss the sanity from my brain, because yeah, what I'm doing isn't smart. I barely know this guy. Am I really going to get naked with him and hand over my virginity?

"Yes," I murmur, answering his question as well as my own. He gives me a nudge with his body, backing me until the backs of my knees hit the bed, and that's when my one working brain cell nudges me. I need to text Peyton. He backs up an inch, reaches over his shoulder and tugs off his shirt, and the second I take in all his hills and valleys, I damn near bite off my tongue. Swallowing hard I lift my phone and he angles his head, confused. "I have to send my friend a text. Girl code."

"Right," he says, and I quickly text—torpedo.

I'm about to set my phone down when an eggplant and a thumbs up emoji pop up. A low chuckle climbs out of Landon's throat. Dammit, he wasn't supposed to see that. I set my phone down on his nightstand, and take a fueling breath as he closes the distance between us. His body is warm, his fingers hot as he pulls me against him again, and I try not to react like the virgin I am when I feel his hardness press against my stomach.

Strong hands tug on the belt holding the dress together, and a jolt of excitement and nervousness rushes through me.

"Fuck," he grumbles, as the dress falls away and puddles around my feet. "I need to see you better."

He makes a move toward his lamp, and I wrap my hand around his arm to stop him. "No lights," I say, and he hesitates again. "I like this mood better."

He runs his knuckles down my arms and goosebumps break out on my flesh. God, I love the way this guy touches me. Although I have nothing to compare it to.

"Yeah?" he asks. "You like it in the dark?"

"Yeah, and I think it will be more fun to feel my way around," I say, and he chuckles lightly as I put my hands on his chest. His muscles ripple beneath my fingers as I begin an exploration, starting with his chest, my fingers moving over all eight abs until I reach his pants. I hesitate for a brief second, and he takes my hand and slides it lower, until I'm cradling his cock through his jeans.

Damn that is nice—and big. What the hell am I supposed to do with that? I guess I'll soon find out.

I take my time to explore him, and a new kind of eagerness builds inside me. Suddenly anxious to see him naked, I pop his button, but he grips my hand and stops me. My heart speeds up as my gaze jerks to his.

"I need my mouth on you before anything," he says, and slides one hand around my body, to pull me against him. His hungry lips find mine again, devour my mouth, bite at my lip. Tomorrow I'll have marks and I'm not even upset about that.

His lips leave mine and travel downward. Using his thumbs, he lightly brushes my hard nipples through my bra and a moan I have no control over rises in my throat and seems to excite him. His soft chuckle whispers over my skin as he reaches behind me and in one swift movement, he removes my bra. Apparently his nimble football hands are adept at many things, but I don't want to think about that right now. Nope, I can't think about it. Not when he's staring at my breasts like they're a big hot fudge sundae and he hasn't eaten in days.

Lord help me.

"Such perfect tits. I might want to fuck these," he murmurs as he holds them and bends to take a hard nipple into his mouth. Mercy. Do all guys talk like him? Do I even like that?

Ohmigod, I do.

His tongue swirls, his teeth nip and I shut my eyes against the onslaught of pleasure. I've touched myself before, of course, but nothing has ever felt this good. The heat of his mouth sears my skin, and I feel the pull all the way to the needy spot between my legs. I breathe in his intoxicating scent as he moves from one nipple to the other. My hips roll instinctively, searching for...something.

Landon's hands slide down my body and grip my hips, his fingers biting into my flesh as he holds me still, like my movements are just too much for him. While I'm not sure if that's true, I work to roll them again, to bump up against his hard cock, and he tears his lips from my nipple.

"You are so fucking sexy and if you keep that up I'll be done before I've even started."

Oh.

I smile secretly, liking this effect I have on him. He stands to his full height, and my body is flush with his as he slides his hands down my back. A hard shiver goes through me as his fingers dip into my panties, and I toss up a silent prayer of thanks that I wore my only pretty pair. Maybe I should have let him turn the lights on and see my body, my lace underwear —my face.

Nope, not going to do anything to ruin this night. I'm still not sure which twin he thinks he's with and I'll deal with that dilemma later. When my body is not screaming for his touch. When my pesky V-card is not begging me to get over myself and make love already.

Make love?

Oh, what a joke. I am not stupid enough to think this is anything other than sex, or that this isn't a one-night thing. The ballers are all a bunch of man whores with revolving bedroom doors. He nudges my panties down, sliding to the floor with them. His mouth is inches from my sex, his breath hot on my mons as he taps my legs for me to lift. I lift them one at a time and he tosses my scrap of lace over his shoulder.

I take a deep breath as his thumb goes to my wet pussy, and he casts a quick glance up at me. Fearing he can sense my nervousness, I put my hands on his shoulders and squeeze, giving him encouragement. But all my unease fades away the second his scorching hot tongue makes contact with my clit.

"Ohmigod," I say out loud and his chuckle reverberates through me.

"Like that do you, Angel?"

"Yes," I pant. "More please."

I catch his grin in the dark before he buries his face between my legs again, and I close my eyes. Angel. Yeah, maybe that's the perfect name because I sure as hell feel like I'm in heaven. I run my hands over his broad shoulders, loving the way his muscles bunch beneath my hands. He tongues me, and I grip his hair, and pull him against my pussy a little harder. Dear God, who am I? I don't know and I don't care.

I want this.

I want him.

Before I even realize what's happening, I'm on his bed, and he's widening my legs with his body, pushing my thighs open until I'm on full display. A loud, tortured growl crawls from the depths of his throat. I wish I could see him. I wish I could see the look on his face as he takes in my nakedness with his fingers. I've never been ashamed of my body. I've just never really been the object of a guy's attention before.

His big hands slide up my thighs, and I let loose a moan as he presses the rough tip of his finger to my clit. I toss my head from side to side, and grip the bedding. "Do you like what I'm doing to you, Angel?" he asks.

"Yes."

"Was this what you were looking for?"

"It was," I admit—to him and myself. What's the point in keeping any secrets? I want everything he wants to give me, and I'm not about to hide the truth when the hottest guy on the planet is doing the most delicious things to my clit. That would make me the world's biggest fool, and while this might not be my smartest decision, I'm no fool.

He inches a finger into me, and I bite down on my lip. He groans. "You are so fucking tight, Angel."

Oh, that's because I'm a virgin.

He goes still, and I can't help but wonder if he just had the same thought. "Not too tight for your cock," I say, surprising myself. Looks like all that porn watching has paid off, because he's back to fingering me, all hesitation gone. I move my body, rock into him, not because it's what I think I'm supposed to do but because I'm so damn needy.

Heat races through my body, centers on my core, and I am only seconds from climaxing. I try to hold back, I really do, but when he takes my clit back into his mouth, sucks hard, like the team's next win might depend on it, the world closes in on me. I take a fast breath and then another as his thick finger strokes the sensitive bundle of nerves inside me. Then suddenly the world stops spinning, time suspends, and nothing but the strong, exquisite sensations in my body matter.

I tug on the sheets, and lift my head as a vortex of pleasure centers between my legs. "I'm...I'm..."

"Yeah, Angel, come for me." The sheer pleasure in his voice brings on another hard explosion. "Just like that."

My hot liquid heat soaks his finger as he continues to move it in and out of me, and with the way he's rubbing his lips against my pussy, I know when he finally comes up for air, his face will be soaked. I have no idea why the idea of that turns me on.

He laps at me, drinking me like I'm the best thing he's ever tasted, and I grip his hair again, wanting his cock in my mouth.

"Landon," I beg, and tug, wanting more...wanting everything, wanting things I probably don't even know about yet.

"Not done with you, Angel," he says and swirls his tongue all over me. He stays buried between my legs, not moving until he's damn well ready, and while I do want to touch and taste his cock, I'm not going to put up a fight.

Ever so slowly he goes back on his heels, and with my eyes completely adjusted to the dark, along with the lamp light shining in from outside, I can take in the motion as he wipes his mouth with the back of his hand. "Wanted to stay down here all night, but I desperately need to be inside you. I think I might just die if I don't get my cock in you within the next few minutes." He brushes his finger along my slit as he takes his cock in his other hand and strokes it from base to tip, and a little squeal catches in my throat.

"Something the matter, Angel?"

"You're just...big." He cocks his head to the side and I mentally scold myself. What a stupid, innocent thing to say.

"I won't hurt you."

As I take in his dark face, the way he's studying me, my nerves relax. While this guy is a man whore, everything in the way he just touched me, pleasured me, reassured me with his words, puts me at ease.

"I know," I whisper. "I...I trust you."

He goes perfectly still and for a second I wonder if he's breathing. God, did I say the wrong thing? Finally, he breaks the quiet and says, "Yeah?" I don't miss the doubt in his voice. But there's something else there too. Something that sounds like pride. He likes that I trust him. What? Do people not have much faith in him off the field? My heart pinches at that. Landon is a lot of things, but underneath it all, I really think he's a good guy with a good heart.

Don't fall for him, girl.

I quickly remind myself this is a one-night thing, and say, "We need protection."

He nods quickly, like my words pulled him back from somewhere, and reaches into his nightstand. Back on his knees, between my legs, he opens a foil package, but I'm fascinated by his cock, the length, the girth and its hardness. I sit up, and adjust my body, putting my mouth close to him, and a growl tears from his throat.

"Angel, you can't—"

His mouth slams shut with an audible click as I take the crown into my mouth, and weigh him in my hands. I'm not an expert at this. Heck, I've never done it before, but judging by his moans, I don't think it matters. I lean forward and he sinks to the back of my throat, and my damn gag reflexes kick in. Dammit. Embarrassment floods me, and he cups my cheeks and pulls me from his dick.

For a second I expect him to laugh at my inexperience, to tease me a bit, but he's dead serious when he says, "You don't have to do this."

The tenderness in his voice messes with me a little, and once again I have to remember I'm just one girl of many in this guy's life. "I want to." How many times does a girl get to learn about sex from a guy who's an expert? A guy she's always lusted after.

I lick his crown, and massage his balls in the palms of my hands, and he grips my hair, curls it in his fingers. He pulls his cock from my mouth as I steal a quick glance up at him, and he leans down and taking me by surprise, presses a tender kiss to my forehead. Warmth moves through me, and I take him back into my mouth again, loosening my muscles so I don't choke again.

I moan without thinking and his loud growl follows. I never knew I was such a tease, but I like watching this man become unhinged.

"Angel...I can't..."

I let him tug himself from my mouth and fall back onto the pillow. His gaze drops to my chest as he sheathes himself. Is he going to fuck me there? He settles his body over me, and his mouth finds mine as he takes my legs and hooks them around his back, opening my sex wide for him.

His thick crown presses against my opening, and I want to slam my eyes shut and hold my breath, but he's watching me, his eyes locked on mine. I take a slow breath as our lips meld and explore the contours and curves of our mouths. Landon watches me I can't help but think he's gauging my reactions, but there's no way he can know I'm a virgin, right?

He tenderly smooths my hair from my face, when suddenly his hips thrust forward. I open my mouth to let out a scream, but no words form as he sinks into me. He fills me, buries deep and goes still for entirely too long. My breathing changes, fast shallow pants as my entire body stiffens.

He curses under his breath, "Jesus Christ, I'm hurting you." When I don't answer, can't find my voice to answer, his chest leaves mine as he inches back, his eyes moving over my face. "Are you—"

I grab him, pull him to me. "Landon," I plead and lift until my lips are back on his. "Please...I want more."

As I rock against him, encouraging him to move inside me, he follows me back onto the bed, his lips kissing mine as he pistons his hips, his big, glorious cock stretching me in ways I've never been stretched. I lightly scrape my nails over his back, and breathe through the sting until my body begins to tingle all over, every nerve coming alive with pleasure.

"Yes," he moans as I rock with him, rising up to meet each glorious thrust. "You are so hot and tight."

"It's because you're so big," I tell him and that seems to satisfy him—probably strokes his ego too. But I don't care. The man's ego deserves to be stroked. Everything on him deserves to be stroked when he can bring this kind of pleasure to a virgin.

His eyes find mine again, and his face is pained. "You are so goddamn beautiful, I'm not going to last."

"That's okay. I want to feel you."

"Not before you come again."

"I don't think I can," I say quickly.

"Yeah, you will," he says and clenches down on his jaw. He looks like he's in total agony, but I do love a confident man with a plan.

"Touch your tits for me, Angel. Rub your nipples. Pinch them."

I do as he says, liking his orders, and the second I pinch my hard nipples, sensations rocket through me, and my eyes widen as an orgasm approaches. "There you go," he says and slides a hand between our bodies to apply pressure to my clit.

"Oh," I moan, my eyes now rolling around in my head. He chuckles but it sounds pained as he continues to pump into me. He lowers himself and braces one arm on the bed beside me. As he uses hard, blunt strokes, movements not meant to finesse, but rather get the job done, I am almost certain I'm fucked. Of course I'm not referring to our physical joining. I'm thinking this guy might be ruining me for anyone else.

I'll worry about that tomorrow, though. Right now, as pleasure gathers in every nerve, my body totally alive, I can't think, I can only feel. His hips piston into me as he flicks my clit, and I play with my nipples and suddenly my body burns, and pleasure moves rapidly through me until I'm coming around his cock.

"Angel," he growls as my muscles squeeze around him and he throws his head back, claiming his own orgasm. I concentrate on the pulsing between my legs, both his and mine, and revel in the euphoric lightheadedness of my brain. I briefly close my eyes as we ride our release and when our bodies stop spasming, he falls over me, pinning me with his impressive weight.

He rolls to the side, taking me with him. Our bodies are warm and damp and oh so sated, I'm not sure I'll ever be able to use my legs again. What the hell. Legs are overrated, anyway. I open one eye and peek at him, completely angry with myself. I mean, I heard sex was awesome. Peyton told me numerous times what I was missing out on, but come on, this, what we did here, makes my piddly little one-handed climaxes a total bore. I should have jumped into sex headfirst the second I arrived my freshman year.

He rolls to his other side, and I hear a snap as he removes his condom. A second later, he's facing me again, his hand is between my legs again, and for a second I think he's already up for round two, but no, he's actually wiping me with some tissues. A hard shiver wracks my body.

"Cold?" he asks.

"A bit." It's a lie, but I'm not about to let him know this was pretty emotional for me, and that it's possible I could fall for the first guy to touch me.

"I'll get you a T-shirt." He jumps up and heads to his dresser.

He grabs me a shirt from his dresser, and comes back to bed. I sit up, and he slides it over my head. As I breathe in the scent on him, my damn heart squeezes tight.

Could the guy be any sweeter?

Okay, come on, girlfriend. Get your shit together. You can't fall for this guy. He says something to me, a grunt of sorts and I can't quite decipher it. Is he asking me to leave? Oh, God, he probably is. I start to get up and go, when one thick arm falls over me, dragging me into his body. He buries his face in my hair and... Wait, did he just sniff me?

Maybe he did and who am I to judge, right? As I come down from my post-orgasmic bliss, my brain cells start working again. I consider where my dress is, and the most efficient way to get into it and out of his room.

Oh, shit.

I'll have to do the walk of shame. I cringe and curl tighter against him, not wanting to move. He mumbles something else, and the next thing I know his breathing has changed. How could he possibly fall asleep so fast, especially when my brain is racing a million miles an hour? Oh, because he's had sex numerous times and this is his M.O.

The party is still going strong, and my sister is down there. Not that it's any of her business, but she sort of made it clear that she was after Landon. Shit. Did I cross a line, claim someone that she wanted first? Although, I've wanted Landon for a long time. Then again, how would she know that? Worry moves into my gut, and my muscles tighten. Did I make a huge mistake here?

Laughter rises up from downstairs making me painfully aware of my near nakedness, that I slept with a football player—had a one-night hook up with a guy I have to tutor for the next couple months. And I don't even like football players, right?

I try to shimmy away, but he pulls me back. Wait, is he sleeping or not? And why is he keeping me here. I know their reputations. Women do not stay over. I settle myself for the time being and a plan comes together. Wait until everyone is gone, sneak out under the cover of darkness and pretend this never happened. It's a good plan, right? Solid.

If I follow it carefully, nothing can go wrong.

6

LANDON

I peel one eye open and then another. For a second, I'm confused. Who the hell is in my bed? I never let anyone stay over. Never. The fog clears from my brain, and my body ignites as memories come rushing back. I glance at the woman beside me. She's anything but 'anyone.' Goddammit, I loved walking into my room and finding her in here. She was snooping, but the second my lips touched hers, it was clear what she really wanted. Hell, what we both wanted.

As she sleeps soundly beside me, I shove the blankets off and take note of my Angel's phone on the nightstand. I chuckle quietly. I'm glad that Ella has a friend who watches out for her, but now she has me, and I'm going to make it my mission to make sure she's always safe and always in good hands—my hands—and stays away from that asshole Cameron.

I push to my feet, and nearly fall to my death when I trip on my shoes. "Jesus," I mumble, and glance over my shoulder, not wanting to wake sleeping beauty. My pulse picks up when she makes a moaning sound and curls deeper into her pillow. That's when another thought hits me. Fuck. I grip my hair and tug. I'd have to be a total idiot to not know that she'd given me her virginity last night. The second I felt that barrier, the tightening of her body, two things happened. One, I fucking hated myself for taking it. And two, I realized that I was the guy she gifted it to and I don't take that lightly. The truth is, the freshman hazing game always made me sick, and I would never want to trick anyone into giving me something so precious. Sure there's crazy chemistry between us, but if she'd held on to it this long, it must have meant a great deal to her, right? So why me? Why did she give me something she's been holding on to for so long? I'm not even certain I deserve it, but somehow, some way, I'm going to let her know what it means to me.

I tip toe to the door, and tug it open. The hall is as dark as my room, and I quietly make my way to the bathroom. It's the middle of the night and I have no idea what time the party died down, I'm just glad the place cleared out. I don't want Ella feeling any kind of shame when she leaves here tomorrow—after I cook her breakfast.

I take care of business in the bathroom, and head back to my room. I shut the door, and snuggle in next to my sweet virgin. Of course, she's not a virgin anymore, but I shouldn't be too hard on myself. She wanted me as much as I wanted her. I slide my hand around her body, loving that she's naked in my bed. I guess she must have tossed off my T-shirt. Unable to help myself, I brush my finger over her nipple, and she makes a cooing sound in her sleep.

My dick instantly thickens, and I'm hoping she's not too sore for another round. "Hey," I whisper into her ear, and she makes a sexy, sleepy sound and turns my way. Fuck, I wish I could turn the light on and see her but at this point it would blind us both. Come morning, however, I plan to look my fill at her beautiful body. I'm about to ask her if she can take me again, or if she's too sore, when her long, sleek arms curl around my neck.

I lean into her, and pull her under my body as my lips find hers for a slow, wake-up kiss. Our tongues tangle, and this time around she tastes like beer. I hadn't noticed that earlier. Probably because I'd been drinking myself, or maybe she got up after I fell asleep and partied a little. Although that does seem out of character for her. As if knowing my body now, and what I'm about to do, she wraps her legs around my back, in much the same way I'd positioned her earlier. She's a fast learner, I'll give her that.

She moans into my mouth and my dick is so hard, I can't wait to get inside her, but I need to make sure she's ready for me. I shift to the side, and run my hands down the sides of her neck, stopping to cup her breasts, and then go lower, until I find heaven. With a gentle touch, I brush her clit, and her moans grow louder. Damn I like how responsive she is. I expected her to be a little sore, but she's not acting like anything hurts, and with the way she's writhing, encouraging me, I dip a finger inside her.

"Yes," she murmurs, her voice a low sleepy murmur that's hard to recognize. Her hips lift and she bucks against my finger, and she's so hot for it, I slide in another. I kiss the soft creamy flesh on her neck and go lower to take her nipple into my mouth. Her hands curl through my hair and she arches into me. Her moans grow louder, unabashed, wanton, without any sort of shyness, and I swear to God, it's the nicest sound I've ever heard.

"Fuck yeah," I say. "Take what you need. You are so sexy when you let go." I nibble on her hard buds, and a whimpering cry fills the air. My God, I'm damn near ready to explode just from seeing her like this, from giving her pleasure. In no time at all, her hot pussy quivers around my fingers as she climaxes. She clenches tightly, her hot heat dripping down my palm. My blood boils, as one thought fills my mind—*get your cock inside her.*

Her spasms stop and I pull my fingers from her pussy, to grab a condom from my nightstand. I rip into the condom, and in the dark I sheathe myself. Once I'm suited up, she pulls me to her, and widens her legs for me as she cups my ass, to pull me inside. I push inside, and as she moves her hips, something tugs at me, something that is just out of reach.

Ignoring that one brain cell trying to tell me something, I fuck the shy girl who had enough balls to show up at the party after we all heard her private conversation. I totally admire her grit. What will the guys think when they find out I fucked her? Not that I care. Well, maybe that's not entirely true. If she's going to be my girl, I want them to like her.

My girl.

Fuck, maybe I'm getting ahead of myself. But I'll think about that later. Ella pulls my mouth to hers and I kiss the hell out of her. Our mouths eat at each other like we're starved, and she nibbles on my lip, hard enough to leave it bruised and swollen. Wow, what has gotten into her. She's a little wilder, a little more brazen in her half-awake state. I don't hate it. It's just different, that's all.

I slide in and out of her, my balls tight, eager for release as she meets each thrust, with a hard one of her own. I want to go slow, want to take it easy on her in case she's sore but that doesn't seem to be what she wants. Long nails scrape over my back, a little harder than she did earlier, and once again, something niggles in the back of my brain.

Taking me by surprise, she pushes on my chest, and rolls me under her. All right, I can get behind this, or rather under this. She sits on my dick, and I grip her soft round hips as she lifts herself on and off of my fat dick, riding me like I'm her damn stallion.

"That's it," I growl and cup her breasts, squeezing her nipples with my fingers. She throws her head back, her hair spilling over her shoulders as sensations pool between my legs. "I'm close," I say, my voice rough and desperate. She makes a whimpering sound and falls forward. Her teeth tug my lower lip as she gyrates, rubbing her clit on my pelvis, and I slide a finger between our bodies to help her along.

"Landon, yes," she cries out, her voice low and full of need as lust pounds in my ears, making it hard to hear anything clearly. She moves against me, and I let out a deep groan, barely able to hold on. She sits up a bit, and runs her hands over my chest and stomach like she can't get enough of me, and I fucking love it. Intense pleasure spreads through me, and I wish I could have tasted her again. I want her sweet flavor on my tongue. I want to taste her in class tomorrow, and after practice. I want to taste her until I can have her again, because dammit, I want more than a one-night hook up. I just pray to fuck she wants the same, otherwise our tutoring sessions are going to be pretty damn awkward.

Her muscles squeeze around my cock, and I wonder what the fuck is wrong with me, because I can usually hang on a lot longer. But none of those girls were Ella. I know she's special, and I'm the luckiest goddamn guy in the world to have this night with her. The first of many, I hope.

"Oh my God," she cries out, loud enough to wake Brady, since he's just on the other side of the damn wall. He's likely out cold though, and probably has some girl in his bed. Unlike me, he doesn't mind sleepovers, and come morning there could be more than just one girl exiting his room. Like I said, we're man whores, and some of us are far too proud of that, but Ella could definitely make me change my ways.

I slide my hands around her waist, as an orgasm rips through me, and I clench down on my jaw as I ride out the pleasure. I gasp for breath, and her breathing seems just as labored as she falls over me, resting her cheek against my chest. My heart pounds against her face, and she makes a soft, sigh of contentment as she circles my nipple.

We stay in that position until I grow flaccid, and I roll her to her side and pull out. "Give me a second," I say and tug off my condom. That's when my damn heart comes to a roaring halt. Fuck, the rubber broke. Panic invades my gut. I never have sex without a condom, and I've never had one break before. Jesus, I hope she's on the pill. She was a virgin so I know she's clean. I'm clean too.

I dispose of it, and wipe myself down. I grab a few tissues for Ella, and she's on her back when I slide in next to her. I wipe her clean and her soft breathing sounds curl around me. I toss the tissues into the garbage can, and she's facing away from me by the time I get back into bed.

"Are you on the pill?" I ask, my voice low, my mouth near her ear.

She goes stiff. "Why?" she asks, her voice husky and low.

"Condom broke. Sorry about that, but I'm clean and I know you're clean."

She goes quiet for a long time, so long I wonder if she's okay, and if I need to apologize a million times. I can almost hear her brain working as she sorts through this situation. Then suddenly by small degrees her body relaxes, and she takes my arm and pulls it around her. "We're good," she whispers.

My heart slows. Thank fuck. I am so not ready for kids. It's not that I don't like them. I do. I have nieces and nephews. I just have a career to think about. I spent my whole life working my ass off to get into the NFL, and I can't let one broken condom interfere with my future. Plus, my father would kick my ass all the way from his car dealership to Mom's church. Mom would be mortified, to be honest, and expect me to do the right thing, but once again I'm getting ahead of myself and Ella just told me we were good, and I trust her.

Trust.

Such a funny thing. For the first time in a long time, I get the sense that Ella is with me, not because I'm a baller but because we had a real connection, and she saw the man beneath the uniform. Okay, it's true, I don't know her really, but I want to get to know the girl beneath the overalls more. With that last thought racing around in my brain, I press a kiss to Ella's shoulder, and breathe in her scent. Odd, she no longer smells like sweet vanilla. Maybe she did get up and party, and maybe she showered before crawling back into bed with me. That would be odd, but I don't think Ella is like the girls I'm used to.

As I drift off, I hear a noise from behind me, a door opening, or something. I'm too goddamn tired to peel my eyes open, and maybe I'm just hearing things. It's probably one of Brady's girls trying to find the bathroom. Wait, are those footsteps in my room? I try to turn, I want to turn, but my body just won't move, and that would mean untangling myself from Ella and waking her. After all that sex, she needs her sleep and after yesterday's brutal game, and fucking this gorgeous beauty beside me, I have zero energy to expel.

"Wrong room," I groan in my semi-sleep state. The footsteps come to an abrupt halt, and I take a deep breath, sleep pulling me under.

"What's going on?" Ella mumbles from beside me and I hear a small gasp, or a shriek or some kind of girly sound from behind me. Obviously she accidently stumbled into the wrong room. The steps go completely still, and just when I think we're alone again, something clunks on my nightstand.

"Go away," I say, and Ella groans. "Not you." I clarify and pull her in tighter. A second later, my door slams shut with a little more force than necessary. What the fuck? Oh well, I don't know who it was, nor do I care—and now they know it too.

ELLA

I kick the blankets off and rub my eyes as I glance around the room. As the world comes into view, a knot tightens in my stomach and I bite my damn lip and work to keep the tears from coming.

What have I done?

I put my feet on the floor to ground myself, and my stupid brain races back to last night—to Landon. My God, I had sex with Landon and I liked it. A lot. Too much. While I knew it was just sex, nothing more—and that today I was going to pretend it never even happened—there's a ridiculous, girly part of me that loved the tender way he touched me. I never should have had sex with him. Never. You know what else I never should have done.

Gone back for my phone!

Yeah, then maybe I never would have known he slept with Ivy after me, and I could have lived in happy ignorant happy bliss for the rest of my life. "God," I say and let loose an agonized moan. Peyton pokes her head into my room.

Her smile drops when she takes one look at me. "Oh, shit," she says, and crosses the room. She drops down onto the bed, and crosses her legs, like she always does when she's ready to go into counseling mode. "Do I need to kill him?"

"No, of course not," I say, and work to get myself together, despite the storm waging war in my head and my heart. Why was Ivy in his bed? Did she go in there, or did he go get her after I left? Did he think he was sleeping with her all along? He must have, and the only thing left for me to do now is move to Canada.

Peyton waves her hand in front of my face. "Ella," she says. "Where'd you go?"

"I'm fine," I lie, but it's futile. Peyton knows me too well.

"Did you not like it?"

"I liked it, I guess. I just...look it was a one-night thing. No biggie."

"So the rumors are false? No biggie?" she nudges me, and I laugh as she tries to lighten the mood.

"The rumors are true," I say. "Although I have nothing to compare it to."

She takes my hand into hers and gives it a squeeze. "You really like him, huh?"

"Nope," I say quickly. Too quickly. "He's a baller and you know how I feel about those guys." My stomach tightens as a measure of guilt moves through me. Is Jacob looking down on me with disgust for sleeping with a guy who jumped straight into bed with my sister afterward? Honestly, he's not done anything to prove he's different from any other jock.

Ugh, I just don't know what to think anymore, and while I don't keep secrets from Peyton, I can't bring myself to say out loud that Landon screwed my sister after screwing me, and that there is a ninety-nine percent chance he thought I was Ivy to begin with.

But you know what is worse than any of that? I knew it, too, I knew there was a chance he didn't know it was me, and I slept with him anyway. What kind of person does that make me? As that knot in my stomach expands, punches into my lungs, I suddenly can't get air. I swallow hard, grip the bed sheets, and work to look normal as Peyton continues to stare at me.

"I need a shower," I say and jump up. The second I do, muscles I didn't know exist tighten, a reminder of the way Landon used my body last night.

"Are you sure you're okay, Ella?"

My muscles bunch under her watchful eye as I grab clean clothes, hug them to my chest, and turn to her. "It's like this. I wouldn't have slept with him if I didn't like something about him, but neither of us were looking for anything more. I had sex, finally got rid of my pesky virginity, and now I'm ready to move on."

"I actually thought there could be have been something more between the two of you. I thought he was different from the others."

"I know you did, but he's no different from any other jock, Peyton." Somewhere deep inside, I thought that too. I mean, I did sleep with him. "Believe me when I say that."

She stares at me for a long moment, and I hold my composure the entire time. Go me. "Okay," she finally says. "Go get your shower. I'll put on the coffee. I have an early meeting with my prof this morning."

"Thanks," I say and make my legs move at a regular pace as I leave the room, when all I want to do is run and lock myself in the bathroom and cry for a few hours. *Get yourself together, girl.* I fill my lungs, and square my shoulders as I dart down the hall, berating myself for my ridiculousness. I'm a college senior for god's sake. Not some giddy high school freshman lusting after the star football player.

I jump into a hot shower, soap up my hands, and wash all traces of Landon from my body. What is it going to take to wash him from my brain? I slide my hand between my legs, and touch my tender sex. I lightly stroke myself, and close my eyes, as memories of last night bombard me. I take a deep breath, and brush my clit. Maybe I'll go out and sleep with someone else. Now that I know how great sex is, and that there is nothing wrong with a girl taking what she needs. Yeah, maybe that will help wipe Landon from my brain. I might have to film him on the field, but that doesn't mean we ever really have to talk or cross paths again. That's my last frat party, for sure.

With a new plan forming, even though I have no desire to crawl between the sheets with anyone else—I wash my hair and body, then turn the shower off. Twenty minutes later, I open the bathroom door fully dressed, make-up free, and with my hair in a braid. I steal one last look at myself in the mirror. Today I look nothing like my sister, and for that I'm happy.

I step into the kitchen and Peyton hands me a cup of coffee. "Have I told you how much I love you?" I take a much-needed sip, as she shoves her computer into her bag and tosses it over her shoulder.

"Lunch later?"

"Coffee shack?"

She blows me a kiss. "Have a good one." She steps out into the sunshine, and I'm grateful she's not pushing for details of last night. But seriously how am I going to face Landon… how am I going to face Ivy? I don't even know if my sister knows that I was in Landon's bed before her. Would it matter?

My phone pings and I glance at it, my heart in the vicinity of my throat. I steal a glance at the screen, see that it's just an alert, and can't quite figure out why I thought it could be Landon. He doesn't have my number. Unless his coach gave it to him for our tutoring session that start later today.

Oh. My. God.

How could I have forgotten that?

Yup, looks like it's a relocation to Canada after all.

I sip my coffee, grab a muffin from the counter, and shove my laptop into my bag. A few minutes later, I'm weaving my way between students and racing to class. I take my usual seat near the front and set my laptop in front of me.

"Hey," a voice says from the aisle, and I don't need to look up to know it's Landon. Honestly, I could smell his freshly show-ered skin long before he spoke. I fiddle with my bag, stalling for a second to pull myself together, and cast a quick glance his way.

"Hey," I return, and resist the urge to pat myself on the back. Way to go, Ella. *You totally sounded casual.*

He scratches his head, his eyes narrow, almost looking confused as his gaze moves over my face. I recognize that pained look. It's the same one he gave me yesterday when I called myself a nerd.

"This seat taken?"

What the hell. Why is he sitting by me? He's the guy who always tucks himself away in the back, and probably sleeps through class. There I go again, judging football players. I shouldn't jump to conclusions. When it comes to them man-whoring, no jumping needed. I saw firsthand that this one at least sleeps around. I still have a sour taste in my mouth from seeing him in bed with my sister. Equal amounts of anger and disgust race through me, and I remind myself that I shouldn't be feeling anything. He isn't mine to judge, and I'm just another stupid girl who knew what she was getting herself into when I entered his bedroom, and stayed.

"Doesn't look it to me," I say in my most bored voice.

He plunks down next to me, and I stare at him. Did he think that was an invitation?

"What?" he asks, and scrubs the scar under his eyes. It should distract from his looks, yet it only makes him hotter.

"How did you get that?" I ask, instead of telling him what I really think of his stunt last night. Honestly, I have no idea how today is going to play out. Do I just pretend last night never happened? Is he going to do the same, or maybe he's not pretending at all, because well, he thought he was sleeping with Ivy? This is so messed up.

"This?" he asks and rubs it.

I take in his brutally handsome face, his hard features and as much as I don't want it to, my body reacts. My damn nipples pinch tight and an ache spreads through my body, settling deep between my legs. What the hell has he done to me? I've never gone from zero to deliriously aroused in five seconds flat in my entire life, let alone with a guy I hate. Okay, I don't hate him. I can't hold sleeping with Ivy against him, especially if he thought it was her all along.

"Yeah, that?" I ask, and take in the darkening of his already dark eyes. Did I hit a sore spot or something? "Never mind, it's not my business."

"I got this at the movie theater. Helping some people," he says, and there's nothing in his voice to suggest he's lying.

"Helping them with what?"

He turns from me, and digs out his computer and I can't help but think there is something he doesn't want me to see. "From getting hurt," is all he says, and opens his laptop.

I turn back to mine, his huge body crowding me, his closeness and scent overwhelming my emotions. I steal another look at him, and he's rubbing his face, like he's in total freaking agony. Damn, I should have just come right out and brought up last night. What was I to say though? *Oh, hey it was me you were fucking, not Ivy. Hilarious, right?*

Nope, not hilarious at all.

He angles his head, and his dark eyes meet mine. I tear my gaze away, and stare straight ahead as the professor takes up position in front of us. Concentrating takes all my effort as Landon's eyes drill into the side of my head. I finally turn to him.

"Is there something you want to say?" I murmur, as my entire body stiffens. God, did I really just put him on the spot like that? Yeah, I did because not knowing is killing me here.

"Yeah, actually," he says, his voice a low whisper. "You want to come to my place later?"

My heart leaps. He knows. He knows it was me. Why then, did he sleep with Ivy afterward? Honest to God, I feel like I need another shower just thinking about that. "Uh," I begin. How do I answer him? What do I say?

"So, you know, you do your tutoring gig and help me study for next week's test. I really need to pass."

My heart stops beating, and my blood drains. I guess he doesn't know. If he did, he'd say something right?

You're not saying anything either, Ella.

"Or we could go to your place, or wherever you prefer." He shrugs his broad shoulders and I try not to act like a love-struck teen. "I only suggested my place because Brady won't be home."

"Fine, we can go to your place," I say. What the hell is wrong with me? Why would I want to return to the scene of the crime? Not that a crime was committed, I realize that, it just feels like he betrayed me. I must be a damn masochist for agreeing to this. "If that's what you want."

"I want to show you my collection of movies. I never got the chance to last night," he says, his eyes moving over my face, assessing me, and I do my damndest to keep my features neutral, even though it feels like someone is filleting me from the inside out.

I guess he was looking for a movie partner, after all.

"Yeah, sure," I say as the room spins before my eyes. I take a breath, and turn my focus back to the prof again. He's looking my way and I straighten myself in my seat. I'm sure he's wondering why I'm sitting next to Landon. The prof looks away from us and continues to talk about Mark Twain, and I make notes on my laptop. Landon sits there like a deer in the headlights, like he can't even figure out what he's supposed to be taking notes on. Things move fast in college, but how he can be failing English when we're not even one month into the semester is a bit baffling to me. Nevertheless, I'll get him caught up tonight, and hopefully that's all it will take.

The ninety-minute class drags on, and it feels like I've been to war and back by the time it lets out. I pack up quickly, and I'm about to slip away when he gives my braid a little tug.

"What's your hurry?"

"I have to be somewhere," I tell him and clutch my phone. He pries it from my hands. "Give that back."

"I will, just putting my number in." His cell rings, which means he now has my number.

He hands it back, takes my backpack from me, and easily slides it onto his shoulder. I hold my hand out, wanting it back, and glare at him.

"I'm capable of carrying my own bag."

He gives me a casual shrug and starts walking. "And I'm capable of carrying it, so what's your point?"

"Give it back, Landon."

"I'll give it back when we get where you're going," he says and walks out of the auditorium.

"Landon," I practically shout, and hurry after him. When I reach the hall, none other than Ivy is standing there. Landon goes perfectly still when she goes up on her toes and kisses him. My backpack slides from his shoulder and I'm not sure if he did it on purpose or not.

"There you are," Ivy says. "I woke up and you were gone."

He clears his throat, and as I pick up my bag, he says, "Yeah, I uh, had class."

"I know. Brady told me where to find you." Ivy turns my way, and gives me one of her dazzling smiles. "Hey sis," she says. "I love your hair like that."

I instinctively grab my braid. "Thanks."

Her smile is bright and genuine. "Now that you dyed the front blonde, we look alike again."

"Yeah, we do," I say, my gaze sliding to Landon's.

"You better dye it back or people will start mixing us up like when we were young," Ivy advises with a laugh.

"We wouldn't want that to happen, would we?" I say.

Ivy sidles up to Landon. "Nothing good can come from that." She winks at me. "Am I right, or am I right?"

I nod in agreement. "Oh, you're right."

Nothing good can come from that. Nothing good at all. Yeah, losing my virginity to a guy who thought I was someone else, and even though I knew there was a possibility he thought I was Ivy, I still went along with it.

Yeah, I'm not really seeing a good side to that.

8

LANDON

I am so goddam confused.

My gaze follows Ella as she walks away, her steps fast, like she can't get away from me quick enough. Last night, I had a few beers, but it was Ella in my bed, not Ivy. At least the first time. I'm sure of it. I have to be. Right? Things felt different the first time, then under the stark reality of morning, when I pulled Ella into my arms, only to discover it was Ivy, the world shifted beneath me.

Yet if it was Ella, wouldn't she have said something? Wouldn't she have... Oh, God, I just don't know. It had to be her, right? I wanted to bring it up, wanted her to bring it up. When she stayed quiet, I just didn't know how to broach the subject and if I was wrong...

Fuck me.

"Are you going to answer me?" Ivy asks, and puts her hand on my face, turning me until I'm staring at her.

"What?" I ask.

She gives an exaggerated sigh. "Are you going to walk me to class? Where is your head today, Landon?" she teases.

"Uh, yeah, sure," I say, and she slides her hand into mine as we move down the hall. My heart crashes harder in my chest, and the hall blurs around me as my mind goes back to last night, to the incredible way Ella felt beneath me. It had to be her.

"What is the matter with you, Landon?" Ivy says and tugs on my arm. "Are you still thinking about last night?"

"Yeah," I say. Not a lie. I am thinking about last night, and wondering what the hell really happened and who I was with. How fucked up is this? She gives me a sly grin full of mischief. Funny, I always found her attractive, always liked her. We got along as friends and I would have loved this kind of attention —two days ago. Before I realize what is going on, she pulls a key out of her pocket, unlocks a door and drags me in. "Where are we?" I blink, and try to see around the dark room.

"Back stage at the theater," she tells me. "I have my own key. One of the perks of being a star."

I struggle to figure out what's going on. Clearly, I'm clueless like that. Well, not usually. But right now, my mind is preoccupied with Ella, and that confused look on her face when she saw Ivy waiting for us.

"Why are we here?" I ask as my eyes adjust to the darkness.

She pushes her soft body against mine, and wiggles her hips. "You seem stressed and I can't let my man walk around stressed, and I know just how to help you."

I take her shoulders about to move her back so I can exit the room when she slides her hands into my pants, and grips my cock. "Jesus Christ," I hiss through clenched teeth. "Ivy, don't. We can't. I don't want this."

"Shhh," she whispers. "You don't want us to get caught do you?"

She strokes my dick and the traitorous prick thickens, grows beneath her small expert hands. "There you go," she says, delight in her voice as she caresses the length of me dipping into the slit or my pre-cum and using it for lubrication. I grip her shoulders, wanting to push her off me, when she drops to her knees, and in seconds flat has my cock in her mouth. She sucks me deep, expertly, and my head falls back, hitting the wall.

I need to stop this and I need to do it now.

"Ivy," I groan, and she takes me deep down her throat. What the fuck? "Please," I say and that seems to encourage her, when I'm really begging her to stop. I need her to stop. I need to figure out a way to get her off my dick without her biting the damn thing off.

I grip her shoulders, but she won't budge. Ivy sucks harder, knowledgeably, and cups my balls with the perfect amount of pressure and before I know it, I'm spurting into her mouth like a goddamn teenager jacked up on hormones.

Fuck. Fuck. Fuck.

Ivy goes back on her knees, and grins up at me as she wipes her mouth with the back of her hand. "Someone was needy," she says.

I take a few fast breaths, hating myself right now as I zip up my pants, and pull her to her feet. "Why did you do that?" I ask, my voice a harsh whisper.

She blinks at me and for a second I feel like a total prick. I slept with her last night—maybe twice—and I should not be treating her this way at all. No excuses.

She sags against me. "Better?"

"Ivy," I say breathless. "We shouldn't—"

"Of course, we should and you can't tell me you didn't like that, Landon." She licks her lips, the proof that I liked it glistening right there at the side of her mouth, and my stomach drops. I am the biggest asshole in the world. "Now, I need to get to class before I'm late. Walk me?"

I grip my hair and tug, hating myself. Christ, I'd kick my own ass if I could. "Yeah, sure. Uh, wait," I say. Fuck, I'm not a guy to take without giving, and this is all fucked up but...fuck.

"I'm good. For now," she says. "Tonight, however."

We step outside and guilt weighs me down as I glance up and down the hall searching for Ella, I don't want her to see me coming from the room with her sister. Ella and I aren't a couple, yet the guilt I feel is real. I'm repulsed at what just happened, because I like Ella and I like to think I'm a one-woman kind of guy.

I walk down the hall, and fist pump a few guys from the team, and note the surprised look in their eyes as their gazes go from me to Ivy. They're not the only ones who are surprised. I'm surprised. Ivy stops outside the auditorium door, goes up on her toes and presses a kiss to my lips.

"Later, babe," she says, and gives a shake to her jean-clad ass before disappearing inside. I stand there for a second longer, my brain not working so great. Someone bumps me from behind and it sets me in to motion. I absently head down the hall until I reach my class. The next few hours go by slowly, as

I sit in class but take in nothing the prof is saying. I'm going to have to ask Ella about last night. I fucking need to know what truly went down in my bedroom last night.

Once my day is finished, I head to the locker room, change into my gear and walk onto the field for practice. I search for Brady, and he comes running up behind me and jumps on my back.

"You disappeared early last night, dude."

"Yeah." I shrug him off.

"Heard you were with Ivy."

"Wow, you guys gossip like a bunch of old women."

He circles me, and narrows his eyes. "What the fuck?" Clearly he's picking up on my mood.

I kick the ground with my cleats. "Listen, you saw Ella there last night, right?" I ask, and he gives me a look like I might have taken a toke from the wrong pipe.

"Uh, yeah we all did. You and I had a conversation about her, remember?"

"Okay, just checking." Good to know I'm not losing my mind or hallucinating.

He puts his hand on my shoulder. "What's going on? I haven't seen you this stressed since..." He lets his words fall off. We don't talk about the incident that left my face scarred.

"Fuck," I say. "I think I slept with Ella and Ivy both last night." I put my hand up, palm toward him, to forestall what I know is coming next. "At different times, but now I'm not sure of anything."

Brady continues to stare at me. "Dude, you're not making any sense."

"My room was dark, and I walked in and found Ella there." I scrub my face. "At least I think it was Ella. Yeah, I'm sure it was. Today, though she's acting like it never happened and I woke up with Ivy in my bed." Brady gives a low slow whistle. "Yeah, I know," I say. "Fucked."

"That's about as fucked as it gets. You're going to have to talk to Ella."

"She's coming over tonight to help me study. You still going out with your Dad for dinner?"

His face scrunches up. He and his dad don't get along, and his dad puts him under a tremendous amount of pressure to make it to the big leagues.

"Yeah, you have the place to yourself. If dinner ends early, I'll go hang out with the guys."

I nod. "Thanks." The coach blows his whistle.

"I'll be okay, Landon. You get this all figured out. Ivy though, hey. I guess she marked you as this semester's boy toy."

"Looks that way. Didn't even think I was her type."

"Don't let the scars concern you. Girls dig them." He touches his flawless face. "Thought about giving myself a few."

I laugh, and throw my arm around him. "You don't want to ruin this pretty-boy face, Brady."

He fake punches my gut as we walk to the coach, and for the next hour we practice. I'm a sweaty mess when we finish, and stay in the shower for an extra minute, thinking about Ella as I scrub my skin clean.

Back at home, I search the fridge and decide to whip up some pasta. I pull the ingredients out and my phone buzzes. My pulse leaps, hoping it's Ella. I pray she hasn't changed her mind on tonight. I swipe my phone from my backpack, and frown at Ivy's message.

Ivy: What time should I come over? You know you owe me.

Me: I actually have to study tonight. Need to pass English or I'll get kicked off the team.

Ivy: Well that sucks. Want me to help you study?

Me: No, Coach found a great tutor for me. I'm good.

She begins to text back, and for a long time I watch the three dots. Her message must be a long one.

Ivy: Raincheck?

Me: Yeah, talk soon.

I guess whatever it was she was going to say, she must have changed her mind. I run my fingers over my phone, and before I can think better of it, I shoot a text to Ella.

Me: Hungry?

I wait a long time, and I'm about to toss my phone, figuring she was either busy or wasn't going to answer, when her text pops up.

Ella: This is why you wanted my number? To check on my appetite?

I grin. Is Ella playing with me? I'm not sure but I'm going to play along.

Me: You're tutoring me tonight. I don't want you hangry. I have sisters, and that never turns out well for me.

Ella: No worries. I always keep granola bars and juice packs in my bag. I won't be hangry.

Me: Ah, to be twelve again. Seriously though, I'm making pasta.

Ella: Carbs, mmm, my favorite.

Me: I knew you weren't like those other girls who only eat salads.

Ella: Are you calling me fat, L?

Fuck. She just called me L. I grin, liking that.

Me: No, I like to keep my balls intact, that's all.

Shit, shit, shit. Why did I bring up my balls?

Ella: Now you're saying I'm a ball buster?

I laugh out loud at that, relieved I hadn't offended her.

Me: You're perfect, E.

I wait a long time, my stomach tight, my breath hissing from my lungs. Did I just blow this?

Ella: Will this pasta be edible?

Me: Only one way to find out. See you in thirty minutes.

Three dots appear, like she's writing a long message and Jesus, I can't believe how fast my heart is racing at the thought of her coming here, of seeing her again. I can't believe Ella is still going to come over, especially after the look on her face when Ivy wrapped herself around me this morning. That thought gives me pause. Truthfully, with a career in the NFL on the line, I shouldn't be involved with any girl. I should be studying, and avoiding any kind of distraction, and that's exactly what Ella is. A distraction. I have no idea why I am pulled toward her, or what it is about her that fascinates me. She's different from the girls in our circle, and I like that about her. Okay, maybe I did sleep with her, maybe I didn't, but either way, it's time to move past that and sharpen my focus on my schoolwork. As much as I hate to admit it, there can't be anything between us, especially after what happened between Ivy and me in the theater. Fuck. That sort of cemented my relationship with Ella right then and there. I don't want to hurt Ella. I won't, which means we can only ever be friends, despite the insane tension between us.

Ella: Later, L.

I drop my phone and stare at it, a stupid grin on my face as I read over our messages. A car horn blaring outside and pulls me back, and I walk into the living room and turn on the music. I head to my bedroom, and stop when I find my bed unmade, having left Ivy in it this morning. I had dressed in the dimly lit room, and ran out like the house was on fire. I'm about to pull the covers up when I notice drops of blood on the sheet.

Shit.

I sink down onto the mattress, and exhale a long breath. Fuck me. Is that Ella's blood, because she gave me her virginity? Shit, I am so not worthy of that gift, and seeing those droplets convince me a little more that it was her in bed with me. Why is she acting like it never happened? Is that what she wants? To just pretend nothing happened, because she doesn't want anything more from me?

I tug the sheets off, toss the comforter back on the bed, and put the sheets in the washer. I go back to my room to change into a clean pair of jeans and a polo shirt that's been in the closet for ages. I'm not much of a collar guy, but I want to dress up for Ella.

I hurry back to the kitchen, and get the alfredo sauce cooking, suddenly grateful that my mother made her kids responsible. We all took turns cooking, and over the years, I've gotten pretty good at it. I check my watch, and get the water boiling when someone raps at the door. My heart leaps into my throat and I work to calm myself. I rinse my hands, and hurry to the door. The second I pull it open and find Ella standing there in a pair of denim overalls, with a daisy on them, I lose my ability to speak. My God, could she be any more adorable? Her long hair is tucked under her ball cap, her freshly scrubbed face makeup-free, and I know in an instant I want to be more than friends with her.

Fuck me.

9

ELLA

"Hi," I say, and stand there trying to remember how to breathe as I take in the nice way Landon cleans up. Unable to help myself, I blatantly admire everything about him, from his scarred face, to the way his polo hugs his shoulders, right down to the loose-fitting jeans. The man has his own gravitational pull, and it's all I can do to stop myself from leaning in. I take in his bare feet, his cute toes, and I swear to God my ovaries just clenched. What the hell is it about a guy in jeans and bare feet that gets to me? Honest to God, I have the strangest fetishes.

"Hi," he responds after a long moment—like he'd forgotten how to talk—as he stands there staring back at me, his dark, haunted eyes a mixture of confusion and angst. Wait, is he having second thoughts on dinner, or me tutoring him? Clearly, he's with Ivy now, and over the last couple of hours, after a few hard lectures, I came to terms with that.

Aren't you tired of conceding to your sister, Ella?

I cringe as that inner voice taunts me. The truth is, Landon and I are from very different circles and Ivy is more suitable for him, anyway. When she slept with him, she didn't know I liked him, so how can I hold it against her? I'm not saying I don't want something with him. I'm not saying I do, either. Besides, I'm not supposed to even like football players, and the fact that I do fills me with an incredible amount of guilt.

But now, as I stare at God's gift to women, I realize we had one night of hot sex. He might not know it was me, but I'll never forget that it was him. From here on out, we can only be friends—and maybe he doesn't even want that. As that reality sinks in, I take a small step back and my knees wobble as I search for the handrail. His hand instantly reaches out and snatches my arm to pull me back. My body collides with his, and his hardness mashed against my softness is a clear reminder of the way he touched me last night.

"Careful," he warns, his warm breath washing over my face. "The railing is loose and I don't want you to fall."

"Oh, thanks." His head dips, and I breathe in the scent of his freshly showered skin. I have no idea what kind of soap he uses, but it's quickly becoming my favorite. His lips linger inches from mine, and if I knew better, if I had one brain cell that worked properly in his presence, I'd step around him, and get straight to our tutoring.

You are just friends.

As I mentally recite that, his head snaps up, like someone just slapped him across the face—or maybe he can read my thoughts—and he backs away from me.

"I hope you like chicken alfredo," he says, his voice husky as he gestures with a nod for me to follow as he heads down the hall toward the kitchen, his bare feet slapping the tile floor.

I kick my shoes off and following him as I rub my stomach, even though he can't see me, and glance at the bare walls. In all the years they've had this house, they don't have a single picture up. The place really needs a woman's touch—it just won't be mine.

"It's only my favorite."

I follow behind him and try not to stare at his perfect ass in those sexy, low slung jeans. It's impossible, so I just go ahead and look my fill. I breathe in the delicious scents when we reach the kitchen and look at the pots on the stove.

Trying for casual, two friends about to have dinner together, I grin. "I'm impressed, Brooks."

He smiles back at the use of his last name, and gives me a little nudge with his shoulder. "You should be, Holmes." I pull a baguette from my backpack, and he glances at the brown paper bag. "That had better be homemade."

I laugh at that. "Sorry, it's not. If you don't want it," I make a move to shove it back into my bag when his hand snakes out to grab it. His fingers brush mine, linger for a moment, and my damn traitorous body tingles from the top of my head to the tips of my toes. He pulls the bread from my hand fast, like his hand was on fire, and puts it on the counter. Alrighty then. No touching. I get it. He's with Ivy now.

"Point me in the direction of the knives and I'll cut this up." He pulls a knife from the drawer, and hands it over. "Cutting board?"

He produces a cutting board and I go to work on the bread as he drops the pasta into the boiling water, and stands beside me, watching me carefully. My body tenses, so aware of the man beside me and the way he's tracking my every movement. I shift, a little uncomfortable under his inspection.

I cast him a fast glance. "Can I ask you something?" I begin and this time his entire body goes stiff. What? Is he worried I'm about to bring up last night? Does that mean he knows it was me?

"Yeah, sure." He shoves his hands into his pockets, pulling his jeans down even more, and my synapses fire erratically at the sexy sight. How the hell does he expect me to carry on a conversation when he looks so damn slurpalicious—as Peyton would say?

The fresh scent of the still warm bread reaches my nostrils, and I poise the knife over the remainder of the loaf. "How well do you know Cameron Reid?"

His eyes darken, and his chest rises and falls with each breaths. There is a dark, warning look in his eyes when he asks, "Why?"

"He texted me."

"Stay away from him. He's trouble."

I shrug. "He seems nice, and I'm a big girl, Landon. I can make my own decisions." Why the hell am I bringing up Cameron? Is there a part of me that wants to see if he'll react? God, have I become that girl?

His knuckles crack as he fists his fingers. "My sisters would tell me to mind my own business too, but I wouldn't want any of them around Cameron either. Believe me, I'd go to great lengths to prevent it." He grabs a wooden spoon and stirs the pasta and I like this protective side of him. "Did you give him your number?"

I cast him a fast glance, and I still the knife so I don't cut myself. "I don't even know how he got my number."

"Well, it wasn't me, if that's what you're wondering."

I shake my head. "No, I didn't think that." We both go quiet for a moment, then I break it by replying, "He asked me if I wanted to go to the Growler and get a drink. I told him I was tutoring tonight."

"Good, stay away from him." The muscles along his jaw ripple as he clenches down. Does he even know he has that tic when he's angry about something?

"What don't you like about him?"

He grabs two plates from the cupboard and puts a strainer in the sink. "He's a fucking man-whore Ella."

My shoulder stiffen at the harshness in his voice, and I resist the urge to say, pot meet kettle. "You really don't like him huh?"

He leans against the counter. "It's more than that. I've watched him chew girls up and spit them out, just for the sport of it and believe me, you're just his type."

"What does that mean?" I ask, lifting my chin in a defensive move. How am I some guy's type? And speaking of types I'm not sure Cameron is mine or even that I have one. One thing though, Landon never seemed like Ivy's type to me.

"He likes the innocent ones. Bedding one is like a conquest to him. When he gets what he wants, he moves on." He opens his mouth like he wants to say more, then shuts it again.

"Sounds like a lot of guys I know, actually."

"Yeah, well at least a girl knows what she's getting into when she's with a footballer," he states, owning up to the fact that he too is a man whore. "We're pretty upfront about that. Cameron isn't. He leads them on to believe he's totally into them, then dumps them when he gets it. He's a sick fuck like that."

"Oh, I get it, and I'm not judging, Landon. I was just wondering what you knew about him."

"Just please tell me you'll stay away from him. If you don't believe me, ask Ivy."

My throat tightens at the mention of my sister, and I ask, "You have sisters too, huh?"

"Yes, and all four of them are a huge pain in my ass." He laughs and it lightens the mood. He goes quiet, like he's remembering a happy time and it's clear how much he loves his family.

"You're all close?"

"Yeah, we are. I'm the baby brother." He shakes his head. "You wouldn't believe the things they did to me, Ella. I mean, we're talking dressing me up like I was one of their dolls. Humiliating, even at three years old."

I laugh at that, and a new kind of comfort falls over us as he laughs with me. "That's pretty scarring."

"A lifetime of damage," he agrees with a grin.

"Tell me," I say, and channel Peyton as I go all counsellor on him. "Have you found yourself wanting to get into a pair of panties or a dress?" I hold my hands up, palms out, and wish to God I hadn't brought up panties. *What is wrong with you, girl?* "Not that there is anything wrong with that."

He laughs hard, then one brow lifts, mischief in his dark eyes. "Are you really asking me if I like getting into panties?"

Oh shit. I shake my head fast. "Wait, I didn't mean it like that." A loud groan crawls out of my throat, and heat moves into my cheeks. He lightly touches my arm, and his smile is playful when our eyes lock. "Foot meet mouth," I blurt out.

"For the record no, I don't wear girl's clothes, but I'm not opposed to seeing them in mine."

I nod, and my mind races back to last night, to when I slid into the shirt he was wearing to keep warm. I still have that shirt, and have no intentions of giving it back.

"Your sisters sound awesome," I say, bringing the conversation back to neutral ground.

"You and Ivy aren't close, are you?"

"Not really. When we were kids, we were close ,but as we got older we grew apart. Other than our looks, we're very different." I crinkle my nose, and shrug. "I'm guessing I'm not telling you anything you don't already know, though."

"Your looks are different, too. I can tell you both apart easily."

My hand stills and heart leaps. Is he saying he knew it was me last night? Do I dare bring it up and ruin this level of comfort we just achieved?

Ask him!

"Is that how you learned to cook?" I query, as I gesture toward the white sauce simmering on the stove.

Chicken shit.

I shut down that inner voice. "Or did your Mom teach you?"

"Mom and my sisters, actually. I like being in the kitchen, though. It actually de-stresses me."

He tears his gaze away, but not before I catch the storm brewing beneath the surface. I remember my mother once said to me not to judge others, because everyone was going through their own battles. Right now, I can't help but think this man has demons.

"It must be hard to be the golden boy all the time, huh?"

His head lifts, and tormented eyes lock on mine, and hold. "Why would you say that?"

I've obviously hit a nerve with that observation. "You play hard, wanting to win at all costs." My gaze moves over his battlefield scars. "It's like you have something very important riding on that."

"Beautiful and smart," he mumbles as his shoulders relax. "I can't let my team down," he says and then in a much lower voice adds, "Can't let my dad down."

I reach out and put my hand on his. This time he doesn't flinch. No, this time he entwines his fingers with mine, holding them like I could very well be his lifeline. Something passes between us. Warmth and understanding, and I realize that I might have judged him too harshly, and there really might be more to this guy.

"Your folks must be pretty proud of you, Landon, and I promise to help you get your grade up so you don't let anyone down, okay?"

He nods, and the genuine gratitude in his eyes tugs at my heart. "Thanks, Ella. I really appreciate it. I feel like I should do something for you in return."

Oh, he did something for me all right.

"You are. You're paying me to tutor you, remember? And I have my eye on a new camera."

He laughs. "Still...there must be something else I could do to pay you back that doesn't involve money."

Another night in your bed would work.

Cut it out, Ella.

"Nope. I have everything I need," I say, and he frowns and glances at his bare feet like I'd injured him. I grab a plate from his cupboard and lay out the slices of bread. "Butter?"

"Fridge."

He drains the pasta as I open the fridge and search for the butter. "Nicely stocked," I say. "Thought I'd find beer and near empty pickle jars."

"Then you've clearly never hung out with footballers before. We need food. Real food."

I put the bread and butter on the table, and he hands me two glasses filled with water. "I'd offer you alcohol, but studying..."

"Water is perfect." I like that he's taking this seriously. I may have misjudged him after all.

He pulls a chair out from the table. "Have a seat, this will be ready in two seconds."

I drop into the chair and he turns his back to me. I use that time to admire his body as he mixes the pasta into the sauce and plates it. I never stopped to think about the kind of training and work that went into his fitness.

"If football doesn't work, you could always be a chef."

"Football has to work," he says and puts our plates on the table.

"Landon, this looks amazing." He drops down across from me, and I study his face. "How did you get into football, anyway?"

"Sundays were the best days growing up." He smiles as he reminisces. "Like I said, I grew up with four sisters, who were loud and overbearing and dominated the entire house with their makeup, clothes and curling irons, but football, that was my time with Dad. The girls hated it, so on Sundays it was just us guys. Sometimes he'd have his buddies over, and I liked that too. We'd eat crap food, and they'd have beer and sneak me cola. Mom never liked us drinking soda. It made me feel like the big man, a part of something really special, you know?" He grins and I smile, loving that happy memory he has.

"I love that, Landon. He sounds like a great man."

He nods. "Dig in," he says as he reaches for his fork. I do the same and as I slide the pasta into my mouth, Landon's gaze drops to my lips as I take my first bite.

"Mmm, this is so good," I rave, and his chest puffs up, clearly liking the compliment. "Tell me more about you and your dad. Did you guys actually play football together?"

"All the time. His dream was to play in the NFL."

"It never happened?"

"Injury took him out his first year of college."

"I'm sorry."

"Thanks."

I fork more pasta into my mouth, understanding this guy just a little bit better. He can't fail. His dad has pinned all his hopes on his son, and is living vicariously through him—which really is unfair, and it puts undue pressure. He doesn't want to let him down. That's a hell of a lot of pressure.

"Tell me about your mom."

"She's an Anglican minister."

I nearly choke on a noodle. "Your mom is a minister?" I laugh and shake my head. "Here they always say the daughters of preachers are the ones to look out for."

He lifts his chin, all indignant like and says, "I don't think I like what you're insinuating, Ella."

I laugh. "I'm not insinuating anything. I'm just hoping she's praying for you." I take another bite. "Seriously though, I'm guessing you have a lot of expectations to live up to."

"Don't we all. How about you? What was it like growing up with a twin, and how did one love being in front of the camera while the other likes to be behind it?"

I angle my head. "Wow, pretty observant."

He taps his head. "Not all brawn."

I cringe. "I'm so sorry. I was an idiot for saying that."

His perfect lips turn down. "Haven't we moved past that?"

"Thanks, Landon." I smile at him, liking that he's not holding that against me, or any of the other dumb things I said.

"Friends?" He holds his fist out.

"Friends," I agree as we do a fist bump...so very different from how other parts of our bodies bumped last night.

Stop thinking about that.

"Okay friend, answer my question."

I chuckle at that. I'm so surprised at how easy he is to talk to. "I'm not really sure, Landon. I really love movies. I was the one watching Disney over and over again while Ivy was putting on princess dresses and dancing around."

"I guess that's why she's in theater, huh?"

"Yes," I say, and run my finger over the rim of my water glass.

"Did that bother you, Ella?"

"Did what bother me?"

He gives me a second, like he's waiting for me to understand, then spells it out. "I'm guessing she got all the attention."

"I didn't want the attention, though. I loved reading, watching movies, and just sitting back. The limelight was never my thing. It was hers, and she entertained us all. I love that about her, it's just not for me."

"What is for you?"

Not you...unfortunately.

"I want to entertain people in other ways. I want to be a great director, and it's time Hollywood had more women directors, don't you think?"

"Yeah, I agree." His gaze moves over my face, and I see appreciation in his eyes. "You're really different."

Heat once again climbs into my cheeks. "A nerd, I know."

His lips turn up at the corners. "You know, you're cute when you blush."

I put my hand up to my face. "No, I'm not and stop looking at me."

He takes my hand from my face and heat sizzles through me as he runs his thumb over my wrist. "I like who you are, Ella. I like that *you* know who you are, and that you're going after what you want."

That gives me pause. No one has ever said anything like that to me before but it's not entirely true. I'm not going after everything I want.

I tug my hand back. "Thanks, and I like who you are too, Landon. I like that we're friends."

"Tell me about your parents."

I eye him. "Didn't Ivy tell you any of this stuff?"

"No," he says, his voice a little rough as he goes back to his pasta.

I take a big drink of water and eye him for a moment, take in the stiffening of his shoulders. "My parents run an apple orchard in San Francisco Bay. Whenever you bite into a Valley Bloom apple…" I pause and point my thumb at myself. "It comes from our trees."

His eyes go wide. "No way."

"Way."

He shakes his head, staring at me in awe, like I'd just told him how to solve world hunger or something.

"You're a farm girl." It's a statement, not a question.

"Born and bred." I flex my biceps. "How do you think I got these?"

"Impressive, Holmes." He sits back a bit in his chair, and his feet touch mine beneath the table. I ignore the shiver that runs up my leg and settles between my thighs as I take in his face, the way it goes from astonishment to some new kind of understanding.

"Now that you say it, I can see it. Not so much in Ivy, though." His low laugh goes through me as he points a finger directly at me. "But you, Ella. You're definitely the farmer's daughter."

"And you're the preacher's son," I shoot back.

"I think there might be lyrics out there about us." I laugh as he gives me a playful wink and adds, "That's not all we have in common."

"No."

"No. After we finish eating, let's go to my bedroom."

I nearly swallow my tongue. "Why?"

"There's something I want to show you."

LANDON

I slip her backpack over my shoulder and Ella looks almost terrified as I head up the stairs in front of her, which makes me wonder if it wasn't her in my bed last night. But what about the blood on my sheets? Jesus, I have no idea what to think anymore and if she's not bringing it up, I'm not going to either. At least we came to a mutual agreement that we'd be friends, and I like that. I like being friends with this super smart girl who has a mind of her own. She's a breath of fresh air, and as much as I want to be with her, I feel like I can't, not after sex with Ivy, and the whole theater room fiasco.

We reach the landing, and I head to my room. She follows along and stops at the door, peering at me like she can't step over the threshold.

"You need an invitation?" I tease. "You like a vampire or something?"

"Or something," she says with a light laugh that seems forced.

Wanting her relaxed, hell I'd never do anything she didn't want to do, I wave her in. "Come on, have a seat. I don't bite." I point to the chair at my desk and she tentatively walks across my floor and sits in the chair. I drop her backpack beside mine at her feet.

"What...what is this?" she asks, and I practically dive to grab my backpack, but it's too late. She's already touched my good luck charm, and no one is allowed to touch it. Call me superstitious, call me ridiculous. Call me whatever you want, but my keychain ladybug and I go way back. "Landon?" she asks, delight in her eyes as I pocket the toy given to me by my sister when I was a kid, just before I made my first touchdown in Atom football at the age of six. I've had it with me ever since.

"It's nothing," I mutter with a shrug. "Just something I rub... Wait that's not coming out right. I mean."

"No wait, I get it. It's a superstition thing, right?" She blinks up at me, her sweet innocence doing strange things to me.

"Yup, my good luck charm, and no one is allowed to touch it."

She pulls her hands back, and frowns. "I'm sorry I did."

"It's fine."

"For the record, I think it's cute."

"It's not supposed to be cute, Holmes."

"Right," she says, desperately trying to hide a smile, but I'm happy that her mood is lighter and I like seeing this playful side of her. "What I meant to say is it's tough. Ladybugs bite, you know. They pinch too, with their legs, and I heard they can be vicious when there's no food or water nearby."

"Heard all that did you? What are you, a ladybug whisperer?"

She laughs. "I had a fascination with bugs when I was young."

"You're a strange one, Holmes." She arches a brow and I add, "That's not a bad thing."

"So uh, what exactly is it that you wanted to show me." She catalogues the room, her gaze lingering for an extra second on my bed.

I point to my bookshelf, but instead of holding books, behind the closed doors it shelves all my favorite movies. "This is what we have in common." I pull the doors open to display my collection. "I'm a huge movie buff." Her body relaxes slightly. "Maybe one day, I'll have one you directed to add to my collection."

"Hopefully." She stands, and comes over to me, and her scent lingers before my nose as she bends to read the titles. With a soft touch, she lightly runs her hands over the cases. "This is what you wanted to show me, huh?"

"Yeah, and I don't show everyone, so keep this between us."

"Are you sharing secrets with me, Brooks?"

"Which means you owe me one in return."

She laughs at that. "I'm afraid that's not how it works. Seriously though, why is this a secret?"

My mouth gapes open. "Really, Holmes?"

"I don't get it."

"I'm a wide receiver on the football team. I have a reputation to uphold. If the guys knew I liked old classics, even romantic comedies, I'd have to cash in my man card."

"Fine then, your secret is safe with me."

"Good, now it's your turn to tell me one."

She stands up a bit straighter, and takes her hair into her hand. She absently touches her hair, and her gaze leaves me, slides to my bed. After a quick intake of air, she glances at her feet. "Okay, then. If you insist..."

My blood stops flowing, and air seizes in my lungs. This is it, she's finally going to bring up last night. We can finally clear the air, and move forward.

"I stole something once, and I've never forgiven myself."

My heart sinks, partly because she didn't bring up last night, and partly because she looks so sad and lost right now.

I lightly brush my knuckles against hers. "That's a big secret." She nods. "Sounds like it's bothered you for a long time."

"Yeah, and I really don't know why I told you that."

"No one knows?" She shakes her head. "Why'd you do it?"

"I was young, and stupid." She gives a humorless laugh. "Now I'm just older and stupider." I frown at her. Was that a dig about last night?

"What's that supposed to mean?"

"Nothing," she says quickly, and walks past me to the window to glance out when a bunch of car horns blare. She spins around, and sits on the window ledge. "We used to work the farm when we were kids, and we got an allowance for it." A small smile touches her mouth, a happy memory, and my heart squeezes as I watch her blue eyes light up. Such vibrant eyes. The ocean during a crisp fall day. Makes me want to snuggle under the blankets, drink hot chocolate and watch movies. Uh, what was that I said about my man card?

"We were about eight, Christmas was coming, and Ivy still believed in Santa. It's true, we were pretty sheltered on the farm. Anyway, I had my suspicions he wasn't real and all she wanted was this silver glittery lipstick, which was quite dreadful." She rolls her eyes and I laugh hard at that.

"Glittery lipstick. That definitely sounds like Ivy."

"Problem was, Mom never allowed us to wear makeup or lipstick at that age, and Ivy was wishing and wishing, and writing Santa letters. I knew she wasn't going to get it, one because Santa wasn't real, and two Mom never would have bought it for her."

"So you did."

"I saved, but do you have any idea how much those brand name lipsticks from Sugar Lips cost?" Her lips part, like she's totally appalled.

"I don't even know what Sugar Lips is, but I'm guessing pretty pricey." That might be a small lie, because Ella here has sugar lips and damned if I don't want to taste them again.

Don't go there, dude.

"Anyway, I didn't have enough money and I didn't want Ivy to wake up on Christmas morning sad. So..." She shrugs. "I stole it."

"Aren't you the poster girl for fucked up good intentions."

She laughs, and I grin, liking the sound. "That's one way to look at it."

She crosses the room, leans against the footboard.

"What did you want, Ella? What did you want that Christmas?"

Warmth passes over her eyes, and a happy smile touches the corners of her mouth. "For Ivy to be happy."

If I wasn't crazy about this girl already, I would be now. I'm pretty sure I've never met anyone so selfless and the sad thing is, I know Ivy—I like Ivy—but I'm not sure she'd put her sister first like that.

"You're a good sister, Ella."

She nods and pushes off the footboard, moving past me to look over my collection again. "You know, today people stream or download...illegally, and to me that's stealing, which..." She turns to me. "I'll have you know I've never done again." She crouches to look at the movies on the lower shelf. "I like that you have a collection, and don't illegally stream, Landon." She runs her fingers over the cases again. "All the old classics. How did you get into these anyway?"

"My grandmother, actually."

She stands, and smiles. "Really?"

"Look at this one," I say and tug out Casablanca. "I think this was the one that started it all. To be honest, I'm not sure if it was the movies I loved, or the one-on-one time I spent with Gram. I was the only grandson, and I'll admit it, I was sort of the favorite. Everyone loved me."

She laughs and punches me in the arm. "What an ego." As soon as the word ego slips from her mouth, her skin pinkens, clearly thinking of the private conversation we all overheard.

I quickly come to her rescue, considering we've moved past her observation that my ego was as big as my cock. Well, that was more Peyton's statement, but still. "Want to watch?"

"Actually, I do, but we have homework." She scrunches up her nose and points to her backpack.

I frown and I'm about to shove it back in its spot when her arm touches mine. "How about this. We study and once I'm convinced you understand Mark Twain, we can watch."

"Deal."

I set the movie aside and drop to my bed. Underneath the comforter there are no sheets. They're in the washer, washing off the blood. Ella takes her place at my desk, and opens her laptop. "Okay, let's start with studying why Mark Twain is important for all generations."

"Well," I begin and recall what I learned in class. "He was a timeless author, and a cultural icon."

She nods and absently coils her hair around her finger and I wish she'd stop. It makes concentrating harder.

"He was definitely those things, can you tell me why?"

I frown. "Maybe I am all brawn, after all."

"Stop, you are not. We all have our different strengths, Landon. Literature isn't yours, and football isn't mine. I'm not all that fond of math either."

"I'm pretty good in math."

"Then if I start to fail, you can tutor me."

"Deal," I agree.

"Wait, why did you wait until your last year to take English?"

"I didn't. I studied Shakespeare last year." I groan, flip to my back, and put a pillow over my face.

"Why are you torturing yourself with more English Lit again if you already have your writing credits?"

I drop the pillow. "I don't know," I say quickly, and don't meet her eyes. "I guess I'm a glutton for punishment, a masochist." We already shared enough secrets tonight. No need to open up anymore. We're not a couple or anything and she might laugh if I told her I wanted to write a screenplay someday, considering how horrible I am in English. "What were you saying about Twain?"

She eyes me, smart enough to know I'm redirecting and I'm grateful when she doesn't push. She glances back at her screen. "Let me tell you why Mark Twain's stories are important for all generations." She points to my backpack. "Get your computer and start making notes." I do as she says and for the next hour instead of taking notes, I simply listen. Ella has a way of explaining things and making them interesting. She tells me how Huck Finn taught young Americans right from wrong, and the importance of country and friendship. I sit there and take it all in, and I love how passionate she is about the subject. I learn that his book challenged the ideals of the nineteenth century American South. It's fascinating really, and has me wanting to read the book again, to see it from a different perspective. She tells me how it challenged racism, taking anti-racism and anti-slavery stances, why the book was banned and why it never should have been.

When she finally stops talking, I get up and leave the room, and can feel her curious eyes drilling into my back. I come back with a glass of water for her and she gives me a grateful smile.

"Thanks." She takes a big drink. "I was parched."

"I figured. You're the girl who likes to be behind the scenes. I bet you can't even remember the last time you talked so much."

She nods and cocks her head, real concern on her face. "Did you understand all that?"

"Yeah, and I'm going to read the book again." Her sweet smile lights up the room.

"Really?"

"I'd start right now, but we have a movie to watch." I wave the Casablanca case toward her.

She nods eagerly and shifts in her chair to face my big-ass wall-mounted TV.

"Do you want to..." I pat the bed. "It's a bit more comfortable, I think."

"Yeah, sure," she answers tentatively, just as my phone pings. I ignore it, but whoever is trying to get ahold of me is pretty damn persistent.

"Go ahead and answer," she says. "I'll cue the movie, and I'm going to need popcorn, and soda if you have it."

"I have it."

"Your mother allows soda now, does she?" she teases with a sly grin.

"She doesn't know," I say, and Ella laughs out loud.

"I'm guessing there are a lot of things she doesn't know and likely never needs to," she says with a soft laugh that slides over my body as I check my phone to find a message from Ivy.

Shit.

I stare at the phone, my blood draining to my toes. How the hell do I handle this? I glance up and find Ella looking at me, and a jolt of guilt grips my gut.

"Ivy?" she asks, and casually brushes her hair from her face.

"Yeah." I put the phone face down on the nightstand.

She points to the door. "If you two are hooking up, I could go—"

"No." I tap the bed.

"Just for the record," she begins and fusses with something in her bag. "You two are a cute couple."

Shit is this her way of saying there can never be anything between us? That I should go ahead and 'hook up' with her sister, because hooking up with her isn't an option? Wait, didn't I just say, after what happened in that auditorium, I could never be with Ella now? Why the hell am I still holding out hope? I can't. I just fucking can't. Everything about this situation is wrong.

Except what I feel inside.

"Since you look like her, are you saying we'd be a cute couple too?" I ask.

"You know what I mean," she grumbles with an eye roll so hard it nearly gives me a headache. "You two just make sense." She glances at my phone again. "Are you going to get that. She doesn't like to be ignored."

"Come sit. I want to watch the movie with you. That was our plan." She hesitates for a second and I add. "I'll be three minutes making popcorn, so don't go anywhere." I jump from the bed, and she sinks down, adjusting the pillow behind her. But fuck, seeing her on my bed and not being able to put my hands on her is going to be torturous.

I hurry downstairs, make the popcorn and grab two sodas. When I step back into my room, Ella is on my bed, surfing through her phone, a very serious look on her face. My stomach clenches.

"Everything okay?" I ask and stand in the doorway.

Her head lifts and when she presents me with a smile, I nearly abandon all rational thought, toss the popcorn away and jump on her. "Everything is fine," she says, her words smacking sense into me and I shake my head to clear the lust. Her gaze drops to take in my bare feet as I stand at the threshold. "What, waiting for an invitation? You a vampire or something?"

"Or something," I tease, and step into my room, the knot relaxing in my stomach.

"Mmm, smells good." She taps the bed. "We better get this movie going. I have more homework tonight."

In three big strides, I'm across the room and I plunk down beside her, putting the bowl between us, partly so we can share and partly because that way I can't get too close. Who knows what I might try? Asshole that I am.

She hits play on the remote and puts her hand in the bowl at the same time I do. Her gaze darts to mine and for the briefest of seconds, our fingers touch, linger. She blinks, pulls her hand back and stuffs a bunch of popcorn into her mouth, like she's totally unaffected, and the truth is I'm not so sure she is. Or maybe that's just wishful thinking. I shove a handful of popcorn into my face and lean back as the movie starts. But it's hard to concentrate with so much sexual tension taking up space between us. Am I the only one feeling this?

I glance at her, and she's engrossed in the movie, like I'm not even in the room. I guess I am the only one affected and maybe I should go ahead and take her advice and hook up with Ivy. Ella's clearly not interested. That still feels like a douche move, though.

"This part." She sits up a little straighter and her hand lands on my arm. "Ohmigod, Landon, it's my favorite."

I smile at the enthusiasm in her voice. "Mine too. Looks like we do have a lot in common," I say, and she gives me a small smile as she takes her hand back. Soon enough we're chatting, talking about our favorite scenes, making comments on settings and design and the filming, and even the controversy behind the film and the rights. It's fascinating to see her point of view as a cinematography student, and the way she breaks it down as a cinematic performance.

"It's a shame it never did play on Broadway," she says with a sigh.

"Hard to believe it was filmed on a set in Hollywood." She nods in agreement and we both settle in to watch the end. About ten minutes before the movie is over, the door downstairs opens and closes with a bang, and Ella nearly jumps from the bed.

"That's just Brady. He was having dinner with his dad tonight. It doesn't always end well."

Her brows furrow for a second. "I didn't know. I'm sorry to hear that." A brief pause and then, she says, "Do you think he's okay?" She averts her gaze for a second, and glances at the door. Worry lingers in her eyes when she focuses back in on me. Her nose crinkles, drawing my attention to those cute freckles of hers. "I should go." I'm about to reach for her, tell her to stay, when Brady comes busting in.

"I need a drink," he grumbles, then stops dead in his tracks when he sees us. "Shit, sorry, man." He tugs on his hair. "I didn't realize you weren't alone."

"It's okay," Ella says, scrambling off the bed. "I have to get going anyway. I still have some studying to do, and I want to get to bed early tonight."

"I'll walk you back," I say and jump from the bed.

"No, it's okay. It's just a few blocks away." She shoves her computer into her backpack, and puts her phone into the front bib pocket of her overalls.

"Then if it's just a few houses over, I'll walk you."

She's about to protest, and I hold my hands up. "My mother is a minister and I have four sisters. If I didn't walk you and they found out." I stop to do a cutting motion across my neck.

I glance at Brady. "Meet you at the Growler?" He nods. My best bud needs to talk, but I'm guessing he wants me to explain first. I see the questions in his eyes as his gaze goes from Ella to me.

I shake my head to let him know it was nothing. "English," is all I say and he nods, but he knows me well enough to know there is more going on—at least on my part. Ella makes it perfectly clear we're only going to be friends, and I can't disagree with that.

I follow Ella down to the front foyer, and reach around her to pull the door open. My body brushes hers and I'm almost certain she just sucked in a tight breath.

Probably your imagination, dude.

We tug on our shoes, and the night is warm as we step outside, and she goes quiet as we follow the sidewalk from my place to hers, a comfortable quiet around us, except for the cars speeding by and the group of girls giggling on the other side of the street.

"I'm sorry Coach blackmailed you into tutoring me," I tell her, just to break the silence.

She laughs. "It was either that or lose the gig taping the games and my class credit, and there is a camera with my name on it patiently waiting for me to scrape up the dollars."

"Tell me about the camera."

Her eyes go big and I can't help but smile as she swings her arms, completely animated as she talks about some fancy-ass camera. After a few minutes, she practically stops walking. "Ohmigod, I'm boring you aren't I?"

"Not at all. I love hearing about it."

"Liar," she says, and touches my arm. "But about the tutoring, Landon. It's not a hardship. I feel like I shouldn't even be paid for it, because I like that I am able to teach in a way you understand."

"Do I detect a bit of ego?" I tease and give her a little bump, only problem is, she was about to take a step and I totally knocked her off balance.

"Whoa," she shouts and tumbles right into a line of bushes.

"Ella, I'm sorry, are you okay?" I squat down next to her, and she groans. "Are you hurt?"

"Just my pride," she says.

I go to my knees, and look her over. My God, seeing her like this, the light of the moon spilling over her body, fucks me over in so many ways. Her plump lips call out to me, and when she wets them, I nearly lose all ability to focus. I lean in and stop when she speaks.

"I'm going to be pulling thorns from my backside for a week."

"Let me help you up."

"Go slow, please," I give her a little tug and she yelps as we both try to stand. "Wait, stop. Every time you tug, there's a branch that tries to molest me."

Unable to help myself, I laugh, and she laughs with me. "I'm so sorry, Ella. This is my fault."

"Damn straight it is."

"I'll make it up to you. I promise."

"You could start by removing that branch from between my legs. I can't get around it."

I shift my stance, and carefully lift one of her legs to move it around the gnarled branch, and slide my hand up her inner thigh, and try not to remember last night, the way her scent and heat curled around me as I take hold of the branch and snap it. The crack fills the silence around us.

"I think I got it." I reach for her hand again. "On the count of three, I'll pull you up."

We count together and I tug on her hands until we're both standing. I take one look at her and now that I know she's okay, I feel a measure of relief. It's hard to hide the smirk when I see twigs and leaves in her hair.

I pull out a leaf. "Do you need me to do a thorn check?"

She shakes her head. "I'll get Peyton to do it, and there had better not be any bugs in my hair." She hops around a bit, and I can't help but laugh.

"What the hell is going on here?"

We both still when we hear Ivy's voice, and I turn to find her staring at us, and that's when I realize the group of girls across the street are all staring, and some have their phones out. Jesus, they had better not put that up on social media. Ella wouldn't like that. She prefers to be behind the camera, and so help me if they make her the laughingstock, I'll kill them.

"Landon, what are you doing, and Ella, why are you making a fool of yourself?"

"She wasn't—" I begin.

"Liam said you were tutoring Landon tonight. I didn't realize you were putting on a show for him too."

"I'm not, I'm just..." Her words fall off as a beetle or some other bug falls from her overalls, and she bends like she's checking to see if it's okay.

"She fell," I explain. "I was helping her up."

Suddenly everything about Ivy softens. "Ella, are you okay?"

She stands. "I am, thanks."

Ivy looks her sister over and begins to brush the debris off her clothes. "You're a mess. You need to get home and clean up."

"I was just on my way, and I fell."

"So clumsy." Ivy laughs like she's remembering something. "Even as a child you were tripping over your own feet."

Ella stands there staring at her sister, confusion in her eyes. Is Ivy making that up about her tripping over her own feet? "I... uh...better get home," Ella says and glances at her place.

I reach for her. "I'll walk you the rest of the way."

"Landon, she lives right there," Ivy blurts out, and Ella quickly nods in agreement.

"It's fine."

I shake my head. "No, I think I should—"

"I'm a big girl. I can get home by myself." Ivy gives her sister a big smile, and Ella returns it.

I know she lives right there, still... "But I—"

"Landon, come on," Ivy tugs me. "Everyone is headed to the Growler." She turns on the charm, and goes coy as she rubs herself against me. "And you know you owe me, after the fun we had in the theater."

Ella backs up, shrinking into herself. It's something I've seen her do before in Ivy's presence. I glance across the street and the girls who were capturing the fiasco are now gone.

I try to shake Ivy off of me. "Just give me a second, Ivy."

"Nope, it's all good." Ella backs up even more, putting both physical and emotional distance between us. "He's all yours, sis."

"Of course, he is," Ivy says and puts her arm through mine. I stand there, watching her walk away, until she's safely inside her place, shutting herself in, and me out.

ELLA

I close the front door tight, and lean my shoulder against it for a moment. My heart pounds in my chest and stupid, stupid tears press against my eyes. Why the hell am I suddenly so emotional? I must be getting my period, because no way could I be crying over Landon. I already came to the conclusion that we can only be friends, but after tonight, the tutoring, the movie, the shared popcorn on the bed, not to mention my side trip to the bushes...I don't know. All those things somehow brought us closer, created a bond.

Or maybe that's just in my imagination. Maybe he doesn't feel a damn thing for me.

I take a breath to pull myself together and push off the door. Wiping my face with the back of my hand, I walk down the hall to the kitchen. The place is spotless. It was Peyton's turn to clean, and she does a way better job than I do. I drop my bag onto the table and pour a glass of water. Walking down the hall, I glance in Peyton's room but she's not there. She has a shift at the Growler tonight. I guess she'll understand my mood this morning once she sees Landon and Ivy together.

My phone buzzes in my pocket and I tug it out, happy it wasn't damaged in my fall. Speaking of Peyton.

Peyton: Hey, just about to get off shift, do want to grab a drink?

I smile and shake my head. Obviously, she spotted my sister and the man who took my virginity together at the pub.

Me: Going to get to bed early, it's been a long day and you know I hate the Growler.

I don't mention that I'll be digging thorns from my ass for the next twenty minutes or so, or that I watched a movie with Landon, in the very bed he deflowered me in.

Peyton: Just so you know, I'm about to spill a beer on Landon. Sorry, not sorry.

I laugh out loud at that. Leave it to Peyton. No matter what, she's always on my side, always fiercely protective. Seeing Landon at the bar with my sister, after learning I slept with him last night, has no doubt set her off. I'm not about to tell her he slept with Ivy after me, and I saw it with my very own eyes. I wouldn't put it past her to neuter him. She might be studying to become a social worker, but like me, she's a hard-working farm girl at heart, and knows how to use a scalpel during castration.

Me: Don't do that. I know he's there with Ivy. We are just friends.

Peyton: You never come out, Ella. You can't go four years at Kingston and never hit the pub. Come for one drink. Lots of cuties here tonight.

In my bedroom, I stand and look at myself in the mirror. Honestly, I'm a little keyed up and once I hit the bed, I'll stare at the ceiling for hours on end, thinking about none other than Landon. I'm sure of it. What could one little drink hurt? Nothing. It will likely relax me and help me sleep. But seeing Landon with Ivy, that might hurt. *Get over it already. Maybe seeing them together, dancing, drinking and laughing might help. Might be just the thing I need to get over it.*

Me: I'm not interested in any cuties.

Peyton: You know what they say about falling off the horse.

Me: I am not climbing back on anything.

Peyton: (eggplant emoji) Get your butt down here. I'm off in five, and the band is kick ass. You're going to love them, I promise.

Me: Fine, be there in a few minutes.

I set my phone down. Am I really going to the pub for a drink? I usually avoid that place. It's nothing but a pickup joint, and a place my sister hangs out. I reach for my phone, ready to tell Peyton I've changed my mind, when a text comes in.

Peyton: You are not changing your mind. I'll drag you here myself if I have to.

Laughing at how well she knows me, I spend twenty minutes picking thorns out of my ass. Then I comb my hair and slip into a pair of jeans and my vintage Rolling Stones T-shirt. Peyton knows I love music and local bands. I often go see them, just not at the Growler, where my sister hangs out. Music is a huge part of my life really and so important in film. And well, maybe I'm crazy, because I think there is a part of me that wants to see Landon and Ivy together at the pub. Maybe I'll see something off, something that proves they don't belong together. Cripes, what is wrong with me? I just said seeing them together would help me move on, didn't I? I definitely need therapy.

I keep my face makeup free, but put on a bit of peach lipstick, not that I plan to jump on any eggplants tonight, but my lips are dry from all the popcorn. I am not trying to impress anyone.

I step out into the night, and a car drives by, a bunch of freshmen hanging from the windows, and I just grin. I feel safe on my street, and the campus is just a few blocks away, but it was still nice that Landon wanted to walk me home. He's obviously a protector at heart, thanks to his four sisters.

I reach the corner and I'm about to cross the street when I hear heavy breathing sounds coming from right behind me. I turn quickly and jump to my left, my hands fly to my chest when the guy coming at me tries to dodge me. I jump again just as he shifts directions to go around me and he crashes straight into me.

"Whoa," he says, his eyes wide as he reaches out to steady me before I get knocked over...again. "I'm so sorry. Are you okay? I thought you were moving left, then you moved right."

Cameron Reid.

"I'm sorry. It's my fault, you just frightened me, and I never was very good at frogger," I tease.

Worried eyes lock on mine. "Are you okay? You seem...upset about something?"

"I'm okay," I say quickly and give a very unladylike snort. "I took a dive into the bushes earlier. Once a night is enough."

He frowns. "Yeah, I saw that."

   CATHRYN FOX

A tortured groan crawls out of my throat. This day could *not* get any worse. "You *saw* that. How did you see that?" I wrack my mind, but don't remember seeing him when I went ass over heels. There was a group of giggling girls across the street. I guess he could have been with them. Landon did say Cameron liked them innocent.

"I don't want to tell you," he says, and my gaze races over his flawless face, his hair still perfectly styled despite the fact that he's out running.

"Ohmigod, someone recorded it, didn't they?" I slap my hands to my face, embarrassed.

"Yeah, they put it on the campus Instagram. It's gone viral. Sorry, Ella."

I groan, and he puts his hands on my hands, removing them from my face. His touch is warm and friendly, and doesn't elicit the things inside me that Landon's touch does. "Want me to go hunt them down for you? Crack a few heads?"

I relax as he goes perfectly serious. I've been fighting my own battles my whole life and honestly, I don't think this one is worth fighting. "Nah, it's okay. Let them have their fun. In eight months, I'll be out of outta here." He grins at me and I take in his classically handsome looks. I can see why all the girls like him, but I guess I'm just hung up on Landon. "What?" I ask as he continues to stare in silence.

"Chin up. I like that attitude," he says.

"I better get going. Sorry for interrupting your run," I apologize, and beneath the streetlight, I take in his hard body.

"Not interrupting at all. Glad I *ran* into you." He grins and says, "See what I did there?"

I laugh. "A baseball star and a comedian. I had no idea." I admire his grin, and as my gaze moves over his face, I ask, "How did you know it was me and not Ivy?"

His eyes narrow in on me. "I can't tell if you're kidding or not."

"Not." I tug my hair. "Now that I have blonde in it, I figured people wouldn't be able to tell us apart."

"Is that what you want, Ella? Is that why you dyed your hair blonde?"

As soon as the words leave his mouth, I nearly swallow my tongue. No, that's not what I want. I want people to like me for me, and when I went to the frat party last night to apologize to the players, I wanted them all to know it was me, Ella Holmes, not Ivy Holmes, right? Ohmigod, please don't tell me there is some small part of me that hoped Landon thought I was Ivy—because the only way I'd ever find myself in his bed is if he thought I was my twin. God, I really do need therapy.

"No," I say. "That's not what I want."

Still deep in thought, I take a step off the curb and he jerks me back fast. I land against him with an undignified thud as a car speeds past. My heart races, as I watch the taillights until they disappear around the corner.

"Gotta watch where you're going, Peaches. The freshmen are a menace to society."

I take a couple fast breaths. "I'm...thanks, Cameron. I owe you one."

"Yeah, you do, and I'm going to walk you to wherever you're going."

"You don't have to do that."

"Move it, Peaches."

"You're exercising."

"And you're exercising my patience," he teases with a wink. "Let's go." Refusing to take no for an answer, despite my protests, he puts his hand on the small of my back and leans forward, almost bent in half, and looks both ways, his eyes big, his actions so exaggerated as he scans the street, it pulls a laugh from me.

"All right, it's clear." I whack his stomach and hit a wall of muscles. "Cut it out."

"Just being careful," he teases, and I study his profile as we walk.

"Like what you see, Peaches?" he asks, a wide cocky grin on his face. What is it with these jocks and their ability to charm without even trying?

Landon warned me to stay away, but he seems nice enough. He was nice at the party the other night too. Wasn't trying to lure me out back or to anyone's bed. Could Landon be right about him, though? Does he go after the innocent and then dump them when he gets what he wants? I like to come to my own conclusions about people, but I'm wise enough to adhere to someone's warnings. Maybe the two have a history that I don't know about. Maybe Cameron stole one of Landon's girl-friends or something.

He arches a brow at me. "You never answered my text."

I shrug in apology. "Been busy studying, filming the team and tutoring."

"That's a yes then. Drinks at the Growler."

"I don't like the Growler."

"Oh, I get it, you're into Brooks. I'm not your type, right?"

"How do you know my type?"

He glances the length of me, and I fidget a bit. "I was there the other night, remember? I saw the way you were looking at Brooks."

I twist my fingers together. "I needed to apologize to him, and everyone else on the team."

"Yeah, heard about that too."

I shake my head. "Is there anything you don't know?"

There's something in his eyes, spreading across his handsome face, that says he knows a lot about a lot of things, maybe too much, and it creates a strange sensation in my stomach. *Always listen to your body and your intuition.* As my mother's words ping around inside my brain, he cracks his knuckles, and his devilish grin full of secrets, widens.

"Star pitcher, Peaches. Gotta know what's going on around me at all times, stay on top of my game."

"Are you saying life is a game?"

He laughs. "Are you telling me it's not?"

I guess I never really thought of life as a game before. "Why are you calling me Peaches?" I ask, and cross my arms. My mind takes that moment to remember Landon's mouth near my ear, the name Angel on his tongue when he entered my body.

He shrugs. "'Cause you're so goddamn sweet, Peaches."

A sound of disbelief rumbles in my throat, and he wets his lips like he's ready to sink his teeth into a big juicy peach. "You don't know me well enough to say that, Cameron."

"I know enough." He skips ahead of me, and starts slow jogging backwards. "Why'd you think I'd confuse you for Ivy?"

I glance at him, take in his lightness on his feet. I can't help but think Ivy was one of his many conquests, or maybe he was one of hers. I snort at that and he angles his head. I tap my cheek like I'm deep in thought. "We're very different."

"No shit."

"Are you and Ivy friends? I take it she's your type."

He laughs. "Nope, not my type."

"Right because she's not an innocent," I mutter under my breath.

Not missing a thing, he lightly pokes my forehead, and I note how rough the pad of his thumb is. Likely from baseball. "Sounds to me like someone's been filling your head with lies. Don't believe everything you hear, Peaches, and don't believe everything you see."

"Sage advice," I say, although there was no denying what and who I saw the other night—in Landon's bed. "I'm a cinematography student. I know better than to believe everything I hear or see. Trust me on that."

"Glad to hear it, but yeah, I like chicks, all chicks. Show me a straight guy on campus who doesn't. But I gotta tell you, Peaches, I don't meet too many girls with balls like yours, though."

"What's that supposed to mean?"

He goes quiet for a long time, like he's trying to figure out how to answer me, then his head lifts, his dark eyes on mine. "One, you turned an entire football team against you, then had the balls to show up and apologize. Two, the guy you like is fucking your sister and you're holding your head high. Like I said, balls."

"I don't have balls, but I appreciate the compliment, I think."

"So whaddya say, grab a drink with me?"

I stare at him trying to figure out his angle. "I'm not looking for any sort of relationship, Cameron."

He holds his hand up, palms out. "Just friends."

"You really want to be my friend?"

"Let's be honest here, Ella. I'd love to fuck you six ways to Sunday," he says and my cheeks heat. "But you and I both know that ain't gonna happen when you're hung up on Brooks."

My stomach clenches, as I think about Landon and Ivy together. "I guess I can't figure out what's in it for you."

"I figure you're gonna be a big director someday." He angles his face and shows me his chiseled jaw. "Figure you might want to put me in one of your movies, after I retire from the MLB."

I laugh at that. "What is it with jocks and their egos? Wait, how do you know what I want to do?"

My question seems to take him off guard for a second, but he quickly pulls himself together and says, "I have my ways."

"Tell me, what this is really about?"

"It's not about anything." He glances around as we hit main street, numerous students milling about. "Where are we going anyway?"

I point to the campus pub. "*I'm* going to the Growler to meet Peyton. And *you're* going back to the pavement to finish your run."

"The Growler, huh? Thought you just said you didn't like the place."

"Well, not normally, but Peyton convinced me to come tonight to listen to the band. In case I might want to put them in one of my movies, when I'm famous." I cheekily grin at him.

He steps close, his body hovering over mine. "Are you easily swayed, Peaches?"

"No," I answer as he looks over my head, a snarl on his face to go with the one in his throat. I have no idea what he's looking at, but whatever it is, he doesn't like it. "I wonder why your sister never told me she had such a pretty twin," he says.

I arch a brow. "Maybe she was trying to protect me from guys like you."

"Guys like me?" He grins. "I'm offended, Peaches."

"You don't look like the kind of guy who gets offended."

His grin is bright and wicked. "You don't know me well enough to say that." I laugh as he throws my words back at me, and he lifts his head, and gestures to the sign above us. "We're here." He pulls open the door and waves his hand. "After you."

"I'm meeting—"

"Not joining you, unless you want me to come in and help make Brooks jealous."

"I'm not into games," I tell him. "Besides, why would me being with you make him jealous? He's into Ivy, not me."

"Fuck, you are so innocent. If you're not careful, some guy is going to chew you up and spit you out."

"I heard that was your specialty."

"Brooks tell you that?"

"Maybe."

His lips twist, like he has a secret. "Maybe he's the one who chews them up and spits them out, Peaches."

"I don't know," I say, my mind racing back to the night I snuck from his bed, only to return to find my sister. Did he chew me up and spit me out or did he think I was Ivy all along?

"And remember," he adds. "We already established that you can't believe everything you hear or see."

"True."

"All right. Go meet Peyton. I'll wait here until you're safely inside. Gotta make sure no bushes or cars take you out first."

I smile at him. "Thanks, Cameron. I'm good now, and walking me here was sweet of you."

"Don't forget saving your life. That was sweet of me too, don't you think?" As he looks down at me with those deep blue eyes of his, music pours out of the club, but that's not why my skin has come alive. I angle my head, and scan the club, almost certain Landon's eyes are on me. Cameron puts his thumb under my chin, and turns my face back to his. "I think there's some proverb that says you're my servant now or something."

I laugh and put my hand on his chest to give him a shove. "Go run."

He takes my hand and gives it a little squeeze. "Not until you agree to drinks, as friends of course." He cocks his head, and looks so damn adorable, I can't help but shake my head at his foolishness. Honestly though, why shouldn't I go out with him as friends?

"Fine. Drinks. That's all, though."

He looks offended. "Did you hear me ask for anything else?"

"Goodbye, Cameron."

"Later, Peaches." I watch him walk away, and as I do, I can once again feel Landon's eyes drilling into the back of my head. Maybe I was wrong. Maybe my day could get worse. What good could possibly come from being here tonight?

What the ever-loving fuck is Ella doing with Cameron again? Jesus Christ, she's laughing and putting her hand on his chest, acting like they're best friends or something...something I don't want to think about. Nope, picturing her with anyone but me is like a good hard kick to the balls. Even though I have no rights, I want to go over there and drag her away from him. That guy is no good and she'd be wise to stay away from him.

Beside me, Ivy says something and lets loose a laugh and she puts her hands on my shoulders, digging her nails in and dragging my attention back to her. "So, do you?"

"Do I what?"

She shimmies closer, and rubs against me. "Do you want to get out of here, go someplace quieter?"

I glance up to see Brady and a few of the guys come in. "I'm just going to grab another beer. The guys just got here." As Ivy whimpers her protest, I make a motion to Peyton, and she brings me a beer, but when she does, she accidently tips it, and it splashes over my shirt.

Her eyes pop open. "Oops, sorry. That one is on the house, obviously."

"No, it's not on the house. It's on me, literally," I tease. As she blinks dark lashes over innocent eyes, a part of me can't help but think I deserve it. Yeah, if I slept with Ella and Ivy in the same night, I definitely deserve it. Don't even get me started on the blow job in the theater. Jesus Christ, I can't be with Ella now. Not after that. She deserves a guy who'd treat her better. Ivy grabs a bunch of napkins and starts dabbing me dry as Brady smacks my back.

"What's up, bud?" he asks, as he takes in the mess that is me, and the way Ivy is touching me all over.

"Hey," I say and angle toward him as Ivy whispers in my ear that she's going to the little girl's room. "How was dinner?" I ask when she disappears, and it's a stupid question. I can tell by the tightness in his shoulders that his father gave him shit again.

"Same old. Same old. I gotta win at all costs, and keep my eye on the prize. I'd like to tell him where to shove it, but he's holding my tuition over my head, like he always does. Man, when I make it, I am going to pay him back every cent and live my own goddamn life."

"Sorry, bud." I hold my hand up and gesture the guy who just replaced Peyton for a couple more beers. "It really sucks."

He runs his hand through his hair. "He just fucking rattles me. Tells me how much he sacrificed for me, and that I owe it to him to make it to the NFL."

"I know," I say and nod, understanding the pressure, but Brady doesn't want advice—not that I really have any—he just needs me to listen so listen I do. He rants a little more, and after a few minutes, he takes a big breath and puts his hand on my shoulder. "Thanks, I feel better."

"Good," I say. I glance past his shoulder as Ella takes a seat at the end of the bar, and Peyton slides her a drink. She takes a sip and leans in, her eyes wide as Peyton tells her something. A moment later, Peyton unties her apron and joins Ella on the other side of the bar. The two completely ignore us and when the band starts playing a fast song, Peyton drags Ella to the dance floor.

"So Ella, huh?" His gaze goes from me, to Ella, back to me again. "In your room?"

"She was tutoring me and then we watched a movie. Nothing happened," I tell him when he raises a brow.

"Maybe not, but you wanted it to."

"I don't know what I want, bro." It's a lie. I do know. "I mean, she wants to be friends, we agreed on that. I still don't even know if I slept with her." I slowly look out to the dance floor again. Jesus, I can't seem to keep my eyes off Ella. The way her hips sway, the way she touches her hair, the way she smiles, tugs at something deep inside of me. I turn to find Brady watching me.

I take a big sip of beer, and drop my glass onto the bar top with more force than necessary. I give an exaggerated exhale and meet his gaze. "What?"

He shrugs. "I didn't say anything."

"Didn't need to. If you got something on your mind, just come out with it."

"If you want her, you should go get her."

"It's not like that Brady. I don't know if I slept with her and even if I did…" I groan and grip my glass. "I can't be with her now." I lean into him, my words for his ears only when I tell him what happened in the dark theater.

"Fuck," he curses and takes a big drink of his beer.

Ivy comes back from the bathroom, with Jaxon tight on her heels. He's wiping his mouth, and she glances at him over her shoulder, grinning. Did those two just hook up in the bathroom? I must be mistaken. Jaxon has a girl, and Ivy wasn't gone that long. Jaxon is also a buddy. He saw Ivy crawling all over me tonight and would never go after another guy's girl. Bro code and all—at least within your own teams. Poaching a girl from the other teams is fair game, and not something I'm ever planning on doing again. That didn't end well my freshman year. Cameron and I both have the scars to prove it.

Wait, is Ivy my girl?

Instead of coming back to the bar, Ivy dances over to her sister as Ella watches the band, hips swaying ever so slowly. Ivy leans in and says something, and Ella hugs herself, tripping backward a tiny bit—a familiar gesture when she's in the vicinity of her sister. Ivy wobbles on her too-high heels, and Ella grabs her seconds before she face plants. I push from my stool and hurry over to them.

"Hey," I say to Ella. "Never seen you in here before."

"Yeah, well this is my week for a lot of firsts," she says, and I can't help but wonder if she's talking about being in my bed.

I put my hand on Ivy's back to help stabilize her as she sways in her ridiculous heels. "Thought you had homework."

"I do, but Peyton said the band was great, so here I am listening." As Ella gives a casual shrug, Ivy throws her arms around me.

"I was just telling Ella about our little trip backstage this morning, and how I helped you destress," she blurts out far too loudly. As heads turn our way, blood drains to my toes, and my stomach knots. Fuck, why would she go and do that?

"I think you should take her home, Landon." Ella's eyes meet mine and real concern lives there. "I think she's had too many shots of Patron."

"Okay." I put my arm around Ivy and anchor her to my body. "Let's get you home," I say, and she smiles up at me.

"That's right, you owe me." She giggles and then hiccups.

"Yeah, right." I have no intentions of taking her back to my place or sleeping with her. "Ella," I begin. "Earlier, I saw you with Cameron."

"Yeah," she says, her eyes wide, like it's none of my business and really, it's not. But it is. I'm pretty sure the reason he's sniffing around her is because she's an innocent, and he saw the two of us together at the party. Yeah, I'm sure it has everything to do with the grudge he's held against me since our freshman year.

"I just...be careful around him, okay?"

"Maybe you should worry about the sister in your hands," she says, and Peyton grabs her and drags her away from me, abruptly ending our exchange. Feeling like a total asshole—I'm responsible for the mess between the three of us—I meet Brady's gaze and let him know I'm taking Ivy home, but will be back shortly. He lifts his beer in salute, and shakes his head at my predicament. I can only nod my head in agreement.

Ivy laughs at nothing, some joke only she's privy to, as I walk her back to her sorority, and hand her off to one of her sorority sisters at the front door. Once I know she's safe, I hurry back to Growler to find Ella and Peyton still on the dance floor. They head to the bar, and both take a few shots. Her gaze lifts as if feeling my eyes on her and I stare, wanting to go talk to her.

She turns from me, says something to Peyton and a minute later she heads outside as Peyton puts her apron back on and goes to the back.

"I gotta go, bro," I say to Brady and he just lifts his glass in salute again. I move through the crowd and hurry toward Ella. "Hey," I call out, and she stops and glances at me over her shoulder.

"Is Ivy okay?" she asks.

"Yeah, saw her home safely."

Her shoulders relax. "What are you doing back here, then?"

"I wanted to make sure you got home okay, too."

"I'm okay, Landon. I only had a few drinks."

With my throat tight, I say, "About what Ivy said, you know, in the theater."

She holds her hands up. "Hey, I don't want to hear it. What you two do is your own business." She waves her hands back and forth between us. "We're friends, but we're not that kind of friends. Tell it to the guys, not me."

"It's not what you think." I touch her arm and she turns into me, her body inches from mine.

"What is it then?" she asks, catching me off guard.

"It's not...Ivy." Fuck, what do I say? "I...I don't know what we are."

She nods, and goes quiet for a moment, and my gaze falls to her lush lips. I dip my head and my heart pounds hard against my ribcage as volatile heat sizzles the air, taking up space between us. Her breathing changes, a soft little whimper in her throat as she stares up at me with those wide blue eyes of hers.

"Then I suggest you talk to Ivy and figure it out. According to her, you two are an item." As her words hit like a kick to the dick, she inches back, and folds her arms over her chest. "I'll see you at the game, Landon."

"Ella," I say as she hurries down the sidewalk. She glances at me over her shoulder. "Thanks for the tutoring, and watching a movie."

"You're welcome."

I stand there a moment longer, and once I know she's safe, I head back into the bar. Peyton is behind the counter again, and she's watching me closely. I guess her replacement never showed and she's picking up another shift. I don't bother ordering another beer. My shirt is still wet from the first one she dumped on me. I find Brady and tell him I'm heading home. He decides to stay out a bit longer, and I jog back to our place.

In my room, I glance around. If I try really hard, I can almost still smell Ella's sweet vanilla scent. I grab my sheets from the dryer, make my bed and take off my wet shirt before I plunk down on the bed. I dig my phone from my back pocket and run my hands over the screen. Don't do it, bro. The urge to message Ella wins out and before I can think better of it, I shoot off a message.

Me: Hey, just making sure you got in okay.

A long moment and then she finally texts back.

Ella: I'm home, and safe.

Me: Okay, good to know.

Me: Are you travelling with us to the Anaheim game Friday?

Ella: Looks that way.

Me: Want to watch a movie after we return?

Ella: Don't you party after a game?

Me: Sure, but we can watch a movie after that.

Ella: I'll probably have homework.

Me: Right, of course.

Ella: I enjoyed Casablanca tonight, though.

I grin, and look around the room to find the case still on my dresser.

Me: Me too. Night Ella.

I set my phone down, and put my hands behind my head and stare up at the ceiling. My dick takes that moment to twitch. I quickly take off my pants, and free my dick. I take it into my hand and rub as I close my eyes and picture Ella in bed with me. I groan as I tug, going from base to crown. My hand picks up speed, and I come all over my stomach in seconds flat. Jesus, I have no idea why I'm acting like a hormonal teen again.

"Fuck," I curse just as my phone vibrates on my nightstand. I grab a tissue, wipe up quickly, and reach for my phone to read the message.

Ella: If I get my homework done early, I guess I might be able to watch a movie.

Me: Great, let me know what you want to watch.

Ella: I'll bring it.

Me: Oh yeah, what are you thinking?

Ella: Don't worry, Landon. It's not porn.

I laugh out loud at that, happy that she can make fun of herself, when I know the whole experience was incredibly mortifying for her.

Me: Not worried. Now go study. I don't want to be responsible for you failing anything.

Ella: See you tomorrow, Landon.

Me: Yeah you will.

13

ELLA

It's Friday afternoon, which means tonight is game night, and the mood on the bus as we travel to Anaheim, our first away game, is thick with excitement and anticipation. From my front seat, I brace my leg on the pipe in front of me, opening my laptop, and glance over my shoulder. Some of the guys are listening to music, some are carrying on with one another, and some are sleeping. One guy in particular is reading Huckleberry Finn and I can't help but smile. I love that he's taking my tutoring lessons seriously and he really is trying.

As though he feels my eyes on him, Landon's head lifts and a smile touches his mouth. I quickly turn away. I don't want anyone on the team getting the wrong idea about us—I don't want Landon thinking I might want more, especially now that Ivy has laid her claim. We're friends, and that's just the way it is, the way it should have been from the beginning. Although, according to Ivy, she hasn't seen him all week, since he's been practicing and studying in the library with me. I thought it was a better place than his bedroom, and the memories it triggers in my traitorous brain. I go back to my computer when my phone pings. I snatch it from my pocket and I'm glad I'm at the front of the bus, where no one can see the ridiculous smile on my face when I see it's Landon messaging.

Landon: Is it lonely way up there at the front of the bus?

Ella: Not lonely at all. Getting lots of work done. How's the book?

Landon: Book is good, but I'd rather be watching a movie with you.

Ella: Are you excited for the game?

Landon: Yeah. How about this, if I score a touchdown, you come party with us?

Ella: Are we doing this again?

Landon: Depends if it's working.

Ella: So, if you don't score a touchdown?

Landon: I'll skip the party and go straight to movie time with you.

Ella: If you win, you have to party with your friends. I'm not going to take you away from that. After what these guys overheard me say, I'm treading on thin water.

Landon: They all like you and movie time with you is still a win for me.

Ella: (emoji, eye roll)

Ella: Go back to studying. We have that test on Monday and you need to pass.

Landon: Wow, you're bossier than Coach.

Ella: Go. Study. Now.

Landon: Make sure you video my touchdown, E.

I shake my head and set my phone beside me, wishing I wasn't so excited about spending time with him. I hate, hate, hate that. Yet, no matter how many lectures I give myself, I can't stop thinking about him, can't keep my mind on my schoolwork. This...right here, is why I kept my head down and my nose in a book for the last three years. I can't take my eyes off my goal, which means guys are a distraction I don't need. Correction. Landon is a distraction I don't need.

Landon: Stop thinking about my touchdown and get to work, E.

I glance at my phone and turn to find Landon grinning at me. I just shake my head again, loving his playfulness, and hating it just as much. Honestly, it would be so much easier if he was just an egotistical jock, out for himself. There just seems to be more depth to him. As I tuck my phone away, I remember the sight of him in bed with my sister, and I take a deep breath, reminding me what's between the two of us is friendship, and he flirts with everyone, and I might be reading him all wrong.

One hour later, we're all piling off the bus, and the guys are running inside to get ready for the game. I notice the way Landon lingers back, and when I hike my camera bag over my shoulder, he takes it from me.

"I'm capable of carrying my own bag, Landon."

He gives me a grin. "And I'm capable of carrying it for you."

"Fine, carry it then," I say as we walk inside. His knuckles brush mine as we both reach for the door at the same time, and I swear to God, his touch is like a spark to dry tinder. My entire body flares hot, and need stirs deep between my legs. Good Lord, who knew one night with this guy would continue to arouse so many things in me. He angles his head, and I pray my cheeks aren't red with heat.

He pulls the door open, and stands there, like he wants my body to rub up against his as I enter. I move past him, and hope he can't see the effect he has on me. We can't be friends if he knows I'm lusting after him. Once we're inside the campus stadium, I hold my hand out for my bag and he slides it off his broad shoulder.

"You better go get ready," I say when I realize we're the only two in the hall and all the guys have disappeared inside the locker room.

"Listen, to be fair you should probably get a few of the other players on the video. Last time, you were pretty focused on me." I stand there slack-jawed as he teases, debating on smacking or kissing that sexy grin off his face.

"I was not." I whack him. "I just have to go where the action is." Shoot. That didn't come out right. "I mean..."

"I know what you mean," he says, and backs up, entering the locker room backwards, like he can't stand to take his eyes off me. He stares a little longer, and I touch my hair, suddenly self-conscious. He must like what he sees, considering he's into my sister and we look alike. I was surprised Cameron could tell us apart when I fixed myself up and went to the Growler. But our personalities, however, are incredibly different. I'm usually in overalls and a ball cap. That's my comfort zone.

Landon disappears behind the door, and I take the equipment to the field to set up for the game. I feed off the energy in the bleachers as I watch the other team run onto the field, and the crowd goes crazy. I scan the field, and that's when I see my sister and the other cheerleaders taking their spot on the field. They traveled on another bus with fans, but I opted to go with the camcorder on the guys' bus. All the girl chatter, talking about the players, gets on my nerves, and there very well could be a part of me that didn't want to hear any more stories from Ivy. She's open about her sex life, and it hasn't been easy for me to wipe my brain clear after she told me about their theater hookup.

As I stare at Ivy, she turns my way and waves her pom poms, and I wave back. Honestly, it's not like she knew I was into Landon. It's not like she jumped in and took something that was mine. I can't be mad at her for liking him too. He's a likeable guy.

Once I'm set up, our guys all come running onto the field and I suddenly find myself cheering right along with Ivy, the rest of the cheerleading squad and the fans. Through the lens, I scan for Landon, and when I find him, he's smiling at me. Busted.

I turn the camera, and for the next few hours I concentrate on the action and capturing all the plays. A little thrill goes through me when Landon makes a touchdown, and turns my way, doing a dance that sends a tingle skittering through me. Ivy screams his name from the sidelines, and I turn to film her. She catches sight of me, and does a little dance for the camera. I laugh and shake my head. That is so like Ivy.

Once the game is over, I pack up and head toward the bus. Ivy comes running up to me, a big smile on her face. "Hey sis, wasn't that a great game?"

"It was." I take in her energy, as she bounces around. "Hey, can I ask you a question?"

"Of course, you can."

"What do you know about Cameron Reid?"

She grins. "Oh, are you interested in him?"

Maybe I sort of want her to think I am. "I don't know. He wants to grab a drink, and I was just wondering what his story is. He and Landon don't seem to get along."

"I don't know the details, really. But I think something happened between them in their freshman year. I think there was a girl involved. Some game they were playing." The word 'game' rings in my head, and I recall my conversation with Cameron. He thinks life is a game.

"Do you and Cameron get along?"

"Yeah, we're friends." She puts one hand on her hip and eyes me, a sly smile on her face. "I had no idea Cameron was your type."

"I don't have a type," I say, with a casual shrug.

"Sure, sis," she teases.

"If we're speaking of types, I thought he'd be more your type." Cameron is attractive, with his perfect features, and he's usually the kind of guy she goes for. I still can't quite wrap my brain around her and Landon.

She crinkles her nose. "Cameron's okay, I guess. I'm more into football players though."

"Yeah, I know." I hike my bag up higher on my shoulder when it slips. "Landon and all."

She smiles, glances around and then leans into me all conspir-atorially. "Don't say anything, but I'm going to ask him to come home with me for Thanksgiving weekend."

I try not to let my eyes bulge out of my head, as my heart nearly misses a beat. "You are?"

"Yup, already talked to Mom and Dad."

"You guys are serious then?" Holy crap, Ivy has never brought a guy home to the farm before.

"He might be the one," she says with a chuckle. Just then all her friends come running over, laughing and cheering.

"Let's get back and party," one of the girls yells, grabbing Ivy's arm, all the while completely ignoring me.

With my stomach in a tight knot, I stand there as the girls all bounce away. A moment later, the guys make their way to the bus, and I jump on first, taking my seat up front, wanting to be alone with my thoughts.

I pull my phone from my pocket, and see a text from Cameron. I scan it as a big, hard body drops into the seat beside me. I don't need to lift my head to know it's my new friend Landon. That thought nearly makes me laugh. For the last three years, I was invisible and now I have two guy friends—two jocks who have their pick of girls, and have never bothered with me before. I should probably spend more time analyzing that.

"Did you get it?" Landon asks.

"Yup, I got all the action." I glance over my shoulder and inch away from him. "Shouldn't you be back there with the guys celebrating?"

His eyes narrow in on me. "Are you okay?" he asks. "You seem upset about something."

"Not upset," I lie, trying to wrap my brain around the fact that my sister is going to ask him home for the holidays. Has their relationship progressed that quickly? Another thought hits me like a punch. I'm Ivy's twin. Perhaps he's only being kind and friendly to me because some day he's going to be my brother-in-law. Ivy is here to get her MRS. She doesn't even hide that fact. Now that she's in her fourth year, she must be buckling down and thinking about cementing her future. Of all the jocks on campus, vying for professional careers, Landon is a sure thing. He's definitely going to make it, and everyone knows it. "I just have some work to do." I lift my phone. "And a few texts to answer."

He frowns, a storm in those dark eyes of his as he stands. "Okay, I'll see you tonight at the Growler."

"I'm not sure I can make it, Landon. I'm kind of busy and I have a bit of a headache." I'm not lying about the headache, and I think I really need to distance myself from this guy. I don't think being near him is healthy for my head or my heart.

He scratches his head, and the little boy lost look on his face cuts into my core. "I can skip the partying. We can watch the movie instead."

"No, I don't want to take you away from your friends."

My phone pings again, and Cameron's name flashes. Landon's entire body stiffens. "Ella, are you and Cameron—"

"Yeah, we're friends. Just like you and I are friends," I tell him. Honestly, I don't have to explain myself to him, and Ivy said Cameron was okay. Do I really have anything to fear?

"Ella, he's not a good guy."

"Whatever is between you two is between you two. He's been perfectly nice to me," I tell him.

"That's exactly how he plays it." Landon snorts and brushes his damp hair from his forehead. "He draws you in and gets you to trust him, because he's only after one thing."

The comment hurts, to be honest. "So, you're saying all I'm good for is a fuck?"

His chest rises quickly as he sucks in a breath, and I resist the urge to ask if that's all I was to him. He probably wouldn't have any idea what I was talking about, though. He thought I was Ivy. Either that, or he drew me in with his charm, because he was only after one thing, too.

"Ella, that's not what I'm trying to say."

"Everyone take your seats," the driver calls out as he stuffs his big body into his seat and closes the bus doors. They clang shut, and a big breeze washes over Landon and sends his scent my way. I try not to breathe in the aroma of freshly soaped skin and shampooed hair, and the way it reminds me of our night together.

"It's not what I meant," he says again, and hikes his bag over his shoulder. The bus starts moving and he grabs the back of my seat, his hand brushing my shoulder as he holds on.

"You'd better take your seat," I say.

He stares at me for a moment longer, and I get the impression that he really wants to tell me something, but he just clenches his jaw and makes his way to the back of the bus.

My throat burns as I fight tears, and I work to concentrate on the text messages. I read the one from Peyton, letting me know she made lasagna, and set a plate aside for me. The next one from Cameron actually makes me smile.

Cameron: Hey Peaches, what's up.

Me: Just sitting on a bus.

Cameron: I hear the guys won.

Me: Yup, it was a good game.

Cameron: Speaking of games, want to play one?

Me: You really into games, huh?

Cameron: Who isn't.

Me: I'm not big into them.

Cameron: That means you don't want to play?

Me: Depends.

Cameron: On what?

Me: What kind of game you want to play?

Cameron: Two truths and a lie?

I laugh at that. I haven't played that game since my junior year of college when Peyton had a bunch of her classmates over and we all drank a little too much wine. That night I learned my virginity was a rarity. Do I regret that I gave it away to Landon? I guess in a way I do, because he doesn't even know it.

Cameron: Bet you thought I was going to say something ridiculous like spin the bottle, didn't you?

Me: Well, no, we're not twelve anymore.

Cameron: Okay, fine. We can play spin the bottle if you want. Geez, I had no idea you were so pushy.

Me: LOL, I am not pushy and wasn't suggesting that.

Me: I was thinking you meant play sports or something.

Cameron: Actually, that does sound like fun. What sports do you like?

As my fingers fly over my phone, I can feel Landon's eyes drilling into the back of my head, and it takes everything in me not to turn around. I concentrate on my answers.

Me: Um well, I'm not much into sports. I'm into cinema.

Cameron: Right, my smart girl.

The word *my* trips me up.

Me: I'm not your girl, I'm your friend.

Cameron: Yeah, I know. What do you do for fun, Peaches?

Me: I take pictures, and videos, and watch movies. You?

Cameron: I play baseball and text beautiful girls.

That makes me laugh out loud. At least he's honest about how he lives his life. He's a man whore and isn't ashamed of it.

Cameron: How much longer before you get back?

Me: We just left, so a couple hours.

Cameron: Hungry?

Me: Starving. Peyton made lasagna.

Cameron: I like lasagna.

I consider that for a moment. Peyton is working tonight and I won't be watching a movie with Landon. Maybe I should invite him over for something to eat. I mean, we're friends, and it's Friday night, and I don't have any big plans for the weekend.

Me: Subtle much?

Cameron: Subtlety isn't really my specialty.

Me: I guess I could share.

Cameron: See you soon.

Me: How do you know where I live?

Cameron: I know everything, Peaches.

As soon as I read the words, something uncomfortable niggles in the back of my brain. Am I being smart? Should I be listening to Landon? He's not given me anything solid to go on, and their hatred of each other was over a girl, according to my sister. I toss that around in my brain, when his message comes in.

Cameron: White or red?

Me: Uh, what?

Cameron. Wine.

Me: Red.

Cameron: Done and once we empty the bottle, you might be able to twist my arm into using it to play spin the bottle.

Me: First, we're not playing anything, and you need more than two players. Second, do you flirt with all your friends?

Cameron: Nope, only you.

Me: How did I get so lucky?

Cameron: You could get lucky if you wanted to. But you need to get over Brooks first.

I shake my head at his teasing, and resist the urge to tell him getting over Landon might be impossible. When I don't readily answer, he texts back.

Cameron: Sorry, not sorry.

Me: See you later, Cameron.

Cameron: I'll be waiting for you, Peaches.

I stare at my phone, waiting to see if Ella is going to text me. She was definitely upset about something, and now she's up at the front of the bus texting away, and I can only assume it's with Cameron. He might be the star pitcher, but I know firsthand baseball isn't his number one game. No, hitting on innocent girls is his game, and I never should have brought Ella into our world.

The bus finally comes to a stop on campus, and Ella hurries off before I can get to her. She disappears inside the recreation building, and I lose sight of her as we all head to the locker rooms. Coach chats with us all, goes over a few plays that Ella recorded, with no extra conversation anywhere on the recording, and once he's done, we head to the Growler to celebrate. I'm just not in the mood to party. But I don't want the guys worried about me, so I decide to go for one beer.

The place is alive with music and laughter and everyone is celebrating our win when we get there. I glance around, hoping to find Ella, but knowing I won't. Peyton is behind the bar, and I take a seat.

"Hey," I say.

"Beer?" she asks with a raised brow.

"Only if you're not going to spill it on me," I joke. She grins and slides a beer across the counter to me. "Where's Ella tonight?"

"Probably home studying. Why are you asking?"

"No reason. Just wondering. She uh, just took off so fast after we got back from the game."

I pick up my drink and turn to face the crowd. My heart jumps when I spot Ella, but then quickly realize it's Ivy. From a distance they really do look alike. In the dark they do, too. But you know what? I'm sick of this. I need to know if Ella was in my bed that night. Maybe it was Ivy. I guess she could have been on her period. I take a big drink of beer, set it down, and dodge Ivy as she comes my way.

Deciding it's well past time to get to the bottom of the matter, I head outside. Darkness falls over me, and the night air is warm as I walk to Ella's place. I knock hard, and my body goes stiff when I hear voices inside. A male voice in particular. Jesus Christ, she's in there with Cameron.

Ella opens the door, and her cheeks are a soft shade of pink, like she's been 'exercising' or engaging in some other strenuous activity.

"Landon," she says as my phone pings, a million texts coming in. "What are you doing here?"

"Yeah, Landon, what are you doing here?" Cameron asks, as he comes sauntering down the hall behind Ella, standing so close to her I want to punch that smirk right off his face.

"I wanted to talk to you," I say, and take a deep breath to control the rage welling up inside me as Cameron hovers close.

Ella blinks dark lashes over vibrant blue eyes. "I have company."

I glare at Cameron. "I know what you're doing. I know what this is about. Why don't you just leave her alone."

"What are you talking about, Landon?" Ella asks as Cameron flashes white teeth in some semblance of a victory smile.

My hands fist at my sides. "He's trying to get back at me."

"For what?" she asks.

We all took an oath, never to tell of our games, but I'm not going to stand back and let anyone hurt Ella. "Freshman year, there was this girl, this thing..."

"Why don't you tell her what the thing was, Brooks. Tell her about the initiation game you footballers play."

"Motherfucker," I say under my breath. "It wasn't like that and you fucking know it. And who are you to talk? Your baseball team is no better."

He laughs in my face, and puts his hand on Ella's shoulder. "If you got something to say, just say it."

Ella stands there for a moment, her gaze going back and forth between the two of us and I can almost hear her brain spinning. "What are you guys talking about?"

"Nothing," I say. Fuck, if she knew the initiation game the teams played during their freshman years, she'd hate me for sure. Cameron fucking knows it. We were nothing but stupid kids, and the game never sat right with me from the beginning. I have sisters, for fuck's sake—and morals. Cameron and I both set our sights on the same girl, Rebecca Holloway. He tried to charm his way into the virgin's panties—like the game dictated—and I'm no better. I did the same. Only thing is, I couldn't go through with it, and ended up falling for her. Cameron was just trying to fuck her for the win, and when she found out about the game, she dumped me, assuming I was playing too. It might have started out that way—and I'm not proud of that—but things changed fast for me. Would Ella believe me if I told her, though? I don't want her to feel like a goddamn piece of meat here, but that's all she is to Cameron—sex and revenge. He's been wanting to get me back for stealing his prey before he closed the deal with her.

I pinch the bridge of my nose, and as much as I hate to do what I'm about to do, I need to let Cameron know she's not a virgin. Maybe then he'll back the fuck off. "The other night, in my bed...us, it was you and me, right?" Shit, I didn't mean to pose it as a question, it just came out that way because I'm still questioning that it actually happened myself.

Her entire body goes stiff, and a strange garbled noise crawls out of her throat. "I have no idea what you're talking about."

"I think you should leave," Cameron says.

"Don't fucking tell me what to do, asshole."

Ella grips the side of the door, her knuckles white as she clutches it.

"Ella, listen to me. He's out for revenge, I promise you." The sadness that edges her downturned lips is like a kick to the nuts. Shit. I don't want to hurt her feelings, or make her think she's anything but perfect and beautiful, and that any guy—besides Cameron—would be privileged to have her. She deserves respect, not getting fucked—as well as fucked over

—so this guy can settle a score is deplorable. "None of this is what you think."

"Why would I be out for revenge, Brooks?" Cameron taunts. "And if I was out to get you, why would you think I'd go through Ella? You two are just friends, aren't you? You're with Ivy, right?" Ella nods like that makes perfect sense to her and panic grips my nuts.

My phone continues to ping, and Ella says. "That's probably her, wondering where you are. Good night, Landon."

The smirk on Cameron's face sets off a storm inside me as Ella shuts her door. That fucker has to know I like Ella. That's why he's doing this. Has he been waiting for four fucking years to get back at me for stealing the virgin he'd been baiting? I turn and punch the side of the house, hard enough to bruise my knuckles.

I curse and shake my hand out. Jesus Christ, I should have kept my fucking distance from Ella. I take a deep breath, and let it out slowly as I stand on her doorstep staring at the closed door, my blood boiling in my veins. So help me God, if he touches one hair on her head, hurts her in any way, I'm going to kill him.

I shove my hands into my pockets and stalk back to the pub, trying to figure out how to get Cameron out of her life. As soon as I enter, Ivy throws herself at me.

"Where have you been?" she asks.

"I was checking on Ella. She's with Cameron."

Something flashes in Ivy's eyes, appearing and disappearing so quickly, I can't quite decipher what it was. If I had to guess, I'd lean toward jealousy, but that can't be right. Ella always takes backstage in her presence.

She gives me a big smile. "Aren't you a nice guy, checking on your girlfriend's sister, but don't worry. She likes him. She told me earlier."

"Really?" I ask, a bit surprised by that. "She actually brought up Cameron to you?"

"Yeah, right after the game tonight. He's so totally her type."

I scrub my face, and shake my head, trying to wrap my brain around that. Jesus, I really never thought a smart girl like her would fall for his charm. He's had three years to perfect it, though, so the blame isn't all hers. "Cameron isn't a good guy, Ivy."

She frowns at me. "I know something happened between you two, but the past is the past. We're all grown-ups now, Landon, and I think he really likes her." I shake my head. Of course she does, that's how he plays the game. "It's time to move on from your dispute, don't you think?"

I look at her. Could Cameron really be interested in Ella? I don't see why he wouldn't be. She's the whole package. Maybe Ivy is right, and it is time for me to move on and forget about our dispute, forget about Ella. Maybe she never was the girl for me. Why then does it feel so damn right when I'm with her? I would never forgive myself if Cameron chewed her up and spit her out, just to get back at me. I spot Peyton, who is taking off her apron and it gives me a measure of relief to know that she'll be home with Ella.

"Come on." Ivy wraps herself around my body. "Let's get you in the party mood, and I bought a little something today that will put a smile on your face," she says and undoes the top button on her shirt to give me a quick peek at the black lace beneath. She orders two shots for us and I down the Patron.

She does the same, and for the next couple of hours we party and drink, until I'm a little numb inside.

The next thing I know, I wake up in my bed, Ivy beside me. I let loose a groan, and wrack my brain, trying to figure out what happened last night. Jesus Christ, I pray to God I didn't sleep with Ivy again. Does it really matter, though? Ella is with Cameron, and I can't be with her anyway, not after sleeping with her sister, and I guess maybe I never slept with Ella in the first place. She straight up told me she had no idea what I was talking about.

I push the covers off and check for a condom. When I don't find one, I tug on my jeans and head to the bathroom. One look at my face, and I groan. Shit, I look like fucking hell. I make my way to the kitchen and put on a big pot of coffee. My thoughts go to Ella as I sip it, and drop down to the table to read over some notes, but can't clear the fog from my brain. I grab my phone, and shoot a text off to Ella before I can think better of it.

Me: Sorry about last night. Can we just forget about it?

Ella: It's fine.

Me: Are you studying today?

Ella: Yeah, going over notes later.

Me: Study together?

Ella: I don't think that's a great idea.

Me: Well you are my tutor, aren't you?

Me: Don't you have a camera with your name on it?

When she doesn't answer, I text back.

Me: I really could use your help.

Ella: Okay, let's go to the library.

Me: See you there.

I start to pack up my books, when Ivy enters the kitchen, looking sleepy and hung over.

"Going somewhere?" she asks.

"Big test on Monday. Got to study."

"Is my sister still tutoring you?"

"Yeah," I say and glance down, not wanting my eyes to give my feelings away.

"Heard she and Cameron did it last night," Ivy says with a wicked grin.

My stomach clenches tight, and my gaze lifts, but she's walking to the coffee pot and pours a big mug and can't see the storm inside me.

I clear my throat, wanting to sound casual. "How did you hear that?"

"Girls talk, Landon." She laughs like it was a silly question for me to ask, and takes a sip of her coffee. "I think they make a cute couple, don't you?"

"Yeah, sure." I take in her kiss-swollen lips. Pieces of last night start to fill in, and I'm pretty certain we didn't have sex. I was so drunk there was no way I could have gotten it up anyway. How then, did she get those marks on her neck, and why does she look like a well-fucked woman this morning?

She walks up to me and puts her arms around my shoulders as she sits on my lap, her sex aligned with mine. "How long are you going to be?"

"A couple hours at least." I tap her backside, to get her off me.

She pouts. "That long?"

"I have to pass English, or I'm off the team."

She climbs off me. "We definitely can't let that happen. My man needs to make it to the NFL. Text me when you're done and tell Ella I'm happy about her and Cameron."

"Sure," I say and storm out of the house. Not even the early morning sunshine or the birds help my mood as I cut across campus and head to the library. The second I enter, and find Ella sitting there, absently twirling her hair in her fingers, my heart misses a beat. Man, I am so fucked. I'm with one twin, sort of—I'm not even sure I was given a choice here—and falling hard for the other. Not that I can do anything about that. She's with douche bag Cameron, and I honestly pray to fuck he's not doing this as revenge, and he really does like her.

"Hey," I say quietly, and her head lifts. The second our eyes meet and lock, energy arcs between us. Jesus Christ, am I imagining this, or does she feel exactly what I'm feeling? I must just be projecting, because she slept with Cameron last night. Her smile is so goddamn warm and inviting as she gestures for me to take a seat across from her, it's all I can do not to lean over the table and taste her sweetness.

I want to ask her how her night went, but it's not my business, and I'm terrified of what she might say, so I plunk down, and pull out my books. "Did you enjoy your second read of Huck?" she asks me.

"Believe it or not, I did, and it made much more sense to me."

"Okay, let's go over what I think will be on the test," she says, and our fingers touch as she reaches for my book. My throat tightens, and I'm pretty damn sure a little breathy sound escaped her lips. "Sorry," she says and pulls her hand back. "Just turn to page eighteen."

I open my book and for the next hour or so we talk quietly, and I have to say, I really enjoy being with her, no one else around but us two. I like closing the world out. Just as we're finishing up, I say, "Can I ask you a question?"

She slides her laptop into her bag. "Sure."

"What movie was it?"

"Movie?"

"Last night, we were going to watch a movie. Which one did you pick?"

She smiles. "One of my favorites. Citizen Kane."

I laugh, and then lower my voice when she puts her finger to her lips. "I love that one. Did you, uh, watch it last night?" Okay, I know I'm fishing for information, but I can't help it.

Her face falls, and she averts my gaze. "No."

"Ella?"

Her head lifts. "Yeah?"

"Is everything okay?"

"Yeah, fine," she says, a little too quickly, and I bite the inside of my mouth to keep myself from asking if she slept with Cameron.

"If you're not doing anything later, maybe we can still watch it."

"I'm sure Ivy has plans for you both. When she texted me from your bed this morning, she told me not to keep you too long."

My heart tumbles into my stomach as Ella stands. "Ella," I begin, wanting to tell her how I feel about her, that it's her I want to be with, but how can I do that to her? Why the fuck would she want a guy who slept with her sister just hours after he took her virginity? She deserves better than that. She hikes her bag over her shoulder, and I stand as questioning eyes watch me, waiting for me to continue.

"What is it?" she asks as I stand there staring at her.

"I got this," I say and take her bag and put it over my shoulder. The truth is, I don't 'got this.' I don't got anything, least of all the girl I want to be with.

No one ever said life was fair, Landon.

15

ELLA

September and October fly by in a blur, between tutoring Landon, and keeping my head down, busy with my own work and filming the games, I've barely had a minute to catch my breath. Honestly though, while I enjoy recording the games and need the credit, it's not easy for me to see my sister all over Landon at every turn, and maybe, deep down, it really guts me to stand back, and watch it happen. But there's nothing I can do about that, and I have to remind myself that she didn't know I was into him, or that I slept with him nearly two months ago. Heck, he doesn't know it either. It boils down to this, we might have a love of movies in common, but she's clearly the girl for him.

My mind goes back to the night Landon came to my place when I was having lasagna with Cameron. My God, when he asked if it was me in his bed, I nearly swallowed my tongue. I was so damned embarrassed I denied it, pretended not to know what he was talking about, and if he thought it was me, if he had one little inkling that he slept with the nerdy twin first, why the hell did he sleep with Ivy afterward? See, none of that makes sense unless he really is an egotistical asshole, and I really have the feeling he's not.

I glance down and find a text from Cameron, and an uneasy feeling closes in on me. I can't quite put my finger on it, but something shifted in him that night at my place after Landon showed up at the door. Or maybe it was my imagination, but the genuine worry, the deep-seated fear in Landon's eyes made me stand up and take notice—pay more attention to my intuition.

I don't consider myself a bad judge of character, and my sister didn't seem to have a problem with Cameron when I asked about him, but still, little warning bells went off in my brain after Landon left, leaving me alone with the guy he clearly hates. Peyton came home right away, and that's when Cameron left. I still don't know what they were talking about, the girl, the thing from freshman year, or why I would be used in some revenge plot. None of it made any sense. I asked Peyton and she was clueless too. Perhaps my sister knows, but I never have five seconds alone with her for a private conversation. But, like Cameron pointed out, if it was revenge he was after, he'd go after Ivy.

We've been texting over the last couple months, but between school, filming the football team and Cameron's baseball games, the two of us have been too busy to meet up, but tonight Peyton is working and there is a good band playing so I agreed to meet Cameron at the Growler.

I make my way home from campus and change into a pair of jeans and T-shirt, and head to the pub. The night air is a bit cooler now that we are into late fall. Thanksgiving is just around the corner, and I hug myself, wishing I'd grabbed a jacket. I hurry my pace and make it to the Growler quickly. Hard to believe I never used to come here and now I'm here all the time. I pull open the door and the place is packed, but then again, it's Saturday night.

I make my way to the bar, and Peyton gives me a big smile as she slides a fruity blue drink across the countertop. "You look hot tonight."

"I was running to get here."

She shakes her head. "That is not what I mean. You look hot in those jeans, and that T-shirt really shows off your tits."

I laugh at that and take a sip. Mmm, I'm not sure what she's given me, but it's delicious. "Thank you but I hardly look hot."

"Uh, yeah, you do." She puts her hands on her hips, daring me to challenge her. "Don't you see all the guys looking at you?"

"They're probably looking at you." I look to my left, find Caleb at the end of the bar. "Actually, Caleb *is* looking at you. What's going on with you two anyway?" Her face flushes and it never flushes. Nothing embarrasses Peyton. "Do you have something to tell me?"

"Nothing. I hate him."

Wow, something horrible must have happened. "Seriously?"

"Yeah, he's a jerk with a capital J."

I give her hand a squeeze and leave it at that. She clearly doesn't want to talk about it. "I know all about stupid mistakes," I tell her.

"Speaking of stupid mistakes, yours is looking at you right now."

Landon Brooks. My stupid mistake. I laugh at that. What else can I do? Cry? Hell no. Peyton gestures with the tip of her chin. I spin on my stool and when my gaze lands on Landon, my breath leaves my lungs in a whoosh. My God, he's so gorgeous, dressed in low slung jeans and a T-shirt that shapes his muscles. You'd think after all the time we've been spending together studying I'd have gotten used to it, but no. I still react like a love-struck teenager. He rubs the fresh bruise beneath his eye. I'm guessing he got that at practice today. I consider his other scars. He never did tell me what they were from.

Landon moves through the crowd and takes the seat next to me. His big body crowds mine, and I try not to react when his thigh brushes against my leg. His fresh soapy scent fills my nostrils and I breathe him in.

"How did you do on yesterday's exam?" he asks.

"Pretty good." I turn to my drink, trying to appear unfazed. "How do you think you did?"

"Not bad, thanks to you." He lifts his beer and clinks it with my glass of whatever it is I'm drinking. "I really appreciate all your help, Ella." The sincerity in his voice wraps around me and I lift my gaze and admire his rough and rugged face.

"I'm glad to help. Getting closer and closer to buying that camera." He shifts in his seat and his leg presses harder against mine. Oh boy. "Where's Ivy?" I ask, a reminder to myself that while I'm insanely attracted to this guy, my body emitting enough energy to light the town, he's with my sister.

He frowns, and I try to think back to the last time I saw her. It was days ago on the field. She wasn't her normal self, less bubbly and vibrant. Did Landon Brooks break her heart? As much as I hope he hasn't, there is a small selfish part of me that kind of wishes they weren't together. Although their separation wouldn't affect me in any way. Landon's not into me.

"I'm not sure where she is. She hasn't been well lately, actually. I was wondering if you knew what was going on."

I sit up a little straighter. "Really? She never said anything to me." My heart starts to race with worry. I glance around the pub but she's nowhere to be found. Maybe she's just exhausted like the rest of us. Midterms were killer, and Thanksgiving is just around the corner. We all need the break. I'm not sure if she asked Landon to come back to the orchard yet, and I have no idea if he agreed. I resist the urge to snort. Some break that's going to be for me if he comes. Watching the two of them together all the time. Maybe I'll stay with Peyton. I grab my phone and shoot her a text.

Me: Hey, Ivy. How's it going?

Ivy: I feel like crap.

Me: Do you have the flu?

Ivy: I think so. I'm going to go to the clinic, I think.

Me: Do you want me to go with you?

Ivy: No, I'm okay.

Ivy: I can't get a hold of Landon.

I hold my phone out and show it to Landon. Air seems to slowly leak from his lungs, he looks deflated, and I can't help but wonder if there's trouble on the home front.

"You guys okay?" I ask.

"I uh..." he hedges, and his words fall off when Cameron takes the seat beside me. From behind me, his legs spread and he puts them around my body. I glance at him over the shoulder.

"Hi," I say. "Just a second. I'm checking on my sister." I turn back to Landon, take in the stiffness in his body, the tightening of his hand on his beer, rage emanating off him in waves. What the hell is going on with him? I realize he doesn't like Cameron, but who I'm with is none of his business. Not that I'm with Cameron. I just want to keep things platonic. "What should I tell her?" I ask.

He pulls his phone from his pocket. "Nothing. I'll text her myself." He climbs from the stool, and I lose sight of him in the crowd.

"What the fuck was that all about?" Cameron asks, and spins my stool until I'm facing him and his legs are wrapped around mine. The position is intimate, too intimate for our friendship, and a little possessive. I try to move, shift a little but he keeps me in place.

"What are you drinking?" he asks.

I glance at the blue magic in my glass. "Not even a clue."

He laughs and Peyton leans into us. "It's a Blue Lagoon."

He makes a face like he might have just sucked a lemon. "I think I'll stick with beer."

Peyton pours him a draft, slides it across the counter and disappears to help the next customer. I turn to take in the bodies on the dance floor.

"Looks like you want to dance, Peaches."

"No, actually I don't." I notice a red haired guy sitting at a table close to the bar, studying me. With a sly grin, his gaze slowly slides from me to Cameron, back to me. Do I know him? I can't quite place him or figure out why he looks so familiar. He's probably in one of my classes.

"Drink up," Cameron says, and tips my glass to my mouth.

"Are you trying to get me drunk?" I tease and once again that uncomfortable feeling takes up residence in my gut. I shift again, and put my hands on his legs to move them so I can turn on my stool. Am I being silly? Reading too much into this? He eyes me, and I turn my focus to the band. "They're pretty good, aren't they?"

"Yeah, pretty good," he says and I look back at him.

"I'm talking about the band."

"I'm not." He leans into me. "Let's get out of here."

"And go where?"

He reaches into his coat, and pulls out a movie. I gasp when I see that it's A Tale of Two Cities.

"Where did you get that? That's one of my favorites." I eye him suspiciously. "Wait, how did you know?'

He grins. "I know everything, remember?"

I narrow my eyes in on him, and something just beyond his shoulder catches my eye. I lift my gaze and find the same guy with the red hair, leaning over the counter, trying to get Peyton's attention. Those little alarm bells jangle again. How do I know him?

"Seriously, Cameron. How did you know?" I ask. He picks up his drink and his eyes go to Peyton. She smiles at us and reaches into the fridge for the orange juice. Ah, that makes sense. He asked Peyton, and really that's kind of sweet. "You really want to watch this?" I laugh. "That does not seem like your thing at all."

"Come on." He takes a big pull from his beer, nearly finishing it, and sets his glass on the counter. A second later he's standing and pulling me up with him. My body collides with his, and I look up, way up, to meet his eyes, but there's no spark to dry tinder. Not like there is when I'm near Landon, or not near Landon. I look over my shoulder, my gaze searching the room...searching for the man who makes my insides quiver without even trying or knowing. My heart sits heavy in my chest, when he's nowhere to be found. I guess I should be glad that he's gone to my sister's rescue and really why shouldn't I do something with Cameron. It might actually help me move past Landon. Or not. Either way, I'm not going to sit here and mope about it.

"Where to?" I ask, turning back to see some heat simmering in Cameron's blue eyes.

"Your place."

I nod. I do feel better about going to my place, and Peyton is off in half an hour, so she'll be home with us. "Okay," I say. We step outside and I put my arms around my body to ward off a chill as the night temperature has dropped with the sun going down.

"Cold, Peaches?"

"Freezing," I say, and he pulls me to him, offering his warmth. I accept it and let him warm my body as we make the short trek to my place. Inside, I flick on the lights, and Cameron sets the lock behind us. The sound of the bolt sliding home sends an odd little shiver down my spine.

I turn to him, unable to dispel those tingles a girl gets when something isn't quite right. Maybe this isn't a great idea. I'm about to ask if we could do this another night, except when I glance at his face, and take in his soft smile, the easy casual way he's moving, like nothing is out of the ordinary as he pulls the movie from the inside of his jacket, I give myself a lecture, tell myself I'm being silly. Whatever beef he has with Landon is theirs. It has nothing to do with me.

We head to the living room, and he goes for the DVD player. "I'll make some popcorn. Do you want a beer?"

"Sounds good." He pulls the movie from the case. I watch him for a second. "Everything okay, Peaches?" he asks.

"Yeah, fine." I leave the room and in the kitchen, I shoot Peyton a text and wait for a response as I shove the bag of popcorn into the microwave. When she finally gets back to me, letting me know she has to take on an extra shift, my stomach tightens. I stare at the microwave and shake my head, convincing myself I'm getting alarmed for nothing. I'm not even Cameron's type.

So why then, is he here?

I fill a bowl with popcorn, grab him a beer, and a soda for myself. His feet are on the coffee table and he's stretched out relaxed on one end of the sofa as the movie begins to play. I

"Didn't think you were coming back," he teases as I hand him the beer and he twists it open.

"Slow microwave," I say, and sit at the other end of the sofa, putting a measure of distance between us. He grins, and arches a brow.

"Afraid of me all of a sudden?"

"No," I say and laugh it off. "This is just my comfortable spot."

One broad shoulder rolls as he tips his beer to his lips. "Suit yourself."

I put my feet on the sofa, and he reaches out and grabs them, allowing me to stretch out. I cast a quick glance at him. "Might as well get comfortable. Looks like this is a long movie." He looks past my shoulders, to my Canon camera sitting on the side table. "That yours?"

I pick up my camera, and look it over. "Yup, it was a gift for my twenty-first birthday."

"Let's see."

I hand it to him and he looks at me through the lens. "Hard to take a selfie with this thing."

I laugh. "It's not for selfies."

He snaps a picture of me. "Don't do that."

"Why not?"

I shrug. "I don't know. I just don't like getting my picture taken."

"What do you like then?" he asks, a strange suggestive edge to his voice when I hold my hand out, and he gives me the camera back. I set it on the side table and try to pull my legs back, but he holds them on his lap.

"I like movies, remember." I gesture to the tv.

He taps his head. "Of course I remember. I remember everything."

For some odd reason, the red headed guy from the Growler pops into my brain. That's when it hits me. Jonny. He's the guy who'd been throwing up in the bushes when Peyton and I were standing outside Landon's house. Why was he staring at me so hard?

"Are you going to watch the movie or are you going to watch me, Peaches?" he asks and I shake my head to clear it.

"The movie. I was just thinking about something." I munch on popcorn, take a sip of my soda, and he starts rubbing my feet, his focus on the TV. I relax slightly, and after I drink the whole can of soda, I grab the remote and pause. "I'll be right back. Too much soda, and all that Blue Lagoon."

He laughs and finishes off his beer. "Just grab another in the fridge," I say and dart to the bathroom. I listen as he walks to the kitchen, and that's when I remember I left my phone in there. I finish up and hurry back to the sofa, and he's sitting there waiting for me with a fresh beer. I check the time.

"Are you sure I'm not keeping you from anything?" I ask.

"Nope. No place I have to be," he says and pats the sofa. I drop down on the other side again, and he gestures with a nod. "Got you another soda."

"Thanks." I'm not really thirsty, but I grab the can and take a big drink, needing to do something. Every now and then Cameron glances at me, and when I catch him looking he just smiles.

"Do you like it?" I ask.

"Oh, I like it." He smirks, but something niggles in the back of my brain, a warning of sorts, that it's not the movie he's talking about. I try to tug my feet back again, unease worming through my veins, but he holds them to him, and starts working his hands up my pantleg.

"Cameron, don't," I growl and try to push him away, but I'm suddenly weak and dizzy.

"Something wrong?" he asks.

"I don't feel the best." I glance at the clock again, counting down the minutes until Peyton gets off. "Maybe I'm getting what my sister has. You should probably go. I could be contagious."

"What does poison Ivy have?" he asks, and before I even realize what's happening, he's on top of me, on the sofa, pinning me with his impressive weight.

"Don't call her that."

"Why not?"

"She's not poison." He gives a low laugh that suggests I have no idea what I'm talking about. I kick at him. "Get off me."

"You know you want it." He runs his hands through my hair, the beer on his breath washing over my face and turning my stomach. "I can smell it on you."

My stomach revolts. "I don't want anything."

"Hot little virgin wants my dick. Come on, admit it."

I push at him, but he's all strength and muscle and I can't budge him. I take a few gulping breaths, attempting to clear the fog from my head. "What did you give me?"

"I didn't give you anything yet," he mocks, with a cruel laugh. "But I'm going to rectify that. Then she'll be happy."

Unable to understand what he's talking about, I push and shove but it's like trying to stop a semi with my pinkie finger. "Stop it."

"I haven't had to work this hard for it since Rebecca left me for your asshole," he mutters. "Fucking virgins."

"What are you talking about?" I shove at his arms, my breath coming in fast pants.

"You still don't know, do you, virgin?" He makes a tsking sound. "So fucking naïve."

"Cameron. Get the fuck off me."

I shift and turn, but he grabs my face with one hand, his fingers biting into my jaw hard enough to leave bruises. "She was my virgin, but your boyfriend fucked her first." My head spins, and Cameron blurs through my tears. "He's not the guy you think he is, Peaches."

My stomach plummets, real fear invading my body. "I'm not....a virgin," I tell him, hoping that will get him off me.

"Yeah, you are. My buddy Jonny heard you tell Peyton you were at the party."

Shit. Shit. Shit.

I'm in real trouble here. Why the hell didn't I listen to my intuition, listen to Landon? Wait, what was that he just said about Landon?

"Who is he?" I ask, hoping if I engage him in conversation he'll let me go.

He lets loose a bark of laughter. "All you need to know is he fucked my virgin freshman year, now it's time for me to fuck his."

"I'm not a virgin. I slept with Landon," I say. "That night, at the frat party. He thought I was Ivy and I slept with him."

He inches up, pins my arms with his knees, but I manage to wiggle one free, and in one fast movement, I reach behind me, grab my camera and crack him over the head as hard as I can.

"What the fuck," he curses and falls to the side, giving me enough room to get out from underneath him.

Dizzy, and weak, I push to my feet, and start for the door, but he grabs my ankles and tugs. I fall onto my face with a thud, and he hauls me back. "Don't believe you, virgin," he yells.

He drags me toward him as I claw at the floor, and the room starts to fade in and out. I need my phone. I need to call someone. As soon as that thought pops into my head, I realize it's already too late. Cameron has me beneath him again, blood coming from the side of his head where I hit him. He pins my arms above my head, his lips twisted, a merciless grin on his face as he inches closer.

"Why are you doing this?" I ask, my voice hysterical.

"Landon took my virgin, and won the game. Now I'm taking his. That's all the story you need to know, anyway." Is he suggesting there's more to it, and what did he mean when he said, then she'll be happy? My thoughts are so scattered, and I'm having a hard time trying to figure out what he's saying. "Usually I can bag the girl before our Thanksgiving deadline, but you've not been making it easy for me, Peaches. Always studying, always working, always drooling over Landon. It's a bit pathetic, don't you think? You weren't seeing who was right here in front of you all this time."

He shifts his weight, and pulls open my jeans. "Stop it," I beg and try to kick at him, but my legs are too weak. "I'm going to call the cops."

He laughs. "What for? We've been seen together, and you invited me to your place, plus everyone knows we've already slept together—supposedly. Jesus, it's so easy to start rumors amongst dim-witted cheerleaders."

Slept together, what the hell is he talking about?

"You'll pay for this," I threaten, but the warning sounds weak, even to me.

"Who's going to believe you? Go after me, Peaches, and see what it does to your reputation. See how far you get in Hollywood." This time his laugh is cruel and dark. "Besides, you should get used to giving it up if you want to make it in the movie industry."

This can't be happening. Anger and fear balloon inside me. As it expands, fight or flight instinct kicks in. He might be stronger, but I'll be damned if I go down without getting a few good hits in. I search the floor, my fingers grasping, reaching, searching, until they connect with my camera strap. Cameron is so busy trying to get my jeans down, he doesn't take notice. I pull it closer, grab the lens, and crack it over his head hard enough to break it. His hold loosens, as a shocked look spreads across his cruel face. With adrenaline kicking it, it allows me to bring my knee up and get him right between his legs.

His face contorts and he lets loose a loud groan and rolls to his side, bringing his knees to his body. "You fucking bitch. You're going to pay for that, and that one will be free."

Free? What is he talking about? I crawl away, and he grabs my ankle, but I kick his side with the last of my strength. Driven by a force I don't even understand, I push to my feet and open my door. With my pants open, I dash outside, and tears falling down my face as I run, heading to God knows where. I swipe at my eyes and continue to run. I glance over my shoulder to see if he's following me, and I run smack into a brick wall.

"What the hell."

Landon.

He puts his hands on my shoulders, and inches back to see my face. "Ella, what the hell?" A sob rips from my lungs, and I slide my arms around his waist, my cheek against his strong heart as I cry and hold onto him like he's my lifeline.

"What is it?" he asks again, smoothing his hand over my back and my hair. "Ella, are you okay? Tell me what happened."

I nod and sniff against his shirt, as his hands encircle me, holding me to him securely. He curses under his breath and pulls me impossibly closer as I cry into his shirt, soaking it, and after a long while, he inches back again to check in on me.

"What's going on?"

"What...what are you doing here?" I ask.

He lifts his head, as I wipe my face with the back of my hand. "I was on my way to see you."

I shake my head, nothing making sense. My legs go weak, and when I sag against him, he scoops me up. "Just rest, okay?" I nod, and bury my face in the crook of his neck, as he carries me down the street.

"Where are we going?" I ask, when I notice he's not headed to my place. I'm grateful for that, but suspect Cameron is long gone by now.

"I'm taking you to my place," he tells me. He hurries down the street, and when we reach his place, he dashes up the stairs, pulls his blankets back and sets me between the sheets. I take a deep breath, refilling my heaving lungs. He tucks me into his bed, and adjusts the blankets around my body. Once he has me mummified, he sits on the edge of the bed beside me, his worried gaze roaming my face.

"I'm going to get you a glass of water."

I tug my hand out, and reach for him. My fingers curl into his shirt. "No, don't go," I beg, my mouth so dry it's hard to speak, but I can't be alone right now. I don't want to be alone.

"Okay," he agrees, and puts his hand on my arm. He gives it a comforting squeeze and we sit in silence as I stare at the ceiling, my brain struggling to keep up.

"Can I have your phone? I don't have mine and I need to text Peyton."

He digs his phone from his back pocket and hands it to me. I shoot off a text to Peyton, telling her to meet me at Landon's place, and not to go home and that I'd explain everything later. I don't hear back right away, so I hand the phone back.

After a long moment, I ask, "Why were you coming my way? Is Ivy okay?"

"Ivy is fine." He takes a fast breath, and rubs the back of his neck. "And I don't know, Ella. I just had this strange feeling. I went back to the pub, and Peyton said you left with Cameron. I don't know, I just needed to see you. Something felt off."

"Cameron..." is all I can manage to get out.

I take in his dark eyes, the worry, and pain lingering there. "I mean, I know you guys are a couple, are sleeping together and it's not my business..."

I shake my head and grab my head to stop it from spinning. "I didn't sleep with him. Why are you saying that?"

His brow furrows. "Ivy said you did."

"Why does everyone think I slept with him? I didn't."

"Motherfucker," Landon barks, like he knows something I don't. "He's a fucking dead man." He swallows hard and looks me over again. "Did he hurt you?"

I shake my head no. "No, I got away." A tortured moan catches in his throat. "I'm going to fucking kill him. You know that right. As soon as you're up for it, we need to call the police."

I tug on his shirt, a tortured sound crawling out of my throat. "I don't want trouble."

"Ella," he says and I take a fast breath, the world closing in on me.

"I'm on a scholarship, Landon. I can't. I just can't."

"He hurt you."

"No, he didn't. He tried, but I hit him with my camera and got away." He reaches out and brushes his hand over my cheek, no doubt looking at the red marks formed by Cameron's fingers. "I think he put something in my drink."

"We should go to the hospital."

"No, I don't want to...I...I invited him over." Cameron's warning comes back to haunt me, and sadly enough, he's a big-ass superstar jock. I'm a nobody. My name will be raked through the mud. "I should have known better. I should have listened to you."

"None of this is your fault, Ella." His eyes slam shut. "Jesus Christ," he murmurs as he works to calm himself down. "It's my fault, not yours."

I blink through the haze, and try to settle my jumbled brain as my body begins to warm beneath his blankets. "How is it your fault?"

His gaze flies to mine, then he turns away, like he doesn't want me to see what's behind those dark, tortured eyes. What is it he's not telling me?

"He was baiting you right from the start. I fucking knew it too. I should have beat his ass a long time ago."

"Baiting me?"

He pinches the bridge of his nose and pushes to his feet. He paces to the window, glances out and comes back to me. "It was a long time ago," he begins, his voice thick with regret.

"He said you're not who I think you are. I don't understand, he said you took his virgin, or something. I don't know, it's all running together now."

"I didn't take his anything, Ella. Rebecca was never his. She was a conquest for him. He was charming his way into her pants. It was all a game. A stupid fucking freshman game that he's still playing to get even with me."

I try to sort things out but can barely think through the blur. Sleep pulls at me, but I force myself to stay awake. The tumblers all begin to align, but I need to hear it from Landon. "What kind of game?"

"It's stupid."

"Tell me."

"The sports teams play it. It's like an initiation, a hazing, freshman year."

"Hazing isn't legal."

"Which is why it's Kingston's best kept secret."

My heart begins to pick up speed again, and I just sit, waiting for him to explain. He finally breaks the quiet and explains, "We see who can sleep with the most virgins. It's a stupid contest."

"A stupid contest? You think?" Rage wells up inside me, and my insides shake, until I feel ill. "Do you play?" I tug my legs to my chest and wrap my arms around them.

"Don't be afraid of me, Ella." He reaches for me and I put my hands up, palms out to stop him. Hurt moves into his eyes as he looks down, picks at some imaginary piece of lint on the bedding. "I'd never hurt you. You have to believe that."

My mind goes back to the night of the party. Did Landon know it was me, know I was a virgin? I can only assume Jonny told Cameron. Had Landon overheard? Heck, was that the reason he brought it up in front of Cameron, to let him know he already bagged me? Won the contest?

Don't think about how tender he was, Ella. You were nothing to him.

I swallow the bile punching into my throat. "Did you play the game, Landon?" For a brief second he hesitates, and that tells me all I need to know.

His head slowly lifts, and when his eyes meet mine, my heart jumps into my throat. "Yes, no. I did. I mean I..."

I push the blankets off me. "I should go."

"Ella, wait, please. Let me explain." She blinks at me, and I stare at her. How the hell can I explain this without sounding like an asshole? "I never participated. I didn't want to participate. I have sisters, for fuck's sake. If any of them were treated that way, I'd fucking kill whoever hurt them.

"What happened with Rebecca?" she asks.

I rub my face. "She was a nice girl, from the Midwest. Really innocent and sweet." She nods, and I continue with, "Cameron went after her, and he was charming her, and I didn't like it. I didn't like him. He was always bragging about how many virgins he bagged—his words, not mine—and Rebecca was really sweet."

"You two got close."

"Yeah, and it might have started out wrong, but I wouldn't have slept with her to win some stupid bet. I really liked her."

"This totally pissed Cameron off."

I nod. "Yeah, I thought we were past it, but then...you."

"Me." She shakes her head. "I'm guessing he knew I was a virgin, and we've been hanging around a lot." She blinks up at me, and I wait for her to mention the night we were together. She opens her mouth, but before she can get anything out, someone pounds on the front door. Her entire body goes stiff, and I put my hand on her arm.

"That's probably Peyton."

"Right." She relaxes, her shoulders slumping.

I stand. "Are you okay alone for a second?"

She nods, and pulls the blankets up to her chin, and every protective instinct inside me goes on high alert. "Yeah, and Landon, thanks. I'm glad you never played the game."

I swallow, hard. "I'm sorry this happened to you, Ella. He's going to pay for this."

She shakes her head. "I don't want that. I graduate in April and this will all be behind us. I don't want this to affect your future, Landon. It's not worth it."

My heart beats against my ribs. "You're worth it, Ella."

The knock comes again, harder this time, and I reluctantly leave Ella to let Peyton in.

"What's going on?" she asks as soon as she sees my face.

"She's okay. She's upstairs. Go on up. I'm going to get her some water."

Peyton nods and dashes up the stairs as I go to the kitchen. Just then Brady comes in through the back door. I turn to him, rub my hand over my face. "Hey bro...whoa, what the fuck is going on?"

"Ella, she's upstairs. Cameron..." I let my words fall off as I grab a glass and fill it with water.

"What the fuck did he do?" Brady asks. He drops down into the chair, and I quickly tell him what happened.

"That fucker is dead," he growls, and I snort, loving that he sees things the same way I do.

"Ella doesn't want me to do anything. She's worried I'll fuck up my career."

His dark eyes narrow, his mouth tight, anger emanating off him. "Yeah, well, she never said anything about me not doing anything." He jumps from the chair and cracks his knuckles.

"Brady, this is my fight."

"Yeah, well we're brothers, so that makes it my fight, too."

"I plan to have words with him," I say.

"I will too, with my fists."

I shake my head, knowing there is no stopping Brady when he sets his mind to something. "Let me get Ella home. I want to check her place to make sure he's long gone."

"I'll come with you."

I glance up when I hear footsteps on the stairs. I head to the hall, and find Ella and Peyton walking to the front door. "Have a drink." I hand her the glass.

"Thanks." She takes it from me and has a big swallow.

"Brady and I are going to walk you both home. I want to make sure the place is safe."

"That's okay, we can get home ourselves."

"I know." I grab a jacket from the closet and drape it over her shoulders to keep her warm, and Peyton gives me a small smile and we all head outside. The girls walk ahead of us as Brady and I keep watch from behind. Once we reach her place, I go in first, and when I find her camera on the floor busted, I pick it up and examine it.

I pick up the can of soda and sniff it. Ella comes in behind me, as Peyton and Brady talk quietly in the hall. "Hey," I query softly. "Are you okay to stay here, or do you want to stay at my place tonight? Both of you, of course."

"I'm okay. I really don't think he's going to try anything again."

"You cracked him with this?" I ask, holding out her broken camera. She nods, and I smile. "Tough farm girl."

"He's probably got a good concussion."

I shake my hands out, and then fist them. "That's not all he's going to have."

"Landon, please. Don't do anything to get yourself in trouble." I'm about to tell her not to worry, when she asks, "Wait, what is going on with Ivy?"

"She's okay. She didn't end up going to the clinic. She started to feel better. It's probably the flu."

"Okay, good."

I stand there for a moment, and glance around, my gut clenching as I envision what happened here, the fear Ella must have felt. I take a deep breath and try to control my rage. It's not what Ella needs from me right now and I want to make sure I direct all of my rage at the right person.

I move my arm, and my knuckles brush hers. "Are you sure you're okay?"

"I am." She nods emphatically, but she's not okay. Nothing that happened here tonight was okay. I understand her reluctance to go to the police. Back in high school, a girl was assaulted, and she became the one who was shunned, and tossed to the curb by society. Life is not fucking fair. "Thanks for being here, Landon."

Guilt sits heavy on my shoulders weighing me down. That's just it, I wasn't there for her and I was responsible for all this. "He's going to pay, Ella." She opens her mouth, and I hold my hands up to stop her. "I won't get into trouble, but he needs to learn a lesson. This is my fault and I need to make it right."

"Landon, please…This isn't your fault." Her throat makes a sound as she swallows. "Don't tell anyone about this. It's…embarrassing."

The worry and sadness in her eyes rips through me, filleting my insides, and I take a step to close the distance. I pull her into my embrace, circling my arms around her small body, holding her close. As I offer all the comfort I can, I say, "You have nothing to be embarrassed about, and you have my word. I told Brady but he won't say anything, and I won't tell anyone else."

"Not even to Ivy?" she asks.

"Not even to Ivy. I promise."

"She said Cameron was okay."

"No one knew he would do this, Ella."

"You did, though. You warned me." She frowns. "I never knew I was such a bad judge of character."

My heart seizes, because if it *was* her in my bed, and I jumped straight into fucking her sister, in my defense I thought it was still Ella, she could very well be talking about me too. I want to ask her, get it all out into the open, but I'm not sure now is the time or place. Instead I just hold her to me, throwing up a silent prayer of thanks that she was able to fight Cameron off.

I kiss the top of her head and just hold her for another minute. Peyton peeks her head in. "Everything okay?" she asks.

I put my hands on Ella's shoulders and back up an inch. My gaze moves over her face, but she just stares at my chest, wide-eyed, like she's reliving every minute of what happened in here, just an hour ago. "You have my number. Call me if you need anything, okay?"

She glances at the movie case, and her voice is low when she says, "He said he wanted to watch a movie." She looks at Peyton and blinks rapidly.

"What?" Peyton asks, her brow furrowed, worry dancing in her eyes as she comes closer.

"Did you tell him I liked old movies?"

Peyton shakes her head. "No, I didn't."

A garbled sound catches in her throat. "He let me believe you did." How the hell did he find out I liked old movies? The only people who know are Landon, Peyton and Ivy. "He had this all planned, and I fell for it."

"None of this is your fault, Ella," Peyton says. "None of it."

Ella nods, looking unconvinced, and puts a hand over her mouth as she yawns. "Come on, let's get you to bed," Peyton says.

Not wanting to leave her, but knowing she needs sleep, I step away, and a few minutes later, Brady and I are prowling the streets looking for Cameron.

We hit up the pub and ask around, but he's nowhere to be found. The chicken shit is probably hiding out, knowing we were going to come looking for him tonight. We search the streets, all his haunts, and when we come up empty, Brady turns to me.

"We'll find him tomorrow. Hell, maybe he's already in the hospital. I saw the camera."

"Thank god it was there, and she's a quick thinker." My chest constricts. "I can't even think about the alternative." My phone pings, and panic rips through me. I tug it from my pocket, and see that it's Ivy. I frown, as I read the message.

"Everything okay?" Brady asks, his steps slowing when he sees that I've stopped.

"Yeah, it's Ivy." I start walking again and go quiet as a group of girls pass us.

"Hey Brady. Hey Landon." They all smile flirtatiously, but I have too much on my mind to flirt back. Even if I didn't, I still don't want to flirt. I think those days are behind me now. Brady gives them a smile and my mind races as he says something to make them giggle. They pass by and we start walking again, the cool night air doing little to tamp down the rage simmering inside of me. "Ivy's not been feeling well again. She wants me to come over."

I stare straight ahead, but can feel Brady's eyes on me. "Are you going?"

We take the corner, headed toward home. "I should go check on her, I guess."

"What are you going to do, bro?"

"About?"

"Come on, you know what I'm talking about."

I nod. "She asked me to go home with her for Thanksgiving."

He gives a low slow whistle. "That's a big step."

"Yeah..."

"What do you want?"

"I want what I can't have," I mumble as another message comes in from Ivy, asking me to bring her some ginger ale. "I think I should go to the farm. You know, to make sure Ella is okay."

"Yeah, I get it." He nods and I'm not sure how he can, when I have no clue what I'm doing. All I know is Ella might need me, and I want to be there for her, and I slept with her sister, and have to figure out what the hell is going on between the three of us.

"I better go. Thanks for your help tonight."

He pats me on the back. "Anytime, bro."

I head to the grocery store, pick up the soda and make my way to the sorority house. One of the girls lets me in and points me to Ivy's room. Inside, I find her on her bed, typing away on her laptop.

"How are you feeling?" I ask.

"Much better." Her gaze moves over my face. "I missed you."

"Been busy."

She cocks her head. "Are you okay?"

I hand her the soda and she puts it on her nightstand. "Yeah, just a lot on my mind." I'm not about to tell her what happened. They might be sisters, twins at that, but I gave Ella my word.

She pats the bed, a wicked grin spreading across her face. "Why don't you come over here, and let me help you forget about life for a while."

17

ELLA

I linger at the trunk of Brady's car as Ivy introduces Landon to mom and dad. When I found out Landon's best friend wasn't going back to Texas to be with his family for Thanksgiving, I asked him to come along too. It's a big farmhouse with lots of rooms and at least he'll be a nice distraction for me, someone I can talk to while Ivy and Landon are off doing their thing. He's nice too. I sat in the front with him during the drive and got to know him a little bit.

"Thanks for driving us," I say as he grabs my bag from the trunk, and hands it to me. I scoop up my camera. It's a replica of the one I smashed over Cameron's head. I just found it on my bed one day. Landon insists he didn't replace the broken one, but I know better.

"I'd have piggybacked you all the way here," he jokes with a grin. "I mean, a home cooked turkey dinner. Yeah, I'd have carried you barefoot over glass to get a meal like that."

I laugh at him, and let my gaze roam over his handsome face, which has brand new scrapes under his eyes. Unlike Landon's scars, his will heal and disappear, and while I want to ask what happened, I think it's better if I don't know. After the incident with Cameron, Cameron went missing for a few days, and rumor is that he had a run-in with Brady. Not that Landon needs anyone to fight his battles, and really, it wasn't even Landon's battle in the first place. I'm just glad the whole thing died down, and Cameron has been avoiding me ever since.

Brady grabs the rest of the bags, and slams the trunk. He glances at me as I give a great big sigh. "Everything okay?" he asks as Ivy glitters and glistens and flutters around Landon, letting Mom and Dad know that he's going to be a superstar. Is that why she's digging her nails in? He's a sure thing, and will give her the lifestyle she wants. Brady here is going to be a star too. I'm sure of it, and with his handsome, chiseled face, and being a quarterback, Brady will get more endorsement deals, and might make more money that Landon in the long run.

I pull up a smile from deep within me and flash it his way. "Perfect."

He shakes his head. "Are you going to say hello to your folks or just hang back here and worship my trunk?"

"I'm just giving Ivy a chance to introduce Landon. I don't want to interfere."

"Maybe you should," he laughs, with a casual roll of his shoulder.

I lean against the back bumper. "What do you mean?"

"Wait, do they think..." he waves his hand back and forth between the two of us, and I just shake my head.

"Don't worry. I told them you were a friend."

"I wasn't worried, Ella." His perfect teeth flash in a smile. "Any guy would be lucky to be with you."

I take in his face, and there is nothing there to suggest he's lying. "Well, that is very nice of you to say, but no one expects me to come home with a guy, anyway."

He nods like he understands and I'm glad I don't have to explain that I'm the geek who gets overlooked for her sparkling sister. "You want to mess with everyone?" he asks a gleam in his eyes.

I angle my head, and shade the sun from my eyes. "What are you getting at?"

"We could pretend we're a couple. Just to shake things up." I'm about to ask why he'd want to shake things up when under his breath he mumbles, "And light a goddamn fire under Landon's ass."

"A fire? What are you talking about?"

"Nothing...just you're sort of stuck with me, as those two figure their shit out." He scowls, all dramatic like, as he nods toward Ivy and Landon. "So let's have some fun with it and put on a show."

"I invited you," I tell him. "I don't feel stuck with you." I grin at him. "Maybe you should be in drama with Ivy." I stand, and hike my bag over my shoulder. He takes it from me and puts it over his shoulder, much the same way Landon always does. "I'm not much of an actress, and I like being behind the camera."

"Come on, it will be fun to mess with everyone." He throws his arm around my shoulder.

"I don't think—"

His smile falls, his voice very serious. "Trust me on this, Ella."

I relax as he tugs me to him. He's Landon's best friend, a nice guy, and I'm completely comfortable with him, although I have no idea why he wants to pretend we're anything other than friends. "Okay, but why?" I ask, not understanding, even though I do trust him. As we walk to where the others are standing, Brady's arm around my shoulder, my gaze lifts to meet Landon's, but he's not looking at me. No, he's shooting daggers at his best friend. What the hell?

"Mom, Dad, this is Brady. Brady, meet my parents, David and Corinne."

"So nice to meet you." Brady gives them a big smile. "Thanks so much for having me. I can't remember the last time I had a real Thanksgiving dinner."

Mom tucks a strand of blond hair behind her ear, and I know she'll take the guys in and treat them like the sons she's never had. Something tells me Brady needs that. "I'm glad you're here." She claps her hands. "I have enough food to feed a football team."

He laughs and rubs his stomach. "Not too sure about that. I eat enough for an entire team." That makes Mom laugh. If there's one thing that gives her pleasure, it's to show love through food.

"Ella!" Mom pulls me into a hug. "I love what you've done with your hair." Her eyes are warm and welcoming as they go back and forth between Ivy and me. "You two haven't looked this much alike since you were kids. I hope I don't mix you two up over the weekend." She laughs, and I tuck my hair behind my ear.

"You'll always be able to tell us apart, Mom."

"I know." She cups my face. "I'm kidding. Anyone who really knows you can never mistake who you are."

"We are so happy to have you boys here," Dad pipes in with a big grin. "How many men get to say their daughters are dating two future NFL players, and they're here for Thanksgiving?"

"Dad, we're not—"

"You like football, do you?" Brady says cutting me off before I can correct Dad, and let him know we're not a couple, because maybe I really shouldn't go along with this. I just don't see the point and I'm seriously *not* into games. I don't get why Brady wants to play this one, but he seems hell bent on it, and what does it matter really? He's a man whore, but he's a really nice guy. During the drive here I learned that he and Landon go way back. He must know about the scars on his best friend's face, but I didn't want to ask questions.

"Big fan," Dad replies, as Mom beams up at Brady. "In fact, every Thanksgiving, all the neighbors get together for a friendly game. I want you both on my team."

Brady laughs. "Landon will just slow us down. Let the other team have him, then we have a better chance of winning."

Landon gives Brady a playful punch to the gut, and Brady lets out an exaggerated grunt. I smile, liking their relationship. It's much like me and Peyton.

Brady glances around the big homestead with the barns, and orchard, tractors and bins of apples. "This place is amazing.

Wait, I don't have to get up and milk a cow at the crack of dawn or anything, do I?" he asks, his body relaxed, his arm still around me as Landon grows tenser. I cast a quick glance at Ivy, and she's looking at me like I might have an apple tree sprouting out of my head. Something tells me she doesn't like Brady hogging all the attention.

"There's a dairy farm down yonder." Dad points. "I'm sure I can hook you up."

"I think I'll pass," he says with a laugh. "Ella, do you want to show me around?"

"Right," I say. "Let's just get this stuff inside first."

"You can put Brady in Granddad's old room, and you know where you can put Landon," Mom says, as Brady and I head inside while Landon collects his bag.

I know where I'd like to put him—between my sheets—but that's never going to happen again.

"Got it." I nod and head inside.

Brady glances around after we enter. "I never would have thought Ivy was a farm girl." In the front entrance, I stop to take a breath as the very scent of home, hearth, and apple pie hits at the same time. "You, though." He gives my chin a playful nudge. "I can see it."

"Is it the overalls?" I ask with a laugh, not really needing him to answer that question.

"And the pigtails." He gives my hair a little tug.

"I like my pigtails." I head up the steps, and he follows behind me.

He chuckles. "I like them too." At the top of the stairs, he peeks into one of the bedrooms. "Tell me I don't have to share with Landon."

"Nope, you guys each have your own room. He's in the loft at the end of the hall." Footsteps pound on the stairs, and Landon and Ivy come up with their bags. Ivy walks into her room and throws herself on her bed. "Landon, get in here," she says, her voice soft, a purr almost, but I don't think Mom and Dad will allow them to share a bed. They'll have to sneak out to one of the many barns if they want to have sex. I just hope I don't stumble upon them.

"Hey, what was that all about?" Landon asks me in the hall.

"Nothing, just Brady fooling around."

"Fooling around?" he asks.

"Shit, man," Brady says. "Your grandfather was a cool guy." Needing to be away from Landon, from the way his heat reaches out to me as he stands too close, I step into Grandad's old room and find Brady looking at the pictures on the wall. I glance over the pictures. Some are of Granddad and Grandma, and some are just of Granddad from the war, some on his tractor, while others are him with a hammer in his hand, building the very house we're standing in.

"He built this place, huh?"

"Yup, the farm was actually his father's, and Granddad built this place on the bare land. I miss him and Grandma."

Brady smiles at me, and gives me another little fist bump on the chin. "You're a good one, Ella," he says. "Is it time to eat yet?"

"Our feast is tomorrow, but if you're hungry, we can go grab you a snack, or we can go get some fruit from the barns."

"Lead the way," he says.

In the hall, I find Landon leaning against the doorjamb as Ivy shows him all her childhood things. "Hey, can I come for the tour?" he asks.

"Sure." I try not to react as I walk past him, my knuckles brushing his.

"Ivy, you coming?" I ask.

"I've seen the farm numerous times." She snorts, gives a big eye roll and puts her hand on her hip, like she's impatient with me.

"Just us then," I say to the guys.

"Hurry back," Ivy calls out, and tosses herself back onto her bed.

Like kids filing from a classroom during a fire alarm, we form a line as we head downstairs, and the smell of cookies fresh out of the oven reaches our nostrils.

"Can I take a rain check?" Brady rubs his stomach. "I believe your mom might need some help in the kitchen."

I laugh at that. "Go, I can show you around later if you want."

"I want," he says, and winks at me. "Does the barn have a hay loft?"

"Oh, please." I give him a little shove. We both laugh. Landon, however, does not look impressed at all.

"Did you invite him here because you like him?"

"Sure, I like him," I say. "And he's your best friend. I didn't want to see him alone."

He gives a small nod as Brady disappears into the kitchen. "That was nice of you."

"Brady thought so too."

I push open the screen door and step outside with Landon. The warm air falls over me, and I breathe in the fresh farm scents. "Can you smell the apples?" I ask him. He nods and I head toward the storage barn. Landon follows me, and he looks like he has something on his mind.

"This place is beautiful," he says. "I can see trees for miles."

"No apple farms in Texas?" I ask.

"I'm sure there are. I've just never been to one."

"You should always take time to stop and smell the...apples," I say to him.

"You're one to talk. I don't know anyone who works harder than you."

Excitement bubbles up inside me, and I glance over my shoulder to make sure we're alone. Call me superstitious, much like Landon with his ladybug keychain, but I've been keeping a secret since this morning, and I don't want to jinx it, but I'm bursting to tell someone. Peyton would be my first choice, but she's home with her family and I don't want to bother her.

"Can I tell you something?"

His face goes serious and my heart thumps when he looks at me with such thoughtfulness. "Sure, anything."

"There were some scouts on campus during the career fair, and I received an email this morning, asking me if I would like to come in for an interview for the summer intern position as production assistant at Paramount." I wave my hands, unable to contain my excitement, and jump up and down. "Don't tell anyone. I don't want anything to ruin this. I just couldn't keep it to myself anymore."

His face lights up as he wraps his arms around me, and jumps up and down with me. "I'm so happy for you, Ella. You've worked so hard for this." He kisses my head, and the giddiness inside me morphs, changes into something I wish it hadn't. I just can't seem to keep control of my emotions around Landon. Our jumping slows, and I become acutely aware of our bodies pressed together, his hands on the small of my back, holding me against his hardness.

My lungs suddenly don't seem to want to work, and I lift my gaze to his, and go weak in the knees when I catch the heat in his eyes as our gazes collide. Without even thinking, I wet my bottom lip, and his eyes darken even more. His head dips, and one small working brain cell kicks in, sending warning alarms flashing through me. There is no denying that there is something between us, that I'm not the only one feeling it here, but he's with my damn sister, and we are not a package deal.

I swallow, and shift back a bit, putting much needed inches between us. His chest rises and falls as he breathes, his eyes never leaving mine. I turn from him to break the moment, and walk up to one of the big apple bins. I briefly pinch my eyes shut, and dig my nails into my leg to pull myself together, and try for normalcy.

"Your folks weren't upset that you weren't going home for the holiday?"

"Yeah, they wanted me there. I wanted to be here, though. I needed to be here."

Yeah, for my sister, I get it.

I nod and grab a Jonagold. "These come from a tree that's been here since the 1800's. Try one."

I hand him the apple, and he takes it, but instead of biting into it, his gaze moves over my face once again, and I feel his assessment all the way to my soul. "How are you, Ella?"

I let loose a slow breath and get the sense he's talking about the incident with Cameron, and not our near kiss. "I'm fine, Landon. It's over. Wait, is that why you needed to be here? To make sure I was okay?"

"It was all my fault. If anything ever happened to you." The sheer worry and agony in his voice cuts through me, makes me wish he was here with me, not Ivy, so I could hold him to me again, longer this time.

"You don't have to worry about me."

He steps up behind me, and his heat and energy sizzles through my body and I bite my lip to stop myself from moaning or physically reacting. "What if I want to worry about you?" he asks, his mouth near my ear, his breath hot on my neck. His fingers find my arm, and he lightly runs the backs of them up and down my bicep.

My entire body burns hot, the blood in my veins sizzle and pools between my legs. "I heard Brady went after Cameron."

"There was no stopping him, and let's just say Cameron won't be bothering you again. I'm not sure why he thought he could in the first place. I guess he figured messing with you to get to me was worth the beatdown. It's the only thing that makes sense."

I just shake my head and catching the narrowing of his eyes, the heat lingering there. "I just want to put it behind me." I want to put my feelings for Landon behind me too. I can't continue to torture myself like this. He opens his mouth like he wants to say more, and I point to the bins. "Okay, these apples are Honey Crisp," I explain and tell him how the Honey Crisps changed the apple industry and brought it back to success.

He backs up, and his voice is tight when he says, "I didn't know that."

"Here, try one," I say and our hands touch, linger as I pass it over. I take a fast breath as his head dips, his body hovering over mine. Jesus, we can't keep doing this. I'm either going to spontaneously combust or melt into a puddle at his feet.

"Ella," he begins. His throat works as he swallows, and he takes a step closer, his scent overwhelming me. I breathe him in deep, my heart pounding against his chest as our bodies touch. "You and Brady, you really were just kidding, right?" he asks, setting one apple down, to entwine his fingers with mine.

I try to sound unaffected when I answer. "I don't know why he wanted to do that."

"I do," he says his voice deep and rough, his breathing shallow. His head dips even more, and his sweet breath washes over my face, reminding me of his tender kisses, the gentle way he took my body.

"Landon," I whisper, wanting his mouth on me again, wanting his arms around me, his cock inside me. I want him. I want him so much it hurts. From the way he's acting, it's clear he wants me too. *Landon wants me too.* But this is wrong. It's so damn wrong, even though everything about it feels right.

"Thanks for telling me about the interview. I like when you share private things like that." He touches my cheek, runs calloused fingers over my jaw. "I want you to take my good luck ladybug when you go."

My heart misses a beat at his thoughtfulness. "I thought I wasn't supposed to touch it," I say, wishing my voice wasn't quite so shaky.

"You can touch anything of mine you want." His voice is soft and easy, sliding over my skin and settling deep between my legs as he cups my face.

"Thank you." My voice is low and quiet, even to my own ears. "That's really nice of you."

"Maybe I'm a nice guy, Ella."

Just then his cell phone pings, and it shocks some sense back into me.

"That's probably Ivy." I step back.

Tortured eyes move over my face, and my throat squeezes so tight it's almost impossible to breathe. "Ella…"

"I'm okay, Landon. If you're worried about me, you don't have to be. Ivy is the one you should be worried about. She's the one you're with, right?"

He stands there for a second, hurt, and something else, something that looks a lot like regret crosses his gaze. There might be something between us, but he can't have both me and my sister, and it's clear he's made his choice.

"Yeah," he agrees, he looks down, like he's remembering something deep and dark, something that weighs heavy on his shoulders—something that makes me think he knew it was me in his bed that night.

"She doesn't like to be kept waiting," I say.

"That's right, I don't," Ivy agrees from behind and then runs into the barn and jumps on Landon's back, staking her claim.

It's okay, sis, I get it. You want him and you always get what you want, no matter what.

18

LANDON

I glance at my best friend as we walk the length of the orchard, until we come to a clearing where neighbors have already gathered for their annual Thanksgiving Day game of football. After Ivy found me with Ella last night, she clung to me like dryer lint and I called it an early night just to get away from her. I've not slept with her since the night in my bed, and well, what happened between us in the theater, and I really don't plan to ever again.

This morning after breakfast, she said she had some errand in town, and didn't get home until a couple of hours ago. Ella spent the day in the kitchen helping with dinner. Brady and I offered to help, but were chased out of the kitchen, so we've been lounging around with Ella's dad, sipping beer and watching football. It was nice to relax, although I've done anything but. No, I'm too wound up, trying to figure out a way to be with the girl I want without hurting anyone in the process.

"I need to tell her," I say to Brady. "Actually, I need to tell both sisters how I feel and I need to do it now. This has to stop."

"Ivy's going to neuter you," he tells me, and I believe it. It's a chance I'll have to take.

"I know, but I can't go on like this. I agreed to come here this weekend to try to figure things out, and to make sure Ella is okay." I lower my voice and glance at him. "It had to have been Ella in my bed, Brady." Something niggles in the back of my mind, I search for it, and pull it to the forefront. "Who did you sleep with that night of the party?"

"Believe it or not, I didn't. Got a call from my father, congratulating me on the game, and then he gave me a lecture. I crashed after that."

I glance at the crowd and find Ella sitting off to the side, fiddling with her camera. She didn't want me to replace the one she broke over Cameron's head, but I did it anyway. "Someone came into my room that night. I figured it was someone you slept with and they were looking for the bathroom." I struggle to remember that morning getting dressed. Was Ella's phone on the nightstand? Jesus fuck, had Ella come back into the room to get her phone, only to find me in bed with her sister. "Holy shit."

"That doesn't sound good."

"I think Ella might have come back to the room, and saw Ivy in my bed."

"When you fuck something up, you really fuck it up, don't you?"

David waves to us, and he throws the ball my way. I catch it, and roll it around in my hand. "Not helpful."

"How do you plan to get out of this mess?"

"I just have to ask Ella straight up, then tell her Ivy was a mistake."

"Was the theater a mistake too?" he asks.

"Yeah, big fucking mistake, one that I can't take back." I toss the ball back and David runs for it. He catches it and does some funny victory dance that gets the others laughing. Many heads are turned our way, no doubt wanting to meet us and I shouldn't be standing back bitching to my best friend.

"Sure you can. Sounds to me like she forced the situation."

I scoff. "Yeah, I can see the headline now. Girl forces guy to let her blow him." I put my hand on Brady's shoulder. "Even I'm not buying it."

"I like Ella, Landon."

My gaze flies to his as my stomach clenches. "Yeah?"

He chuckles. "Not like that, but I like her. She's different, and I think you guys could be really good together."

"That's why you were all over her? To get me to finally make a move?"

"Thought you needed a glimpse of what's slipping from your hands."

"She's not going to want anything to do with me if she saw me in bed with Ivy."

He catches the ball when David throws it back. "Why don't you leave that up to her."

"Yeah," is all I mutter.

"Do it after we get dinner," he says with a laugh. "I don't want to be kicked out without a full belly." He laughs and takes off running and I just shake my head. But he's right, I don't want to screw up Thanksgiving dinner tonight, and ruin it for everyone, especially my buddy, who chose to come with us and support me, instead of going home. Not that I can blame him. He doesn't need a weekend with his parent riding his ass. Brady is under enough pressure as it is.

I reach the group, and note Ivy sitting off to the side, plucking at the grass. "Hey," she says when she sees me.

"Are you playing?"

"No, I'm going to sit this one out."

"Not feeling well again."

"Something like that." She nibbles her bottom lip, like she has something very important to tell me. I guess it will have to wait. Her father is already putting the teams together.

"Landon, son, come over here, you're on my team, and Brady you're with the others."

"I thought you wanted your team to win, David," Brady jokes with a smirk as he's introduced to his team members. I'm introduced to mine, and I catch the way both sisters are sitting on the sidelines, opposite each other.

"We're a player short, with Ivy sitting it out," someone on the other teams calls out. "Hey Ella, get on in here."

"I do not play football," she says. "I don't even know the rules."

"We don't have too many for the game this year," her dad says with a laugh. "Just get the ball over to the other side of the field. Come on, we need you."

She grumbles, sets her camera down and pushes to her feet. "Fine, I get out of dish duty tonight if I do this."

"I'll do the dishes for you," Brady says.

"I'll help," I call out and she arches a brow at me.

She points to us. "I am not interested in eating dirt today."

"Then you're on the wrong team," I say, and she glares at me.

"Landon—" she begins, and I have to say, I like seeing this playful side of her.

"I got you, Ella," one of the guys on her team says. As jealousy rages through me, I size the guy up. He looks to be about my age, and size, although stockier, and his muscles weren't built in a gym, they were grown on a farm. I hate the way he's standing so close to Ella and toying with one of her pigtails. He puffs his chest out. "They'll have to go through me to get you."

Oh, is that right. Challenge accepted.

"Brooks," Brady yells, likely to snap me out of my trance. "Prepare to be annihilated."

"Want to make it interesting, Parsons?"

"Sure, I've got nothing to lose. Right, team?" Everyone is laughing and smiling, enjoying our good-natured ribbing. "What do you have in mind?"

"Whoever loses cooks and cleans for the next month."

He throws his arms out, and his face twists in playful disgust. "Then I have to subject myself to your sub-par meals. How is that a win?"

I laugh and toss the ball at him. "Let's play."

For the next hour, we have a blast, playing fast and loose with the rules. This game is just about getting out, spending time with friends, and forgetting about the score. Although we are up, and I can't seem to help the competitive streak in me.

We all line up again, and the guy with the cannon arms, I think his name is Titus or something, stands close to Ella as they break from their huddle. He says something to her and she smirks. Okay, so she's the one to watch. Not that I haven't been doing that all along.

With the ball in motion, Ella starts running toward me, and I stand there, ready to block her when she turns around and holds her hands out for the ball. Okay, I have two choices here, let her get a touchdown, or tackle her to the ground. While tackling sounds like a hell of a lot of fun, I don't want to hurt her, so I try to block her. She darts around me, and the ball zings over my head. I could easily have stopped it, but the smile on her face is all the win I need. She catches the ball, and jumps up and down, and my heart swells inside my chest with all the things I feel for her.

"I got a goal," she says and dances around.

"You got a touchdown." I give her a high five.

"Wait, how many points is that?"

"After all the games you've recorded for the team, you still don't know?"

"Sorry, not sorry," she says and I laugh.

"Six points, Ella."

Her big blue eyes go wide. "That means we won. We won, Brady!" she calls out and he runs across the field and picks her up. Her team goes crazy and I just laugh as I watch her peacock around the field. With the game over, we take a few minutes to give everyone our autographs and spend a few minutes talking to the families, as Titus drops down into the grass with Ella as she fusses with her camera. It's easy to tell he's sweet on her, and she's so incredibly nice to him. Would Ivy be so nice? I already know the answer to that, and once again, the question of *why me* pops into my brain.

We say our goodbyes and we all head back to the homestead, everyone happy and tired. Ivy lags a bit behind, texting. She pretty much texted the whole game, and I honestly hope she's feeling okay.

The delicious smells hit as we enter, and I stretch my arms out, desperate for a shower. Ella groans as she catches her reflection in the mirror. "I need a shower."

"Go on up," Corinne says. "Dinner will be about thirty minutes. That will give you all time to shower, and Ivy can help me set the table. Maybe that will get her away from her phone for a minute. What could possibly be so important, anyway?"

I was beginning to wonder the same thing. We all head up, and Brady heads toward his room. "I need to call home. Dad sent at least a dozen texts," he moans with a frown as he checks his phone. Ella and I stand outside the bathroom door. "You go first."

She arches a brow and toys with the doorknob. "You know, you didn't have to let me win."

I lean a little closer, let her sweet scent tease my senses. "You think I let you win?"

"I think you easily could have tackled me if you wanted to."

"Are you saying you think I didn't want to tackle you?" I tease.

"I don't know what I'm saying, but now you're stuck cleaning and cooking for an entire month."

"I don't mind. It's better than taking a chance on hurting you."

Her eyes drop, her face falling, a good indication that I already hurt her, which leads me to believe all the more that she'd come back for her phone. Fuck, I want to apologize, I want to explain, I want to make things right between us, but she backs up and closes the door, abruptly ending our conversation. As I stand there staring at it, I vow that before the night is over, I'm going to get everything out in the open.

After she showers, and heads back to her room, I jump in and pinch my eyes shut, trying to dispel the image of her in here naked, or think about the fact that the soap I'm using on my body had just been on hers. A groan crawls out of my throat and I resist the urge to tug one out in the shower. Brady is waiting for his turn, and it probably wouldn't take long, but I'm going to wait. I'm going to make things right with Ella and she's worth the wait.

I finish up, dress in a pair of nice pants and a button down, and meet everyone downstairs as Brady gets himself ready. Ivy and Ella are both in dresses, and her folks are dressed up too. Tonight, Ella has her hair down, and I love the way it frames her pretty face.

"How about a beer, son?" David asks as he cracks the can and hands it to me. I take a long pull, as Corinne pours three glasses of wine. She clinks glasses with Ella and Ivy and everyone takes a sip.

"I love having the house full for the holidays," she says. "You know you're all invited back for Christmas."

"I'm sure their families will be expecting them home for Christmas," Ella says, and as I look at all the food on the counters, Ella continues with, "Mom, did you know Landon is a great cook?"

Her mom's eyes light as Ivy snaps, "How do you know that?"

"Oh, once when I was tutoring, I had some of his pasta."

"Are you done tutoring?" she asks.

"When this term ends, I will be," Ella says, and I catch something that looks like possession with a hint of anger in Ivy's eyes before she quickly blinks it away. What the hell? I must be mistaken. These girls are sisters, and Ella would do anything for Ivy. Even steal, which of course is a big secret. She said the only thing she wanted that year was to see her sister happy, but I can't help but wonder if there was something she wanted from Santa, and if she got it. Brady comes downstairs, interrupting my thoughts, and we all get ushered into the big dining room as Corinne carries in the dishes.

We talk about nothing and everything as we gorge, and underneath the table, Ivy puts her hand on my lap. My gaze instantly goes to Ella, but she's busy saying something to Brady. I'm not with Ella, but I feel a huge amount of guilt at the way Ivy is touching me. I ignore it and take a big swig of beer, as conversation turns to Ivy and theater. I don't follow along. No, I can't settle myself, can't stop thinking about what I have to say to Ella once the dinner dishes are cleared and I can get her alone for a minute.

Soon our plates are empty, and Corinne smiles at us all. "I hope you all left room for pie."

"I'll get it." Ivy jumps up. Everyone seems surprised by that. "Landon, will you help me?"

"Sure." I push from my seat and follow her into the kitchen. Once we're alone, she tugs me to her. "About time I got you alone," she says and I put my hands on her shoulders, about to push her away, tell her I can't go there with her, but what she says next, the two little words that slip from her lips, turn my world inside out and prevent me from speaking. I grip the counter to stop the spinning, to stop myself from falling as my rattled brain works to catch up. Fuck. This changes everything. Like every fucking thing.

So much for talking to Ella after the dishes are cleared and getting everything out in the open.

ELLA

"What's taking them so long?" Mom asks, and I cringe to think they're in there making out. She reaches for the water pitcher. "I'm getting thirsty."

"I'll get it." I jump up. One I don't want Mom walking in on them, and two, I'm a masochist at heart, obviously that's already been established.

I catch Brady's eye, the curious way he's watching me, and as I walk to the kitchen, my legs are stiff, everything about me suddenly self-conscious, like I'm being judged. The French door leading from one room to the other is open, and I push through it, only to come to a resounding stop. What the hell? My throat tightens as I listen to them talk in whispered words, and a part of me hopes, prays, I'm hearing them wrong.

Ivy is pregnant!

What the ever-loving fuck. My sister is pregnant, and the man I've been crazy about forever is going to be her baby daddy. I must be hearing things. How can this be real? *Oh, because they've been sleeping together, Ella.* A noise I have no control over crawls out of my throat, announcing my presence, and as my brain kicks my ass into gear, I plaster on a smile and bounce into the room, pretending I haven't heard anything. Yeah, I'm good at pretending. Good at pretending that I don't care about Landon, that we didn't sleep together, didn't share many moments over the last few months, or the real biggy, that I didn't witness Landon and Ivy in bed together. Who knew I was the award-winning actress in the family?

"Are you going to share that pie or eat it yourselves?" I joke, my voice light and chirpy despite the storm raging inside me. I walk around them and fill the pitcher, hoping the running water will drown out the sound of my heart crashing against my ribcage.

"On it," Ivy says, one set of footsteps on the floor as she heads to the other room. I don't need to turn around to know Landon is still standing there, probably shocked in place.

"Are you coming, Landon?" Ivy asks.

"Ah, yeah. Ella, do you need help with the water?"

"I scored a touchdown," I remind him, attempting a light-hearted tease. "I think I can handle a pitcher of water." What I can't handle is seeing Landon's face right now. I might just burst into tears. How could Ivy have gotten herself pregnant? For as long as she's been sexually active, she's been on the pill. I snort. What the hell am I saying? Why am I putting the blame on her? It takes two. This is just as much Landon's responsibility as it is hers. Another thought hits. What the hell does this mean for the future, for their careers? Will she keep it? Does she want it? Does he? Are they going to tell my parents this weekend?

I'm about two seconds from dumping the entire pitcher of water over my head to slow down my thoughts, when laughter comes from the other room and shakes some sense into me. Clearly, they're not in there sharing the news, because I don't really think this is a laughing matter. How either of them can go back into the dining room and pretend all is right in the world is beyond me. I know I can't pull it off. I guess the Oscar really does go to Ivy.

I try to keep my hand steady as I carry the pitcher of water to the table and set it down. "Are you okay, Ella?" Mom asks, as she blinks up at me.

"Just so tired. It's been a long semester, and a long day. Is it okay if I call it a night? I'll do all the dishes tomorrow."

"You don't have to do that. You helped enough today." Mom stands, and in typical Mom fashion, she puts her hand to my forehead. "You are feeling a bit warm. Go lie down and we'll take care of this. I'll come check on you later." I give her a kiss on the cheek, and keep my eyes off everyone else as I walk through the dining room and head for the stairs. I dash up them, push open my bedroom door and throw myself onto my bed.

With my insides tight and tears pounding behind my eyes, I stare at the ceiling for a long time, until the sun sets and the house settles. I roll to my side, and look at my phone through the blur of tears. Reaching for it, I run my finger over the screen, wanting to call Peyton and tell her. Heck, I tell her everything. But this isn't my news to share. I groan, and indulge in a pity party for a little longer, then push to my feet, and work to ignore the ache inside my body, right around the vicinity of my heart. Hugging myself, I walk to the window and glance out into the dark night.

I guess Ivy is going to need me now more than ever, and I can hardly believe I'm going to be an aunt. Dammit, I'm going to be the best aunt. If she decides to keep it, that is. Landon's mother is a minister. I can only imagine she'd expect Landon to do the right thing, and have the child. My God, does doing the right thing involve marriage too?

My forehead thumps against the cool window and I pinch my eyes shut, considering all the scenarios. My phone pings and I nearly jump out of my socks. I hurry to it, and scoop it off the nightstand as I plunk down on my bed. My pulse jumps when I see a message from Landon.

Landon: How are you feeling?

Me: Much better, thanks for asking.

Landon: Is there anything you need?

Another groan crawls out of my throat. There is plenty I need, but I don't think we get to do a do-over in this lifetime. Landon slept with Ivy, and now she's pregnant. The sooner I accept and deal with it, the better.

Me: No. I'm good. Why are you still up?

Landon: I could be asking you the same question.

Me: I'm just getting ready for bed. You should do the same.

Landon: In bed. Can't sleep. Lots on my mind.

I run my finger over his words, touching them. Do I ask him what's on his mind, and pretend not to know?

Landon: I was thinking of a walk through the orchard. Want to join me?

I stare at my phone, and while I want to say yes, in my heart I know I need to say no. The less time I spend with him the better. Then again, if he's going to be a part of the family, there's no escaping, is there?

Landon: I'm afraid I'll get lost in the orchard and never find my way out.

Me: Okay, meet me by the apple bins.

Landon: I could meet you in the hall.

Me: I don't want to wake anyone. Just meet me outside, and go out the front door, the back screen door squeaks.

I stand, shove my phone into my back pocket and tug on a sweater. This is a mistake. I totally know it, but I suspect he might need someone to talk to.

I stand at my door listening, waiting for him to make it downstairs, and then quietly open it. Keeping the lights off, I make my way down in the dark. I step outside and take a big breath of night air, letting it soothe the anxiety inside me. I peer into the dark, and can make out Landon's shape out near the barn. I head toward him, the night sky bright with stars.

"Hey," I say when I reach him. I can't quite see his face in the dark, but can hear the stress in his voice when he says hello. "You want to go for a walk?"

"Sure."

Grass and hay crunch beneath our feet as we head out into the orchard. A comfortable quiet surrounds us as we walk, both lost in our own thoughts. Finally I break the quiet and say, "Most of the trees are picked clean by now, but a few of the later apples are still on them. Want to go grab one?"

"Sure," he says and I chuckle. "What?"

"That seems to be your word of the night. What happened to that great vocabulary of yours?"

Our knuckles brush, and I can almost feel him relax beside me. "Just a little lost for words tonight," he says and I nod in the dark, even though he can't see me.

"Come on," I urge, and take his hand, sensing he needs a reprieve from reality, if only for a little while. "Let's go do something fun."

"Fun is good."

We walk and walk and walk, until we reach our neighbor's farm. I put my hand to my lips to make sure he stays quiet. "Where are we?" he asks in a whispered voice. I take my phone out and put on my flashlight app. I shine it on the corn stalk maze.

"My neighbors set this up every year for the kids."

"It's a maze?" he asks.

"Yeah, want to do it?"

He scratches his head and when I shine the light on him, he says, "Can you turn that off?" He used those exact words when I shone the light on him in his bedroom that first night, the night that feels like it happened so long ago.

"Sorry," I apologize and turn it off. I run into the maze and he curses under his breath as he follows behind me.

"Where the hell are you?" he asks, and I run, loving the wind in my face, and just wanting to be twelve again, no worries, no hurt...

"Marco," he calls out and I laugh.

"Polo," I say and run around the stalks, coming to a dead end. I turn and take the right when I spot his shadow in the distance.

"Marco."

His voice is close, and I keep running. When I get to a safe distance away, I whisper, "Polo." I can't stop the chuckle in my throat. It rises up and gives away my location as I try to get past him. He reaches out and snatches me by the waist.

"Got you," he says, and tugs me to him. The chuckle dies on my lips as his heat reaches out to me, the space between us filling with want, need, and volatile energy.

"Ella," he whispers in the dark, and I wet my lips, wanting his mouth on mine.

"Yeah?"

He pushes my hair back, and tucks it behind my ears and my entire body tingles, from the top of my head to the tips of my toes. His finger lingers near my ear, and trail down along my neck. His touch is like fire on my skin as I pull in a fast breath. A noise sounds in the distance, an animal scurrying in the night, but we continue to stand there, face to face, our bodies close, aligned perfectly. Before I can think better of it, I put my hands on his shoulders, just for one second—one last time—wanting to feel him.

He leans into me, and his warm breath washes over my face. I wish I could see his eyes. But I'm being selfish, taking what isn't mine even though it seems to be what we both want. Sometimes life just isn't fair. I drop my hands, and step into him, pressing my face against his heart. His hands close around me, like he too knows we can't do this. In the dark of the night we stand there, two lost souls.

"Ivy's pregnant," he finally says, his voice low, soft...afraid.

I inch back, and as his features form in the dark, I tell him, "I know."

"You heard?"

"I didn't mean to. I was coming into the kitchen to get the water." Suddenly feeling confined in the maze, I take his hand and lead him out. We walk in silence again until we reach our farm and I drop down and press my back against an apple tree. Landon sits next to me, and I stare at the stars as his thigh presses against mine. I like him next to me like this, like we're the only two people in the world awake.

"I'm...scared," he admits, and his honesty, his fear, rakes me raw inside. "Here I never thought I could be more frightened than I was that day at the movie theater."

"What happened?" I ask quietly. His hand goes to his cheek, to his scars, and I adjust my position and sit cross-legged facing him. "You don't have to tell me the details, if you don't want to."

He shifts positions, and sits cross-legged to face me. "It's not something I talk about. Not something I want to relive. I wouldn't even go to counselling. I just wanted to forget it."

"It's okay, you don't have to tell me." I put my hand on his legs and he gathers it up. His warm palm closes over my smaller hand. He holds me like that for a long time, and I just absorb his heat, feeling closer to him than I ever have before. His head lifts and when his dark eyes meet mine, something passes between us, and brings us closer together. My heart beats heavily in my chest, and I shift, just to get a little closer.

"It was crazy," he begins, and I suspect opening up like this is hard for him. I remain silent, letting him tell his story his own way. "Brady and I skipped class and went to the movies. It was a kids movie, but we didn't care. We were in grade nine, and anything beat English."

"You were fourteen?"

"Yeah."

I smile at him. "You hated English back then too, huh?"

He snorts. "Yeah, I guess." His lips go tight. "The theater wasn't that crowded. Just some teens skipping school, some elderly people filling their day, and some kids there with their parents. There was this one couple, early twenties, and I remember thinking they seemed out of place. Later I came to learn they were in the dark theater because they didn't want anyone to find them."

From the way he shakes his head it's easy to tell this is the story, this couple is what caused the problem. "Cheaters, huh?"

"Yup." I go quiet again, and let him talk. "This woman's husband was on to them, though. He showed up..." He stops to give a low, slow whistle and I stare at him, take in the twisted agony on his face. "He was totally armed, Ella. Knives and guns, and he was taking everyone out with him that day."

"Jesus," I whispered. "That must have been horrifying for you."

"He killed his wife and her boyfriend first." He holds his hand out and makes a noise like he's shooting a gun. "He didn't even talk to them, just bang bang, and they were dead. Kids started screaming. Everyone started screaming, I was fucking screaming, and he continued to take us out one by one. Brady called 911, but I knew...I knew the cops would never reach us in time, and all those kids were going to die. The exit was behind the gunman, and we were stuck. As soon as I realized that, I reacted. I don't even really remember reacting, but I did." He squeezes my hand a little harder, and closes his eyes, and I hate this trip down memory lane he's taking. I shouldn't have opened the door, shouldn't have asked, but there's a part of me that thinks he needs to get this out.

"What...what did you do?" I ask, and close my hand over his, my throat tight as goose bumps spread across my arms.

"I ducked down, crawled to the other side of the aisle, and just as he pointed the gun at Brady, I jumped him. The gun went off, and he dropped it, and I was so goddamn frightened that he got Brady. The guy grabbed his knife and started stabbing at me over his shoulder. It was like something straight out of a bad horror movie. I held on, though. I don't even know how."

"You were so brave."

He shrugs like he wasn't. "When I was young, I used to watch MMA in secret. Mom didn't like it. But I learned some moves, and I just kept my arm around his neck, squeezing and squeezing while he cut me."

"Landon...I can't even imagine. Did he hurt Brady?"

"No, and while I choked him, Brady got the kids and elderly out safely."

"How did you get out?"

"He passed out and went down. I still kept strangling him, until Brady eventually pulled me off, and dragged me outside. It felt like it went on for hours. The police showed up, and it was total chaos."

"So scary." I free one of my hands and lightly brush his scars.

"It could have been worse. He could have damaged this pretty face."

I stare at him, and it takes a full five seconds to realize he just cracked a joke. "I happen to like this face, Landon."

He grins. "I've never told anyone that story. Never thought I could. Brady relayed the events to the cops, and our names were never released to the media. None of us wanted reporters parked outside our houses." A long pause and then, "Anyway, that's why I take so many English classes."

While that makes little sense to me, everything about him relaxes, like getting that off his chest was a healing balm to his soul. "What do you mean?"

"I thought one day I might like to write a book, or a screenplay."

My mouth drops open. There is just so much more to this guy than I ever realized. "Maybe someday I'll produce it."

He grins. "Yeah?"

"Yeah," I agree and shift positions until I'm leaning against the tree.

He moves in beside me. "You saved a lot of people. You saved Brady."

"He's my brother. I protect those I care about, Ella. Fiercely."

I nod, realizing that about him. "It's nice that you two have such a tight bond. Peyton and I are close like that, and when the baby happens, you won't be alone. Brady will be there for you."

"Yeah, he will be." His head nods, his mood thoughtful. "That makes me feel a little less frightened."

Our thighs touch, and I just want to snuggle in next to him, hold him close and tell him everything will be okay, although I'm not sure it will be. "I'll be there for you too, Landon."

"You will?"

"Yes. You've got me," I say. Truthfully, he had me long before he ever came over to talk to me on that football field that fateful day, long before I ever fell into his bed. Now however, is not the time to tell him. The chance for us is long gone.

LANDON

E ight months later:

After a long tiring day of training beneath the Atlanta sun, I throw myself onto the bed and glance around the hotel room Brady and I are sharing. With both of us now playing for Atlanta, and spending so much time here, we need to soon find permanent residences. After signing our contracts, we bought homes in California, where we want to be off season, and of course, Ivy and my daughter Piper needed a place to live. I'm not about to shirk my responsibilities.

I pull out my phone and stare at the screen saver and admire the image of my little girl, with all that red hair and stark blue eyes, wrapped in a pink blanket. My heart squeezes in my too tight chest as I look at my baby, and consider where my life is today. I'd never given a whole lot of consideration to being a dad—my whole life was spent trying to make it into the NFL —but I'm trying like hell to be the best dad for my girl. I'm also trying to do right by Ivy, and everyone else, but some-times it's not easy.

Everyone expects us to get married, and as the only boy in the family, Mom gave me grandma's ring. I can't quite bring myself to put it on Ivy's hand. I have to do the right thing. I know that, although Ivy told me straight up she wants to lose her baby weight before we get engaged, or married. She wants the perfect engagement pictures for Instagram. Honestly, everything happened so fast and I never even considered us a couple, then or now. Ivy would tell you differently, but I've been so caught up in the whirlwind of her pregnancy, finishing college and signing on with Atlanta, that I don't know if I'm coming or going anymore.

How can I possibly ask Ivy to marry me when it's not what I want, when I'm in love with her sister? That night under the apple tree, the connection Ella and I shared, the deep bond that blossomed between us, I knew for sure it was her in my bed, and that she'd seen me with Ivy. I can't even imagine how awful that was for her, or what she thought of me afterward. But she stood by my side and watched as Ivy gave birth to my little girl.

She's been my rock. Always there for Ivy and Piper, and even more so now that I'm away at training camp. She also supported me when Ivy started suffering from post-partum depression right after Piper was born in early June. Ella basi-cally took over the care of my child. Heck, she's crazy busy herself, interning at Paramount, and she's practically raising Piper all on her own. As for Ivy, after college, and the baby, she pretty much lost interest in everything except her friends, who she's still going out with, and I guess that is good for her mental health. I mean, she loves Piper. I can see it in her eyes when she looks at her and I'm trying to be a good partner.

Ella and I have gotten her help. The doctors say with the right medication and therapy, she'll come back around, and settle into parenthood. In the meantime, I'm counting on my sister-in-law to take care of my almost two-month-old more than I really should. I'm going to have to talk to Ivy about getting a nanny. Maybe she'll be more responsive to it now. She probably wouldn't want to appear to the world like she isn't the one taking care of Piper, and she'd just say Ella will help her.

I put my arm over my forehead and am about to flick the TV on, to watch something mindless as I fall asleep when my phone pings. I sit up a little straighter as Ella Facetimes me.

"Hey," I say after swiping my finger across the screen. Ella comes into view, and my stupid heart beats that much faster, the way it always does when we talk. "Everything okay?"

"Everything is fine," she assures me, but I'm worried about her. She's been burning the candle at both ends, and no amount of makeup can hide those dark, sleep-deprived smudges under her eyes. A good indication that Piper is keeping her up at night. But she's a great aunt, and will do anything for her niece, her sister, and for me.

"She's doing great." She turns the phone so I can see Piper sleeping in her cozy bassinet.

"How are you doing?" she asks, her eyes narrowing in on me and I appreciate her genuine concern.

"Good. Tired."

"Training is going well?"

"Coach is kicking my ass, but I'm not complaining. I'm learning a lot."

"Let me know when you play in a game. Piper insists on watching, which will, of course, force me to suffer through a game." That makes me chuckle and she laughs right along with me. "I bet you're doing great, Landon. You're the golden boy."

I'm living my father's dream, but it's my dream too. There isn't anything else I'd rather do. Then again, how would I know? I was steered into football since I was born. But I never wanted to let my father down. I never wanted to let my mother down either, which is why I have to do the right thing and put a ring on Ivy's finger.

But is it really the right thing for you, Landon?

"How is Ivy?"

Her smile dissolves. "She's okay." She glances back at Piper, and when my sweet girl makes a cooing sound, she tucks her blanket around her tighter. "She's out again tonight. Aunty Ella is on duty."

I scrub my face. "Where did she go this time?"

"She didn't tell you?" she asks, and I hate to admit that while Ivy and I have a child together, dialogue isn't our strong suit... not much is, actually.

"No, I haven't heard from her." I've sent a few texts, but she hasn't answered. I really hate how much she puts on her sister, but I'm trying to understand postpartum.

"She met up with some friends from college." She gives a casual shrug but it's easy to tell she's not happy about the whole thing. "I think they went for drinks. Maybe it will be good for her, you know. Help her mental state."

What about Ella's mental state? Who the hell is there for her when she needs help? Goddammit, none of this is fair.

Ah, but you learned a long time ago life isn't fair.

"Yeah, maybe." I shift my pillow and adjust it behind my back. "I'm sorry, Ella. I'll be home in four days, and I'll see about hiring a nanny if Ivy isn't back to herself." Honestly, training camp can't end quick enough. I don't have a lot of time off before our season starts in September, but I'll have a few days to spend with family.

"Don't be sorry." She leans in and drops a soft kiss onto Piper's forehead and my breathing changes, becomes a little ragged. I hate being away from them. "I don't mind spending time with this cutie. Tomorrow we're going to the pier to get Christmas pictures."

"Ah, it's July."

She laughs and my heart swells when she smiles at me. "I take it Christmas in July isn't a big thing where you grew up."

"Not at all." I shake my head and laugh. Honestly, what would I do without Ella? Over the past eight months, she's been rock solid. That day under the apple tree, she said she'd be there for me, and she wasn't lying. My gaze moves over her face, a little thinner now, her cheekbones more defined. She touches her hair, which is darker now and cut short to frame her gorgeous face. It looks good on her. She retired her overalls and now dresses professionally. But I liked her in her overalls. I liked her in everything, especially my arms.

"How's work?" I ask, and glance at my ladybug keychain, needing to occupy my mind with something else. I love that she took it on her interview, and won the intern position. "Spielberg finally realize your talent and come looking?"

"Hardly."

"He doesn't know what he's missing."

She chuckles. "Men can be so dense sometimes." She turns the phone to show me a pile of books and papers on the sofa. "Work is good, though. Really busy, and while it's not my dream job, it can help me get there."

"You deserve to have all your dreams come true."

She smiles, but I know her well enough to know it's forced. She points a finger at me. "I'm still waiting on that script from you."

"I've been trying to write it out, in between touchdowns," I tease.

"Someday, Landon." Her voice goes soft, intimate almost, and I grip the phone tighter, cradle it in my hands. "I've been talking about you to Piper." She crinkles her nose. "I've been telling her all about your famous touchdowns." Her soft voice curls around me, through me, teasing the deep longing inside me that won't go away.

"I appreciate that," I tell her. I smile and think about the touchdown that brought Ella to the party at my house last year, the same touchdown that led her to my bed later that night. As my body warms, remembering her soft skin, and enticing scent, arousal hits like a two-hundred-pound linebacker, but I quickly shut it down.

I clear my throat and struggle to marshal my thoughts. "Want to watch a movie together, or do you have to get to work?"

A knock sounds at her door. She glances away and then answers, "I actually have to work. That's Nathan. He's here to go over some work things with me. But don't worry, I won't take my eyes off Piper."

A wave of jealousy I have no right to feel kicks me in the nuts. Jesus, what the hell is the matter with me? I want her to find someone. I want her to be happy, to have a family of her own. Ella deserves that more than any woman I know.

"Okay, and Ella, thanks again. You're the best."

"My pleasure, Landon." She gives me a soft smile and points the phone at Piper again so I can say goodbye. I blow her a kiss and then Ella ends the call—to go let asshole Nathan in so they can work. He's probably not an asshole. I'm just in a shitty mood now and that's selfish on my part.

I drop my phone and stare at the ceiling. I'm about to put a pillow over my face and try to fall asleep without my thoughts on Ella when Brady comes bursting in. He takes one look at my pathetic self, and goes still.

"Everything okay?" he asks, and shoves his phone into his back pocket.

"Yeah, was just talking to Ella. She has Piper tonight."

"Piper is good?"

"Yeah."

His eyes narrow in on me, and sometimes I hate how well he can read me. "You good?"

"I don't know." I grab a pillow, put it on my lap and give it a little punch.

He stares at me for a second longer. "Come on, we're getting a drink."

I'm about to protest but he has that look on his face that says he won't take no for an answer. "Shouldn't you be off with a girl or two by now?"

"Not when my buddy needs me."

"Fine." I throw my legs over the side of the bed and grab my wallet. Twenty minutes later we're in the hotel bar, sitting at a table where I'm nursing a beer. I stare at my best friend. He doesn't think I should marry Ivy, not when I'm in love with her sister, but how can I let everyone down, including my child? I need to step up and be the man everyone needs.

What about what Ella needs?

Two women come over, their eyes wide with recognition. "Great practice today," one says, and puts her hand on my arm as she sits down next to me and leans in to showcase her cleavage. The brunette cuddles up next to Brady.

"Thanks," I say. If there's one thing I've learned it's that cleat chasers don't care if I'm a dad or not. They all still want a piece of the player, but I'm not a cheater. Never was and never will be. But would I really be cheating? Ivy and I aren't engaged or married. But I feel I have to be committed to her, which Brady thinks is crazy.

"Why don't you girls grab a seat at the bar, and I'll meet you there in a minute," Brady says. "My buddy and I have something to discuss. Tell the bartender to put your drinks on my tab."

"Don't be too long," the blonde purrs with a giggle. The two stand, head to the bar and I shake my head at Brady. "Aren't you getting tired of that?"

"Don't be mad that I'm getting laid and you're not."

"Have at it, my friend," I say, even though I get the sense that he's getting a little played out. Marriage would look good on him, but his parents' loveless relationship is likely scaring him off.

"Speaking of getting laid, you—"

I hold my hand up to cut him off. "Don't want to talk about it."

He sits back in his chair and picks up his beer. "Aren't you getting tired of living a life that makes you miserable?"

"I'm not miserable." It's a lie. I am miserable. "I love my daughter."

"I know you do. But that's not what I mean. You don't have to marry Ivy. It's not the 1950s, for Christ's sake."

"My mother is a minister, Brady," I say for the umpteenth time. I am so tired of this same old argument. "There's no escaping it."

"I love your mother and honestly I don't care if she's the pope. She shouldn't be pushing this on you."

"I don't want to talk about it."

"You can still go after the girl you want. Jesus, Landon. I see the way you two are together. The chemistry, the way you both look at each other. Even after all this time. That's the real deal, my friend."

I take a long pull from my bottle. "Why me? Why not you?" I ask, bringing up another subject that we've beaten to death. "Ivy never paid any attention to me until I showed interest in Ella. Why did she even climb into my bed that night?"

"Those are questions for Ivy," he says. He's right, and I've never really asked too many questions. She was sick for nearly her whole pregnancy, and now she has post-partum. We never really talked, and truthfully, once she got me, it seemed like she no longer wanted me. Maybe she just wanted to secure her future with an NFL player, which once again leads me back to Brady. He was the kind of guy she went for, but he never seemed to want to hook up with her. I'm not even sure if he likes her, and he once tossed out the theory that she was jealous of Ella—wanted what her sister had.

I still can't quite wrap my brain around that. Ella always stood in the shadows for her sister, always let Ivy shine, she fucking stole lipstick for her, for Christ's sake. Sisters care for one another, stand up for each other, and always want what's best for the other one, right? That's what my sisters do. That's what Ella does, but I've never seen Ivy stand up for Ella. All I know is Ivy wasn't as liked as I thought she was, not like Ella. Yeah, everyone likes Ella. Me, though. I don't like Ella. Nope.

I fucking love her, and I'm so fucking tired of doing the right thing, which doesn't feel like the right thing at all.

So what the hell are you going to do about that, asshole?

21

ELLA

"Hey sweet girl," I coo to Piper as I put her in an adorable red and white dress, with an equally adorable Santa's hat. I'm going with Ivy today to the pier to get Piper's pictures taken with Santa for the big Christmas in July festival, and I just love the outfit Ivy purchased for her.

I check the time as Ivy comes downstairs, dressed in a sexy little cocktail dress that showcases all her curves. Over the last month, she's been working hard to lose her baby weight, and there are times like now, and I feel like crap for saying this, but I can't help but think her mental state of mind is just fine, and she's taking advantage of me. Ugh, I feel so horrible for thinking that, and really I've never had a child and don't really know what she's going through. One thing I do know is that her dress is a little over the top for visiting Santa.

"She's all ready," I say and scoop little miss Piper into my arms. I adjust her hat over her abundance of red hair, and she sticks her tongue out at me. Not on purpose of course. She's not quite two months old yet.

Ivy takes her from me, and rubs noses with her. "How is my beautiful little girl?" she asks and I smile and Piper coos and giggles at her mom. "Were you a good girl letting Auntie Ella dress you while Mommy got ready?" My heart fills with love as I watch mother and daughter. The bond between them is strong and it makes me want a family of my own. Only problem is, the man I want to father my children, has already fathered my sister's child.

"You ready to go?"

She holds her daughter. "Actually, something's come up," Ivy explains quickly and averts her gaze like she can't meet my eyes. What the hell? She steps up to the hallway mirror in Landon's gorgeous Santa Monica home. Over the last couple of months, I've spent more time here than in my own apartment, what with Landon in Atlanta and Ivy needing help with a newborn. "Would you mind watching her?" she asks, as she gives herself a once over in the mirror.

My heart dips into my stomach. Ivy is great with her daughter, but she's putting more and more responsibility on me. At first she was so excited to get pregnant, but now that the baby is here, and while she loves her madly, she's less than thrilled with the responsibility. Heck, I'm working full time and up through the nights with her more than Ivy is. Am I enabling her? Jeez, maybe I am.

"What's up?" I ask, and cuddle my sweet cooing niece as Ivy hands her over.

"Job interview." She smiles widely as she teases a few blonde curls.

Okay, now that's a big surprise. "I didn't realize you were even looking for a job."

"A friend put me in touch with this director. We're meeting for dinner."

"That's amazing, Ivy. Congratulations." I glance at the big clock on the wall. "But dinner at two o'clock in the afternoon? That seems odd."

"Directors are busy people, and if you prefer you can call it a late lunch." She pouts at me, the same pout she always uses to get what she wants—even with me. "Would you mind watching Piper tonight as well? I'm just not sure what time I'm going to be back." I take one look at my sister in her sexy dress that does little to hide her abundance of cleavage and the salad I'd eaten for lunch sinks like stone in my gut. An uneasy feeling creeps through my veins. I don't like the looks of this. Not one little bit.

"I can watch her," I say, and mumble under my breath. "It's not like I have a life or anything."

"What was that?" Ivy asks as she swipes a bright red lipstick over her lips.

"Nothing. I don't mind watching her. Go ahead. I'm sure you'll do great. Is there a particular part you're up for?" Ignoring me, Ivy drops the lipstick back into her purse, gives Piper a big kiss, leaving her lip marks on her cheek, and is about to walk away when I ask, "Have you talked to Landon today?"

She turns to me, her eyes narrow. "No, why?"

"I don't know," I adjust the bow on Piper's dress. "He's home in three days. Will you be able to pick him up at the airport? I mean, I can if you can't. I can help out." Shit, shit, shit. Do I sound anxious to see him? I lift my head and another burst of unease worms its way through my body when a flash of anger—at least I think it's anger—blazes in her eyes. Why the hell would she be angry? Maybe it's not anger, maybe it's something else that looks like anger. Something like jealousy. But that doesn't make sense. She has everything I want, it's not the other way around.

"I'm pretty sure I can pick up my lover," she bites back, her choice of words stinging a bit.

"Okay, just checking." I swear I'm more excited to see him than she is. A knock comes on Ivy's door, and I say, "That's probably Peyton. She wanted to come to the pier with us."

I open the door, and Peyton tugs on Piper's hand. I smile at her, and she seems much happier and more confident now that she's shed her college weight. "How's the little chicken nugget?"

"Don't call her that," Ivy snaps and Peyton raises her brow at me. "She's a beautiful little girl."

"She's in a mood," I whisper under my breath. Clearly, asking about Landon set her off. I don't know what is going on with them, but suspect I talk to him more than my sister does. Peyton walks into the house, and gives a low slow whistle when she sets eyes on Ivy's dress, or lack thereof.

"You're going to make Santa one happy man when you sit on his lap."

Ivy twirls, obviously loving the compliment. "Thank you, but I have an interview. Ella will explain. I have to go. I'm running late." She flies past us, stopping for a second to give Piper another kiss and heads out the door.

Peyton jerks her thumb over her shoulder. "It's nice to see her smiling."

"She does seem to be doing better." I frown. "I think."

"What's this interview she's talking about? I didn't realize she was going to work. Who's going to take care of Piper?"

"That makes two of us and I have no idea what the position is for, or what she plans to do with Piper."

"Girlfriend, no one dresses like that for an interview, and the only position—"

"Stop," I blurt out, but suddenly can't stop visualizing Ivy in all kinds of positions, and none of them sit well with me.

Peyton, ever astute, which is what makes her a great social worker, gives a slow shake of her head and I can almost hear the wheels turning. "I don't like this. Something is off here."

My heart drops from my stomach to my toes, because it's not the first time I thought things were off. Ivy and I both have naturally dark hair, and so does Landon. Piper's stark red hair seemed a little off, but Landon said one of his sisters was a redhead. Still, there's just something that doesn't sit right with me.

"I was thinking the same thing," I admit. "Do you think she's...seeing someone?"

"I don't really know. But she's pretty dressed up, even for an interview, don't you think?"

I nod, unable to deny it, but I don't like drama or trouble, and something tells me it's lurking right around the corner. "She's been going out a lot with the girls, too." I purse my lips. "I've been babysitting this chicken nugget a lot. I practically live here now."

Peyton takes Piper from me, and talks to her softly as she walks to the living room and drops down into the sofa. Her head lifts. "Landon is home soon?"

"Three days." I grab a clip from my purse and pile my hair on the top of my head. I've had very little time for selfcare lately. Is it any wonder I can't get a date? Then again, have I really been putting myself out there?

"Do you think they're having problems?" Peyton asks.

"No clue. I really try to mind my own business. I have to, otherwise I'd go insane."

She gives me a consoling smile and I let out an exaggerated breath. "This isn't easy for you, Ella."

"Ivy is my sister and Piper is my niece. I have to be there for them."

"Your sister stole the man you were, or rather are, in love with right out from underneath you."

"That's the thing, she didn't know." She arches a brow like she doesn't believe that for a hot second, but I like to give my sister the benefit of the doubt. "She can't steal what was never mine, now can she?"

"He was yours. He slept with you that night. He chose you, Ella."

"Then why was Ivy in his bed after me?"

She gives a frustrated groan. "For the life of me, I can't understand why you two refuse to talk about what happened." I open my mouth, about to explain, when she cuts me off. "He had to know it was you. Anyone with half a brain can tell you two apart, even in the dark, and Landon is no dummy."

I check my watch. "Doesn't matter now, though, does it? He's with Ivy now."

"Is he, though? I mean she lives here with his child, but that doesn't mean they're a couple."

"Ivy is waiting on the ring, Peyton. Don't think for a minute she's not."

"What's Landon waiting for then? If he plans to marry her, wouldn't he have asked her by now?"

"Something to do with her baby weight," I say.

"Maybe, but maybe there is another reason he's waiting. Maybe he's waiting for a sign from you, and believe you me, he will not put a ring on her finger, or do the right thing by her if you tell him how you feel or if he finds out she's cheating," she says.

I bite my lip, hard. "Jesus, if she is, do I tell him?"

"Of course."

I give a fast shake of my head as my pulse leaps at the thought of going behind my sister's back. It's not right, but if she's cheating, that's not right either. "I don't know, Peyton...I..."

"Fine, I'll do it for you. Wait, do you think he could be cheating on her? I mean, you know these girls hang out at training camp just to sleep with the players."

"No, he's not a cheater," I say vehemently.

Peyton gives me a look like she just won the lottery—like she just made a huge point. "Exactly, Ella," she says, going into professional mode.

"I'm not one of your patients, Peyton."

"He's not a cheater. You just defended him. Vehemently. That means you don't think he would go from you to Ivy in the same night."

Ohmigod, can we stop this constant back and forth battle? "Because he thought I was her to begin with."

"You know I don't believe that. I've told you that numerous times."

"And in numerous ways," I remind her, but that just results in a knowing smirk from her.

She stands and I take Piper from her. She fusses in my arms, and I hold her against my chest and rock with her the way she likes. Peyton stands there staring at me, but honestly, what is the point of all this now anyway? He's with my sister. I grab the diaper bag and put it over my shoulder. "We better go."

We head out into the gorgeous sunshine, and after I buckle little Piper into her seat, I pull into traffic. We drive through the downtown core, on our way to the Santa Monica Pier.

"Why don't we go to Third Street Promenade? I hear they're doing a fun parade and have a really good Santa."

I cast a quick look Peyton's way. "Yeah, how do you know that?"

"Clients. We talk, you know."

I laugh at that. After college, Peyton got an amazing job at a behavioral health clinic, working with kids of all ages. She loves it, but I'm sure I'd burn out in a heartbeat. "I don't know. Ivy wanted to take her to the pier."

"Do you see Ivy anywhere here?" Peyton blurts out.

I cast a quick glance her way, and take in her raised eyebrows. I think she's tired of my sister running off and leaving me with the responsibility of her child. "No."

"Then trust me on this." She wiggles and settles herself in her seat.

"When did you get so bossy?"

"I've always been bossy," she says. "Caleb is the only one who has ever had a problem with it."

At the mention of Caleb, I cast her a glance. She's not brought him up in a long time, and I can't help but wonder if there is more going on, or if she's seen him around or something. I'm about to ask, but she holds her hands up to stop me. She always did know what I was thinking.

"The Promenade Santa is better, and you want Miss Piper to have the perfect first Christmas photo, don't you?"

I let it go. "As long as I'm not in it, I'm happy." I take a left, changing direction, and as we drive by a downtown hotel, I glance out my window. "What the hell?"

"What?" Peyton asks and glances around.

I slow down and point. "Is that..."

She peers out the window. "Yeah, it's Ivy."

My heart beats a little faster in my chest, as I watch my sister hand her keys over to the valet at one of the posh downtown hotels. "Do you think that her interview is in the restaurant there?"

Peyton gives me a look that suggests I might be dense. "You can't be that naïve."

"I just don't want to think…" I grip the steering wheel tighter, until my knuckles turn white. "I don't want Landon hurt."

"I know. You love him."

I don't deny it. I do love him. I've always loved him. Hell, I tried dating. I even went out with Nathan a few times, but there was no spark, no sizzle, just friendship. I'm pretty sure one night with Landon has ruined me for any other man, and that's just not fair.

"We need to go back," Peyton says as she cranes her neck to keep an eye on Ivy. "Turn the car around."

"No, I can't do that. I don't want to spy on her. It's not my place. Whatever she is doing is between her and Landon. Not me."

She reaches for the door handle. "If you don't stop, I'm going to jump."

"Good Lord, Peyton." I catch the fierce look in her eyes. If there is one thing I know, it's that I can always count on my best friend, and she'll always have my back. She'll even go so far as to jump from a moving vehicle to see Landon and me together. "Stop it before you hurt yourself."

"I'm going to count to three."

"Oh God." I can't take a chance that she won't do it. I slow the car down and pull over. "What are you going to do?"

"I'm going to walk into that restaurant like I own the place and have a look around."

I put one hand over my tight stomach. "What if she sees you? She knows you were going with me. She'll know we've seen her."

"Here's the thing, Ella. She's not going to see me, because she's not going to be in that restaurant. She's fucking some guy in that hotel and when I get the proof, I'm going to tell Landon, and then you two can be together, finally."

My body begins to sweat and it has nothing to do with the glorious afternoon sun "It's not that easy, Peyton. There's a baby..."

"You go to the Promenade and get the pictures. I will text you to keep you up to speed and then you can pick me up when you're done, okay?"

I stare at my friend for a moment, not knowing what to do, when Piper starts fussing in the back seat. She lets loose a cry and I make the split-second decision to let Peyton investigate, even though I don't feel right about it. "Okay, fine."

She jumps from the car, and casts a fast glance my way before closing the door. "I know this is hard, Ella. I know you are a mess inside, and have been for a very long time. I've watched you suffer in silence, but if there is one thing I know, it's that you and Landon belong together. She was never right for him, and I don't know what kind of game she was playing, still is, but she's never played fair when it came to you and she's not going to come out of this the winner. Not in the long run anyway."

"It's not a game, it's life, and life isn't always fair." Haven't I been telling myself that over and over for the last year? It's pretty much been my mantra. But I can't forget that I have so many other amazing things in my life: my family, my best friend, my job.

"I know," she says, "And I love you." The door clicks shut.

"I love you too," I call out as she hurries down the sidewalk toward the hotel. With my insides shaken and stirred, I pull back into traffic as Piper's cries grow louder. Just then my phone rings, and my heart jumps when I see that it's from Landon. I press the button on the steering wheel and put him on speaker.

"Hey Landon," I say and inject a bit of enthusiasm into my voice.

"Ella hi, how are you doing.?"

Piper goes quiet in the back seat when she hears her father's voice. "Great, just taking Piper to get her Santa pictures done." He goes silent on the other end, and my throat tightens. God, what do I do, or say, if he asks about Ivy? I have a feeling he knows nothing about this job interview—and I pray that's what this is—and it's not my place to tell him.

"Is Ivy with you?" he asks, some kind of noise in the background. I hear an announcement of sorts.

"No, she had some things to do."

"What did she have to do?"

"She was meeting someone." I stop at a red light, and tap the steering wheel as a crowd crosses the street.

"Do you know who it was?"

"No," I say with a breath of relief. I actually don't know, so I'm not lying to Landon.

"Not with friends then?"

Shit.

"You'll have to ask her."

He goes quiet, and I can hear his breathing change, come a little bit faster. "I would, but she's not answering. How is Piper?"

"She's great. Happy as ever. Where are you?"

"At the airport. I'm coming home early."

My heart leaps. "I'm so glad. Ivy and Piper will be thrilled."

"What about you, Ella?" he asks, his voice an octave lower. The whispered sound goes through my body, awakens needy parts of me. "Will you be thrilled?"

Oh, God, how do I respond to that, and why the hell is he asking? "Yeah, sure," I answer, and he goes silent again.

"Ella."

"Yeah?"

"We need to talk."

22

LANDON

I sent Ivy a couple texts, asking her to message me, but I've yet to hear from her, and she has no idea I'm coming home early. Something in my gut warned me not to tell her, because there are two things I'm not. One, I'm not an idiot, and two, I'm not a cheater. Thanks to the surprise text I received earlier, I now know that Ivy thinks I *am* an idiot, and she's definitely a cheater. Maybe she's right. Maybe I am stupid, or at least naïve, because I didn't really see this coming. I've been trying to be there for her and my child as much as I could have.

I gather my things from the carousel, I snag Brady's bag as well. As I hand it to him, he looks me over. "You sure you're okay?"

"Yeah. I just have a lot to deal with." I hike my bag over my shoulder, and he puts his hand on my back.

"Anything I can do?"

"No." Honestly, I'm not even sure what I'm going to do. All I know is I need to talk to Ella, once and for all, and clear the air with Ivy. I can't marry her. I just can't. There's also a part of me that can't blame her for cheating, since she's not really getting what she needs from me. I've always done right by everyone, or at least I've tried to, but staying in this relationship, or whatever it is we're doing, whether she cheated or not, is definitely not the right thing to do.

I've always felt it, but my talk with Brady the other night really drove it home and snapped some sense back into me. We only get one chance at this thing called life, and we have to make the right decisions if we want to make the best of it. I've been making wrong decisions that will only end up hurting others in the long run. How can my little girl grow up to be healthy and happy if she's raised in an environment that's the opposite of that?

We head outside and since we both live close to one another, we share a cab. I stay quiet on the drive back, and Brady leaves me to my own thoughts. The night is dark when the driver drops me off first. I say goodbye to Brady and promise to give him a call if I need him. This, however, is something I have to figure out on my own.

I head up the dark driveway, and pull my key from my pocket. The house is quiet when I enter. I quietly set my bag down in the front foyer, remove my coat and kick off my shoes. Moonlights slants off the walls in the living room, giving enough illumination for me to see Ella sound asleep on the sofa, a baby monitor in her hand. I take a fast trip through the house. Ivy is nowhere to be found, but at least Piper is sound asleep in her crib. I give her a kiss, pull out my phone and try Ivy again. She's breathless when she finally answers.

"You're calling late," Ivy says.

I pinch the bridge of my nose, my throat tight. "You haven't answered any of my texts today."

"Been busy," she responds, her voice edgy, like she's hiding something, but she's not hiding anything from me. I already know she's at a hotel with some guy.

"Where are you?"

"Just out with friends."

My heart beats a little faster in my chest. While I don't want to do this over the phone, I need to do it more than I need my next breath. Just then I hear a man's voice in the background, then everything goes muffled, like she's covering the phone.

"Are you with someone, Ivy?"

"Just ran into an old friend."

"Ivy, you and me. I can't do this anymore. I can't be what you want me to be, and I don't even know what that is, but I promise to take care of you and Piper. You guys can stay in the house, and I'll find somewhere else to live."

"You can't be serious," she screeches, her voice bordering on hysteria, and I clench down on my teeth. I'm worried about her mental health, and I don't want to hurt her, but I can't...I just can't.

"I am serious. You know we don't work as a couple as much as I do, so I don't know why you'd want a future with me." It's something I've never understood.

Once again I hear a man's voice, a little closer to the phone now. Ivy's voice is muffled as she answers him.

"We'll talk about this when you get home," she responds, and I get the sense she's not about to be an adult about all this.

"Goodbye, Ivy."

I end the call, leaving her with whoever she's with, as a sense of relief washes over me. She doesn't even know I'm home, and when she does eventually come back to the house, we'll definitely talk. But I won't be saying anything different than I did to her on the phone. I take a long time to get my thoughts in order, and quietly head back downstairs to see Ella. One word dances in my mind as I gaze at her: breathtaking. Call it cliché, call it whatever the hell you want, but when I look at her, it's hard to fill my lungs.

I step closer, breathe in her scent as I take in her sleeping beauty. My heart squeezes in my constricted chest as I gaze at her, consider how close we've grown over the year, how much we've been through—good and bad—and how much she's always supported me, and her sister. Everything about her, from the top of her head to the bottom of her toes is goodness. She is selfless to the point of endangering herself, always forgoing her own needs for the needs of others.

I drop down onto the coffee table and just look at her a little longer, let myself bask in her sweetness. As if feeling my eyes on her, her lids slowly open. At first she stiffens, afraid, but the second she realizes it's me, a wide smile splits her lips. My pulse jumps in my neck, and I can't even begin to tell you how incredible that wide smile, her genuine happiness to see me, makes me feel. In that second, as I look at her, I see the woman I'm in love with, everything in me reaches out to her and I can no longer hold it back.

I need her.

I want her.

I can't fucking live without her and nothing is ever going to keep me from her again.

"Hi," I whisper softly, and drop to the floor on my knees as she sits up, and brushes her mess of dark hair from her face. She blinks dark lashes over sleepy eyes, and it's all I can do not to lean in and claim her mouth, and kiss the living hell out of her.

"How long have you been sitting there?"

Her mouth falls open when I slowly widen her legs and push my big body in between them. I put my hands on her thighs, clamping her thighs around my body, and for one second, she blinks up at me, desire all over her face.

"Long enough for the world to right itself," I tell her, meaning it. As I sit here, wrapped up in her body, the world as I know it is right.

She blinks again, and glances down, that blatant desire turning to confusion, and then understanding spreads across her beautiful face. She puts her hands on my shoulders and shoves me but she can't budge me. It would take a freight train followed by a dozen eighteen wheelers, as well as the entire football team, to pull me away from her. Even then I'm not sure it could happen. I am so crazy about this woman.

"I'm not Ivy," she says, and swallows hard.

"I know." Sheer disappointment spreading across her face. She's not disappointed that she's not Ivy—that I might think she's Ivy. She's disappointed because she wants me to want her for who she is, and I do. "I've always known, Ella," I say and take her hands from my shoulders, to press soft kisses to her palms.

"What are you talking about?"

"I've always known it was you. Now, and back then," I tell her finally getting the truth out there. My shoulders relax slightly, like a load has been lifted.

Her lips quiver. "You mean..."

I put my hands on her legs, lightly brushing my thumbs over her jean-clad thighs, my cock urging me to get her out of them, but I need to take it slow with her.

"Yes, I mean back in college. You gave me your virginity that night you snuck into my room. I didn't take that lightly, Ella. But the next day, you pretended we never happened, and I took your lead, never knowing how to broach the subject."

She swallows, hard. "Landon..." Her voice is as shaky as her hands as her gaze searches my face for answers.

"I know what you saw that night, or what you think you saw when you came back for your phone."

"You knew?" Her lids fly open. "You knew I'd seen you and Ivy, then?"

"I figured it out, and I wanted to talk to you. Wanted to get everything out in the open. I planned to do that during Thanksgiving. I didn't go to the farm to be with Ivy, I went because I wanted to be with you." I take one of her hands and press my lips to her palm.

"You did?" she asks, her voice low and strained.

"Yes, but then Ivy announced she was pregnant and everything changed." I touch her mess of hair and tuck it behind her ears. She leans toward me, and I breathe her in, take everything she is willing to give. "I know what you saw, or what you think you saw."

"You and Ivy," she murmurs quietly. "In bed...that's what I saw. You told me to go away."

"I was telling whoever entered my room to go away, because I thought it was you tucked in beside me." She sniffs, and I hurry on with, "The second I walked into my room that night and saw you, I swear to God I knew it was you, and I was the happiest man on the planet. I wanted to be with you, Ella. I think I fell for you that first time I set eyes on you by the football field, when you called yourself a nerd."

"I am a nerd."

I laugh. "That's what I love about you, and the fact that you showed up at the party to apologize. That takes balls. The second you walked into the party, I was a goner."

She blinks, and I swipe at the tears that falls from her eyes, "But Ivy..."

I exhale. "Ivy." I shake my head. "I thought she was you. It was late, I was tired, yet something deep inside me knew it wasn't. I didn't invite her to my bed, and yes, I slept with her, but you have to believe me, I thought I was sleeping with you."

"Did you not use protection?"

"We did, but the condom broke. She told me everything was okay, so I assumed she was on the pill."

"She was, as far as I know." She glances down for a second, and I give her a quiet moment to process.

"I pretended the next day. I didn't know how to act, or feel, so I just convinced myself you thought I was Ivy all along." The sadness in her voice tears me apart inside. "I should have said something."

"I should have too." I can hear the panic, the need in my own voice when I continue with, "We lost so much time, Ella." I take a fast, unstable breath as my entire body shakes. "I don't know why she came to my bed. I don't know why she started paying attention to me, but it happened that day on the field, after the game, when I was watching you film us. It snowballed from there, and I was caught up in the avalanche, and with not knowing for sure if it was you...I mean I was sure, and then I wasn't. I was so fucking confused, and then we pretended—"

She puts her finger to my lips to hush me. "You said you loved that I was a nerd."

"I do..."

"Does that mean..."

"It means I love you, Ella. I love you so fucking much that I'm empty without you. I'm so damn lost that sometimes it's all I can do to put one foot in front of the other. But I don't deserve you. After sleeping with Ivy, and well, she told you that night at the Growler what happened in the campus theater. I didn't want it to happen, I just. I don't know. There's no excuse."

"Landon, you're with Ivy now though. I can't be that other woman. I won't."

"It's over between Ivy and me. I called her and told her that. Honestly, it never really began with us. We don't belong together, and I think she knows it as much as I do. Back then, after she said she was having my baby, I got caught up in a windstorm, and wanted to do right by everyone, but I wasn't doing right by you, or by myself, or even by Piper. I was coming home to talk to you tonight, and not just because I found out Ivy was cheating on me."

Her eyes go wide. "Peyton told you. I didn't think she was going to. I told her to sleep on it."

I shake my head. "No, not Peyton. An old buddy of mine saw Ivy get on an elevator with a guy at the hotel. You told me you were watching Piper. I couldn't get hold of Ivy earlier, and she hasn't come home yet. I can put two and two together like that. See not all brawn and no brains," I say, and I'm rewarded with a wobbly smile.

"I never meant that."

I push her hair back and cup her face. "So you knew about Ivy?"

"Just today. Things didn't add up, something was off with Ivy. Then we drove by the hotel and saw her getting out of her car. Peyton wanted proof, and she went to get it. I would have told you, or Peyton would have. I couldn't let you go on like that. It wasn't fair, but how do I go against my sister? Landon I never understood why she went after you either."

"Hey," I say, teasing. "What's not to like."

She lightly pounds her fist into my chest. "You know what I mean?"

I run my thumb over her cheek. "I know."

"Landon," she murmurs, a hiccup sob catching in her throat. "I'm sorry."

"You have nothing to be sorry for. You've been my rock, and now I'm going to take care of you. Not just today, Ella. Forever. I want us to be a family. I want you to wear my grandmother's ring."

Her eyes light up and I'm unable to wait one more second. I cup the back of her neck and press my lips to hers, and the second I do, I swear to fucking God, fireworks go off in my brain, and my throat squeezes tight. We lost so much goddamn time.

I break the kiss and her throat gurgles, a mixture of pain and joy in her eyes. "I don't want to hurt Ivy."

"I don't want to hurt anyone either but Ivy and I are done. She's with someone else right now, and this isn't wrong, Ella. This is right and has been a long time coming."

"Piper..."

"She's my daughter. She is my heart. Nothing can change that. We'll work this out, and know this. Everything worth having is worth fighting for. I know we've had a long and convoluted road to get here, Ella. But without it, I wouldn't have had Piper and I would never want to change that." I pull her up, and put my arms around her. "I just hate that I didn't fight for the girl I love earlier."

"You mean me, right?" she asks with a chuckle.

"Yeah, I mean you, and if it's okay with you, I'd like to take you upstairs, get you out of these clothes and spend the rest of the night and the rest of my life showing you how much I want you, how right we are together."

She puts her hands on my shoulders, and she pushes me back. My God, have I read this all wrong? Does she not want what I want?

"Ella?"

She holds her hand out. "I'm Ella Holmes," I stare at her outstretched arm for a second and tension leaves my body as a laugh bubbles up inside me. I take her hand, bring it to my mouth and kiss it.

"I know who you are."

"Just getting that out in the open, Landon." The joy and lightness in her voice fills my heart with all the love I have for her. She angles her head, a small smirk on her face. "Just want to make sure we're on the same page here."

"I'm Landon Brooks. The guy's room you snuck into. The guy you gave your virginity to."

"That night…it was wonderful." She puts her arms around me, and lifts her head, her mouth poised open for me, and the welcoming sight nearly makes me fucking sob with happiness. "I never regretted that decision."

"You have no idea how honored I was. But I wish I'd known. I would have been easier with you."

She glances away. What is she hiding from me? "Ella?" I ask and turn her face to meet mine. "No more secrets okay. None."

"I haven't been with anyone but you."

My heart nearly explodes in my chest, and I swallow against a painful throat. This woman is a gift, and I plan to treasure every inch of her. "I didn't want to be with anyone else."

I gather her in my arms. "Tonight, I'm going to give you an entire year's worth of orgasms to make up for your long wait." I stand there with her in my arms, admiring her strength, beauty and honesty. I don't know where I would have been without her in my life, or how I got so lucky.

"Landon?"

"Yeah?"

"Can we get on with that?"

My heart is beating so wildly, I'm sure it's going to burst from my chest. I take a second to center myself, breathing in through the nose and out through the mouth. I close my eyes. Dear God, do not let me be dreaming on Landon's sofa. I open my eyes again and I can't help the ridiculous smile I can do nothing to hide.

"You're still here."

He chuckles. "I'm still here. You're not getting rid of me that easily."

"I don't want to get rid of you, Landon. Right here, in your arms. It's where I want to be. Its where I've always wanted to be." Happy tears I have no control over spill down my face.

"Hey, why are you crying?"

"I'm just so overwhelmed, and happy and this has been such a long hard year."

"I know it has, Angel," he groans, and I suck in a breath. "What?"

"You called me Angel. That's what you called me that night…"

"I know."

"Wait, do you call everyone you go to bed with Angel?" I put one hand over my face, hating that possibility. "Am I being a silly, naïve girl again?"

"You were never a silly, naïve girl, Ella. You were and are perfect. Then and now." He quietly opens the door to the spare room, the one I've been sleeping in.

Landon places me on the bed, standing back to gaze the length of my body. He studies me so long and hard, I shift a little, feeling uncomfortable. Without thinking, I cross my arms, and he shakes his head.

"I want to see you, Angel. All of you, every inch." He walks up to the lamp and turns it on. "Last time it was in the dark, and while I enjoyed feeling my way around, I need to see you."

"I need to see you too," I tell him. I sit up, put my feet over the edge of the bed, and reach for him. He pulls me to my feet. "I want to undress you."

His groan tells me all I need to know. I slide my hands under his T-shirt, and a shudder goes through him as my fingers connect with his hot skin. I spread my fingers, eager to touch all his rippling abs and they tighten beneath my searching fingers.

"Jesus," he murmurs. "That is so damn nice."

I stand, and drag his shirt up, and he helps me get it over his head. I give a very contented sigh as I take him in, thankful for the lamplight, and he grins, clearly liking the appreciation written all over my face.

"I can't believe this," I murmur under my breath as I breathe in his fresh soapy scent, still trying to wrap my brain around everything we've been through that took us to this very moment.

"Believe it," he responds, his voice so gruff and needy it seeps through me, and settles deep between my legs. "This is happening, Angel, and it's been a long time coming."

I nod, and release his pants, and he groans as I work to free his beautiful cock. He tugs his pants down just a bit, to release himself from his boxers. His long, thick cock pulsates before my eyes and I take him into my hands, moaning at the softness of his skin. Wrapping my fingers around him, I run my hand from base to crown, and I'm rewarded with a beautiful droplet of pre-cum, which glistens in the lamplight. My mouth waters, and I drop to my knees to drink him in, and he grips my hair, pushes it to the side and lets loose a tortured growl as he takes in the sight.

"Fuck, Angel. That is so good. Only with you is it ever this good."

I'm not a girl to believe easily. I've learned a few lessons over the last year, but I believe Landon. He's always tried to be honest with me, and vice versa, and I get what he's saying. He's been my only lover, but I'm not sure the sex could ever be this good with anyone else, and the honest to God's truth is, I don't want it with anyone else.

"I need to touch you," he murmurs as his big hands lightly caress my neck. I whimper as his thumbs brush my nipples through my shirt, and I arch into him, needing more, needing everything from this man. "I've missed you, Ella."

"I missed you too," I tell him. He pulls me up, peels my shirt off and drops it to the floor. His gaze drops takes in my heaving chest, and nipples pressed tightly against my bra.

"You are so fucking perfect."

In a quick move, he removes my bra and leans into me, his breath hot and erotic on my flesh. His lips close over one nipple as his fingers toy with the other, and I grow impossibly wetter between my legs.

"Landon," I cry out, and run my fingers through his hair, holding him to me. He moans louder, liking when I let go and show him what I need. He nibbles on my nipple, biting and teasing and tasting and soothing, and I swear to God if he doesn't touch my sex with his fingers, I'm going to die right here on the spot. A hard quake goes through me, and his soft chuckle vibrates through me.

"Someone's a needy girl."

"It's been so long."

He inches back, and his dark eyes lock on mine, and the intensity there pulls the breath from my lungs. "I'm not going to make you wait another second." He pops the button on my pants, and slides his hand in. He cups my hot sex through my panties, and gives a little squeeze. "I'll never make you wait again, Ella. I vow for the rest of our lives to give you every-thing you need."

"I need you. I only need you, inside me."

He tugs my panties to the side and his eyes shut as his thumb grazes my soaked clit. "Jesus," he murmurs, that one word drenched in joy at finding me so ready for him. "You waited for me for so long. I can't even tell you what that does to me."

"Show me," I boldly challenge him. He drops to his knees and takes my pants down with him, and I lift my legs, one at a time, so he can remove my pants. My panties come down a little slower, and it's easy to tell he's savoring this moment, like it's been a long time in the making, and he doesn't want to rush it. I don't want him to rush it either, but I can barely stand on my quivering legs as it is.

"Ella, baby, you are mine." He removes my panties, parts my wet lips with is finger, and leans in to swipe his hot tongue over me. "This is mine."

"Yes, it's yours. I'm yours."

He goes back on his heels and I run my fingers through his hair as he glances up at me. "I'm yours. I've always been yours. Nothing can ever take us away from each other again."

"Nothing," I promise.

"We can fight anything."

I nod, tighten my fingers around his head, and pull him back to my sex. He chuckles at my brazen neediness, and goes back to licking me. My entire body quivers as he slides a thick finger inside me, and while I've used my vibrator for the last year, nothing, and I mean nothing, compares to this man's touch. My imagination isn't this good, and I have no idea how I'm going to hold on. Then again, who cares if I don't. He's offering me a lifetime of orgasms and I'm ready to accept them.

"Landon," I cry out as his tongue centers on my clit, and his finger works some kind of magic inside me. My body pulses, spasms, and a little yelp climbs from my throat as I climax all over him, my hot juices pouring down his hand, covering his face.

He groans and circles his head, his tongue taking in every drop it can find. I continue to clench around his finger, and after some time, the world around me finally rights itself. I chuckle slightly, realizing exactly what he meant when I woke up and found him by the sofa watching me sleep.

"I love you, Ella. I fucking love you," he says as he climbs up my body and finds my mouth. I taste myself on his tongue as he devours my mouth with his lips, his tongue probing, eating at me like he can't get enough—like he's trying to make up for our lost year. I kiss him back, delirious with need, pleasure, happiness and hope. Our bodies tangle, as we cling to one another like our lives depend on it, and I wrap my legs around him.

He walks to the bed, and falls over me. We kiss as he centers me on the mattress. "Condom," he murmurs, and makes a move to go, but I hold him to me, unable to let him break the contact, the intimacy.

"I'm on the pill. I promise," I say, and he exhales.

"I believe you, Angel. Of course I believe you. I'm clean."

I nod and let my thighs fall apart, welcoming him into my body, my heart and into my soul. The next thing I know he's inside me, filling me, stretching me, making me the happiest woman in the entire world. I love this man. I trust this man, and none of those things come easily to me, but he's always been there for me, even back in college when Cameron tried to assault me. Only Landon, Peyton, and Brady were there. They're my family. They're the ones who truly care about my wellbeing. I see that now. I see that Ivy hasn't been a good sister.

"Touch me, please," he says his voice low, full of need and agony. I run my nails down his back and his muscles bunch.

"Yes," he murmurs into my throat as he peppers hot kisses over my damp flesh, loving me with his hands, mouth and cock.

He powers into me, going so deep he hits my cervix, and a new kind of sensation rockets through me. I've read about full-body orgasms before, but never until this very second did I ever think I could have one.

"Landon, ohmigod, that is so good."

"Yeah?" he asks and continues to slide into me with deep, blunt strokes meant for my pleasure. I claw at him as another orgasm grows, expands and pulls me under until I'm drowning in bliss. He continues to give it to me the way I need it and somehow slides a hand between our bodies to stroke my aching clit.

"Yes," I whimper, my voice a low keening cry that does something wild to him. He pumps harder, faster, taking me to the precipice where he does not leave me hanging. No, he promised he'd give me everything I need, and he's a good man, a man of his word, who takes to heights I've never even dreamed about.

This is right. Everything in my heart and soul tells me so, which means everything else will follow and this thing we call life will all work out the way it's supposed to, as long as I have Landon by my side and he has me by his. I hug him tighter, as I tighten around his pistoning cock, fresh tears fall as my heart fills with all the love I have for this man.

"I love you," I whisper into his ear as he swells even more inside me.

"I love you too," he declares and closes his mouth over mine, kissing me thoroughly, deeply as he fills my body with his seed. My chest squeezes, my heart so full of love, I'm ready to explode. He shifts my body to put his arms around me, and we both hold each other so tight, it's a wonder we can get any air. But who cares? Air is overrated. He buries his face in my hair as he continues to deplete inside me, and when he's done, he collapses on my body, pinning me with his impressive weight.

I cry a little more, let the tears fall freely, and revel in the pounding of his strong heart against my chest. This is where I'm meant to be, yesterday, tomorrow, forever. No regrets.

After a long moment, he inches back, and his eyes are glossy so damn expressive and full of love as they meet mine. "I didn't hurt you, did I?"

I grin, loving the way he's checking in with me. "Only in the best ways."

The corners of his mouth turn up. "Why don't we take a shower, and then I'll come back here, and kiss all the places that hurt."

"There are a lot of places," I fib. Nothing hurts, in fact everything, for the first time in my life, feels wonderful...perfect. He slowly inches out of me and I yelp a little at the loss. He puts his hand between my legs, and lightly touches me, soothing any sting left behind.

"Do you hurt too much, my sweet virgin?"

"Never," I say with a chuckle. "I no longer think we can say I'm a virgin again, though."

He goes serious, and blows out a breath. "Are you really okay?" His dark eyes narrow in on me. "I tried to go slow, but Jesus, Ella, I wanted you so much. I still do." He pushes my hair back with both hands and cups my face. "I'll never stop wanting you."

I'm about to answer, to tell him I'll never stop wanting him when I hear my sister at my bedroom door.

"What the fuck is going on here?"

LANDON

"Shit," I curse under my breath as Ella stiffens beneath me, a little gasp catching in her throat.

"Shit is right," Ivy shoots back. "What the fuck? I'm gone one night and you fuck my sister? What are you even doing home anyway?"

"It's over between us, Ivy. You know that." I slide off Ella and sit upright as she tugs the blankets to her neck. Ella groans, and sinks into her pillow. She hates this. So do I. But this isn't a mistake and neither of us should have regrets.

"It's not over until I say it's over," Ivy shoots back and takes a step closer to the bed. She glares at Ella. "Are you just going to hide there, Ella? Pretend to be the sweet innocent girl that fools the damn world so she can get what she wants?" She gives an unladylike snort. "Is that act still working for you?"

Ella makes a move to sit up, and I put my hand on her, my way of letting her know this is my battle, but the pain in her eyes is a wake-up call that it's her battle too, so I back off.

"What do you mean by that?" Ella asks.

Ivy's mouth drops open. "Really, you're going to play stupid? I'm your twin. I can see right through you."

"She's not playing stupid," I say through clenched teeth.

"You're both stupid. I want you out of here. Right now."

"I live here, Ivy. You're the one who wasn't here when I got home. Care to tell me where you were or who you were with?"

She turns her glare to me. "You don't get to ask me questions when I come home and find you in bed with my sister."

"We're not together anymore, Ivy. We never really were together."

She points to the door. "I said I want you both out of here."

"Let's talk, Ivy."

"About what? How my asshole sister always gets what she wants? How she puts on that ridiculous sweet and innocent act, and gets all the attention and love, especially from Mom and Dad? Well, you know what, Ella? I'm sick of it, sick of you."

Ella goes cold beside me, and I glance at her, note the paleness in her face. Her eyes are wide, stark against the whiteness.

"I have no idea what you're talking about, Ivy. I've never put on any act. I've always stood back to let you shine. You're the actress, not me. I was happy to be in the background."

"Oh, for fuck's sake, drop it already."

"Drop what?" she asks, as my insides turn to ice. Ivy has venom in her eyes, and whatever she's about to say or do, it's not going to bode well for Ella. With my protective instincts kicking into high gear, I pull Ella to me.

"You two disgust me," Ivy spits out and stomps from the room. "Get dressed and get out of here. Both of you."

I jump from the bed, and gather up our clothes. We both dress quickly, hurry downstairs and find Ivy pouring wine into a glass. "You're still here?" she asks, her words high pitched, and laced with anger.

"Drop what?" Ella asks, not about to let this go, and while we need to get to the bottom of matters, I'm afraid Ella's going to get hurt in the process.

"You're such a fucking little bitch. I'm so sick of you," Ivy says, as wine sloshes over the rim of her glass.

"She's been nothing but good to you and Piper."

She gives a humorless laugh. "And don't forget you, Landon. She's obviously been very good to you. I guess you haven't been fucking me all this time because you've been fucking goody-two-shoes."

"I haven't been fucking you, because there's nothing between us, Ivy. You honestly can't say there is." I rub the back of my tight neck. "I can't even wrap my brain around us together. In all the years in college you never paid me any attention until I met Ella. I have no idea why you're holding on to this, or me. Is it because of Piper?"

She takes a big drink of wine, and my insides tighten. I'm honest to God worried about her mental health. There's fire in her eyes, and her hand is gripping her glass so tightly, I'm afraid she's about to become unhinged, I can't help but worry she's going to have some sort of breakdown. Has she always been this unstable, and I've been so preoccupied with other things I haven't noticed?

Ignoring my question, she glares at Ella. "The way you looked at Landon, and the way he looked at you. Disgusting. You got what you deserved, sister."

Ella slowly sinks down into a chair as the blood drains to my feet. "What are you talking about?" I demand.

"Sweet little virgin, thinks she can wave her innocent snatch in front of all the guys and have them come running." Her smirk raises the hair on the back of my neck. "Cameron was supposed to fix that."

I grip the back of the chair hard enough to break it as the pieces fall into place. "No," I groan, a low tortured sound rising from the depths of my throat. Ivy set Cameron up to fuck Ella? I can't be right. I just can't be.

Ella swallows so hard and loud I'm sure the neighbors can hear it. "You...you wanted Cameron to hurt me?

She waves a dismissive hand. "He wasn't supposed to hurt you, just deflower the virgin." She shakes her head. "You even screwed—or rather not screwed—that up."

"I wasn't a virgin, Ivy," Ella says, sitting up a bit straighter, trying to present strength when this has to be hurting every fiber of her being. "The night you crawled into Landon's bed, I slept with him first."

Her face falls, her blue eyes wide and wild. Clearly she didn't know that I was with Ella first. "That's not true."

"It's true. Landon took my virginity at the party. He caught me snooping in his room, and after sex, I snuck out. I forgot my phone and when I went back, I found you in bed with him. What I want to know is why you crawled in bed with him in the first place, especially if you knew we liked each other?"

"You didn't belong there." My God if looks could kill, Ella would be six feet under. "For the first time, I had my own friends, could shine without you always stealing my thunder."

"I never stole your anything." Ella shakes her head, the pain in her eyes raking my insides raw. "I can't believe this. I can't believe you went after Landon because you knew I liked him."

Before I can interject, Ella puts her hand on my arm, and her voice is low, so goddamn tortured when she asks, "Why, Ivy? Why? I'm your sister."

"My sister!" She makes a face like she just sucked on something distasteful. "The only thing you are is a fucking cunt, Ella. Stepping into my territory with Landon, making every member of the team love *you,* even after you called them names. Then you come to the party all sorry and sweet. Please. You had to learn a lesson."

"Your territory?" I spit out, barely able to see through the anger pulsing behind my eyes. How could she set out to hurt her own sister? How did I not see any of this?

"That's right, and I had to show her what happens when she crosses the boundaries. She had Mom and Dad, always the favorite, always so goddamn smart and sweet. She wasn't coming in to my territory and taking over. I had to do something about that." Ivy glares at me.

"You figured if Cameron fucked her, I wouldn't want her?"

"I know the game you guys play." She focuses in on Ella, a smirk on her face, like she really wants to hurt her even more. I'm not sure that's possible, though. "Did he tell you he liked to fuck virgins, Ella?"

"I know all about the freshman game," she answers quietly.

"You thought I liked her because she was a virgin?" I ask, unable to wrap my brain around any of this. I don't give her time to answer. I already know the truth. "So what you're saying is, you wanted to put Ella in her place, make her pay for trying to invade your territory?" I do finger quotes around the word territory.

She snorts. "That beating you guys gave Cameron, that cost me big time."

Is she fucking serious right now? She and Cameron were working together to destroy her sister? "Why all the way to living together, and wanting an engagement, Ivy? If you never loved me, why go through with it?"

She gives a casual shrug. "I was pregnant, you were going to be a good provider and give me everything I needed. But you certainly failed in the bedroom department, which is why I had to get my fucks elsewhere."

Her words hit like a slap, and Ella covers her mouth, tears filling her eyes. I put my hand on Ella's shoulder and this seems to fuel Ivy's rage.

"Speaking of Piper, you're a shitty father."

"He's not a shitty father," Ella snaps back, quickly coming to my defense.

Ivy shrugs again, and says, "Not that it really matters."

My blood runs cold and I suspect she chose those words carefully, wanting to hurt me. "What the hell is that supposed to mean?"

"She's not yours anyway."

I stumble backward, the room going blurry before my eyes. "That's not true. She's mine, Ivy. She's mine. She's my goddamn heart." Rage builds inside me, until I'm seeing red. "Don't you dare try to take her from me."

Ivy laughs almost hysterically and takes a sip of wine. "Take your whore and go. Piper isn't yours and you're never going to see her again."

"She's mine."

"Didn't you ever wonder where the red hair really came from? Which jock could be her real father?"

I take a step toward her, and Ella stands between us. "Let's go," she says.

"That's right, get out of here."

I shake all over, like I'd just taken a tumble in the dryer. "Piper is mine."

"Get a paternity test if you want. Won't change the fact that she's not yours."

I try to breathe, but my lungs are so damn constricted I can't seem to fill them. "Ivy, please don't do this. Don't take her from me."

Ella holds me and I swear to God if she wasn't helping me stand right now, I'd fall to my knees. "Landon, let's go."

With my heart pounding hard against my chest, Ella grabs her purse and my suitcase, and leads me outside, and we both blindly walk to Ella's car. "I'm the father, Ella. I have to be."

"We'll get this straightened out," she says, and I sense she doesn't think I am the father. I walk her to the passenger side, and open the door for her. Before she gets in, she wraps her arms around me, and we hold on to one another.

She finally breaks from the circle of my arms and slides into the car. I walk around to the driver's side, get in and start the car. I stare straight ahead, not knowing what to do next.

"Let's go to the farm," Ella says. "I want to talk to my parents."

I nod, and back out of the driveway. We mostly remain quiet the entire drive, but our hands continue to touch. Many, many hours later, as the sun begins to rise on the horizon, we pull into the farm. We both sit there for a long time, staring at the farmhouse until it's drenched in sunlight.

"Okay, let's go do this," Ella says with a fast intake of breath.

I exit the car, circle it, and take Ella's hand. She gives me a reassuring smile, but I'm not sure anything is ever going to be okay again. I can't believe the lengths Ivy went to just to hurt her sister.

We climb the stairs, and as soon as we reach the porch, the door opens, and Ella's mother stands there, an anxious look on her face.

"Mom," Ella says and when her mom opens the screen door, Ella breaks down. I exchange a worried look with her mother as she leads us to the old farmhouse kitchen, and we sit at the table. David comes into the room, takes one look at us, and fine lines crinkle around his eyes as he too displays worry.

He steps up to the counter. "I'll make some coffee."

"Lots of it," I say.

Once the coffee is made and we are each cradling a cup, Ella tells them everything, and I mean everything. Right from the first time I took her to my bed. But her parents sit there and listen, no judgement on their part and when the truth is finally out there, David and Corinne exchange knowing glances.

"Mom?" Ella says.

Her mother takes Ella's hand and pats it. "None of this is your fault. Who you love is not your fault, but who you hurt is."

"I never meant—"

"I'm not talking about you, dear. I'm talking about Ivy. She purposely hurt you two." Another glance between David and Corinne.

"What are you not telling me?"

David refreshes Corinne's coffee and says, "We've always gone out of our way to make Ivy feel special. Ever since she was a child, she was jealous of you. She started acting out, acting up, for attention. We gave it to her, thinking it would help. We've not always made all the right decisions, but you and Ivy were so different. She resented you being the teacher's pet, always coming home with the high grades. She made up for it by being louder, flamboyant...extra."

Ella stares at her mom like she can't believe she just used the word extra. "I had no idea," Ella says. "I stood back, happy to let her have the limelight."

"The more you retreated, the more you gave it to her, the angrier it made her. She didn't like that you weren't envious of her the way she was envious of you."

Ella shakes her head, her eyes wide and sad. "I didn't know any of this."

"We thought she'd outgrow it in college. She always thought you were our favorite, and when you got a scholarship..."

"She didn't like that," David says. "So, we paid her way, and she got into the best sorority. We thought all that would make her feel special, but obviously it didn't."

Ella looks down, and my heart aches for all she's going through. I can't imagine the pain, the anger, to be hurt by someone she's always stood by, always loved.

"We need to get her help, Mom," she says, her words rushed and anxious. "She needs to be there for her daughter, and I want Ivy happy and healthy, and I want her to live a long life, and find someone who will love her and support her the way she needs. She's family, and I want us all to be a family, no matter the past. I just want to move forward to a better future."

I breathe deep, even though it hurts my chest, because what I'm seeing here, the love, compassion and empathy for someone who hurt her deeply, is the most beautiful thing I've ever seen. But I shouldn't have expected anything different. Ella is one of a kind, and she's mine. I'm the luckiest guy in the entire universe.

"I'm sorry I couldn't be that guy for Ivy," I pipe in quietly.

David shakes his head. "We don't blame you for any of this, son. This is not your fault, or yours, Ella. Ivy needs help. We've known it for a long time, we just hoped with you both on different paths in college, things would get better. It was our responsibility to get her help and we didn't. We will now, though."

"From the first time I saw you both together here at Thanksgiving, I could feel the love between you two," Corinne says. "Then the baby..."

As her words fall off, Ella begins crying into her hands and with my heart pounding like a drum in my chest, I step behind her chair, and hug her. Her mom and dad give me a warm smile.

"We're going to get her all the help she needs, Ella," her mom says as she puts her hand on Ella's arm. "I just wish we would have done it sooner, before she really hurt you."

Ella sniffs. "She said Piper wasn't Landon's."

"She is, she has to be," I whisper, my own tears threatening.

"She's going to try to keep her from him. I just want us to all be a happy family."

I might be in love with Ella, but despite everything Ivy has done, I still want her healthy and well, and I want us to all somehow figure out a way to be a family. If it's what Ella wants, it's what I want too.

"We can have a paternity test done." David eyes us.

"No, she's mine. I don't need a test to prove it."

David nods at me. "Why don't you both go get some sleep?"

"I should go back," Ella says quietly.

"I'll go," Corinne says as she stands. "I'll stay with her until we can get her the help she needs."

"You're not going alone, Corinne," David says and puts his arm around his wife.

"Thank you both," I add, as Ella sags against me. "But I should go...Piper." Worry worms its way through my veins.

"She loves Piper, Landon," Ella reminds me. "If I thought Piper was in any jeopardy, I never would have left."

"I love her, too." I hug Ella to me. "She's everything to me."

"I know she is. You're a good dad," she says, and I know Ella loves Piper as much as I do. She loves her sister too, and would never in a million years do anything to hurt her, despite everything Ivy's done.

I breathe her in. "Maybe I shouldn't have said anything to you. Maybe I shouldn't have made love to you last night. Maybe I ruined everything between you and your sister, me and my daughter." I take a shaky breath and add, "You and me." I inch back and my heart shatters as tears spill from Ella's eyes. Fuck, I don't mean to hurt her, but having her in my life as a friend is better than not having her at all.

"You didn't ruin everything. It obviously wasn't good between you and Ivy or me and Ivy. She'd written off our relationship years ago. But we're going to make this right, Landon. We have to."

What if we can't, though?

What if I lose the two women who mean the most to me in the whole world?

More importantly, what if Ella does?

ELLA

ive Months Later:

I kick off my blankets and stare at the ceiling, much like I do every morning since Mom and Dad have been getting Ivy psychiatric help. They're with her this weekend, and according to them, she's doing much better, but she's yet to speak to me, despite all my calls and texts.

The hardest part of this is not knowing who Piper's father is. Landon doesn't want to take the test. I get it. He's afraid, and in his heart, Piper is his. He hasn't seen her since that night Ivy walked in on us, and the only times I get to see her is when Mom and Dad babysit her at the orchard. A week after that night when we drove here to talk to my parents, Landon left for Atlanta, and only returned home two days ago for Christmas break.

We spent most of the last two days in bed, and when we weren't wrapped up in one another, we talked, walked the orchard, and fell deeper in love. All the while we worried about Ivy and Piper. Many more things make sense though, things like Cameron, and what he said about Ivy being poison, and how he was taking Landon's virgin and that was all I needed to know. He didn't tell me that Ivy had put him up to it, but when I look back, it makes sense, especially the way he exited my life as quickly as he entered it.

"Hey," Landon says from beside me. His hands seek mine and he tugs me to him. I collapse on his chest, and press my ear to his strong heartbeat. "Happy Christmas Eve." He places a soft kiss onto my forehead, and my body warms with all the love I have for him. Just the other day, he asked me what I wanted for Christmas, but he can't give me my family around the tree, happiness and laughter as we open gifts. Just like I can't give him the papers saying he's Piper's father. I wish I could. "Sleep okay?" he asks.

"I got a few hours. How about you?" I run my hands up and down his body. He's wanted to put a ring on my finger for a long time, and as much as I want that, I can't. Not yet. Not until Ivy is well, and can accept the love Landon and I have for one another. I don't want to hurt her, despite everything.

"Not bad." On the nightstand, his phone pings, and he gently moves me off him to read the text. I'm not sure what's going on with him, but he's been on his phone a lot since he's gotten back, talking in private. I want to ask who he's talking to, but there's this ridiculous part of me—the insecure little girl part—that is too afraid of the answer. I've always been in the shadows, always stood back to let Ivy shine and take what she wanted. What if now that she's doing better, she's taking Landon back? What if he's agreeing, to keep the family peace? He's a man who always wants to do the right thing. But that's no longer the right thing, and he knows it, right?

I summon every ounce of courage I can, and ask, "Who...who is it?"

He takes a breath, and says, "It's Ivy."

I sit up a little straighter, my stomach growing tighter by the second. "Is she okay?"

He nods, and I don't miss the hint of guilt in his eyes. "I messaged her every day when I was away. To see if she was okay, and if she and Piper needed anything. She's only started answering me since I've been back. I didn't want to say anything, Ella. I know she's not answering you yet."

After everything that went down, he's still a man who cares, and my love for him grows just a little more. "How is she? How's Piper?"

"They're both in good hands." His fingers fly across the screen and I drop down onto my pillow, because whatever he's texting her is not meant for my eyes. Just then my phone pings, and I snatch it off the nightstand to find a message from Mom letting me know things are going well. I text back that I'm happy to hear that, but can't shake the uneasy feeling mushrooming inside me.

Landon puts his phone down, and stands. "Come on."

"Where to?"

"You need a distraction. Let's go shopping. Sitting around here worrying isn't helping you."

I shake my head, even though Landon standing before me naked is all the distraction I need. Over the last year, his body grew harder, more defined. "No, I'm not in the mood for shopping."

"Christmas is tomorrow, Ella." He takes my hand and tugs it until I'm standing. "Have you bought gifts for your family?"

"No, but—"

"Then let's get dressed. We'll grab something to eat in town, and hit the mall."

I groan. "The mall the day before Christmas. Are you insane?"

His grin is wickedly mischievous. What the hell is he up to? "That's one of the nicer things I've been called." He puts his arms around me, buries his face in the crook of my neck and inhales me.

"What's the point, Landon?" I sag against him. "No one is going to be here for Christmas."

He inches back. "Hey, you don't know that for sure."

I shrug and gesture to my phone. "I kinda do. Mom would have said they were coming back for Christmas. They're not going to leave Ivy and Piper, and I'm sure Ivy doesn't want to see us together."

"I think we should go sit on Santa's knee and ask for this Christmas miracle."

I laugh at that. "I am not sitting on some random dude's knee."

"Fine, then," he laughs, and plunks himself down onto my bed, and pulls me onto his lap. "Ho. Ho. Ho. Now tell me little girl, what would you like for Christmas?"

I grin, loving that he's trying to lighten my mood and help me through this, when he too is in so much pain. "I want my family around the tree."

"Santa will see what he can do."

I shift, put my legs around him, and press my lips to his. We exchange long, passionate kisses, and cling to one another. Landon finally breaks the quiet, and tucks my hair behind my ears.

"Okay, let's move it, because if we sit here any longer, I'm going to throw you down and take you hard."

"Hmm." I tap my chin. "I'm not sure you're selling that right, because I'm not opposed to that idea at all."

He smacks my ass. "Later, I promise. Right now, we have to go."

"Have to? What are you up to, Landon Brooks? Why do we suddenly have to be at the mall, and since when did you like shopping?"

He frowns. "I just think we should get gifts, in case your wish comes true."

I stand, and hug him. "I want your wish to come true too."

"Piper is mine. She has to be."

With that, we both shower, lingering in the spray far too long, dress and head to the mall. There is a new lightness in my step as I take in all the faces, everyone rushing about, purchasing gifts for their loved ones. After a while we make our way to the food court, and grab a couple slices of pizza. Landon's phone pings as we eat, and he pulls it from his pocket, and checks the display.

"I have to take this," he says and stands. "Do you have any more shopping to do?"

I nod, and put on a smile despite the anxiousness inching its way through my veins. "Yeah, there's a couple more things I want to grab."

"Meet me at the car in thirty minutes."

I nod, and glance around the food court, noting the way he's garnering so much attention, despite the ball cap pulled low. Sometimes I forget he's a big superstar, a man who could have any woman he wants, and chose me. I smile at that, as he disappears around the corner, his fingers flying across his phone.

Thirty minutes later, after I grab a few more presents, even though my wish can't possibly come true, then I meet Landon at the car. I know him well enough to know he's up to something. That smirk he's trying to hide says it all, but I'll let him have his secrets, for now.

Back at home, as the sun begins to set, we plug in the tree and snuggle on the sofa, as we watch our favorite Hallmark movie, and of course when I say *our* favorite, I mean *mine*, but he's sweet enough to watch it with me and pretend he likes it. As the hands on the clock approach midnight, we head up to bed, and snuggle under the blankets. While I love being with him, there's still a measure of guilt inside me. There shouldn't be, I realize that, but I can't help it. I won't be whole again, until my sister is better. Sleep pulls at me, and I'm so comfortable in his arms, I drift right off.

A loud bang pulls me awake, and my lids fly open. I turn to find the other side of the bed empty, and my throat tightens. I kick off the covers and check the time. What is Landon doing up at five in the morning? Tires crunch on the ground, and my stomach lurches. Is he leaving? He was so worried about ruining everything, there's a part of me that's worried he's running away, distancing himself because he thinks he's the root of our problems. Apprehension worms its way through my veins, and I walk to the window.

"Ohmigod." I blink once, and then twice, sure I must be seeing things. I pull a robe on over my pajamas, and hurry downstairs. When I reach the bottom, the fresh scent of coffee reaches my nose. I dash into the kitchen, but find it empty. Voices trickle in from the living room, and I tighten my belt and quietly leave the kitchen to find my family, everyone, including Landon, standing before the Christmas tree. Tears pound behind my eyes, and when Ivy turns my way, sweet Piper in her arms, I can't hold them back any longer.

I cry, and cry and cry some more. So does my sister, and when she hands the baby to Landon, it's all he can do to keep his tears at bay. "Landon," I choke out.

"Merry Christmas, Ella." His smile is soft, warm and shaky when he adds, "See I told you, Christmas miracles do come true."

"You...you arranged this?" My gaze slides to Ivy. Does she even want to be here? Silence deafens me as we stare at one another, and after a moment, she takes a step toward me, and I falter backward just a bit, but she reaches a hand out to me, and I freeze, not knowing what to do, or what mental state of mind she might be in. I never meant to hurt her. I would never do it on purpose.

"Ella," she whispers softly, and without thinking I reach for her too. She steps into me, puts her arms around me and we hug. The sound of Mom's tears reach me, and I close my eyes, my heart hurting in my chest. "I'm so sorry, Ella."

I sniff, and inch back. "I'm sorry too."

She shakes her head. "You have nothing to be sorry for, and I want you to know that I'm doing so much better. Thanks to Mom and Dad, and all the work I've been doing with the doctors." She touches her head. "I wasn't right in here, and I didn't want to return your calls or messages until I was, and then I wanted to see you face to face, and tell you I'm sorry for hurting you. I can't ever forgive myself."

"I forgive you," I say.

"I don't deserve your forgiveness." She sniffs and glances over her shoulder. "I'm sorry for hurting Landon too."

Landon takes Piper's little hand, brings it to his lips and kisses it. My heart squeezes so tight, I can hardly breathe. He did this. He arranged for this beautiful, perfect Christmas gift, for me. I wish I could give him something equally important.

Ivy turns, exchanges a look with Mom and Dad, then focuses in on Landon. "I wasn't sure if she was yours or not. I slept around, wanting to get pregnant. For reasons I'm not proud of."

"She's mine," he says. "No matter what. I don't want to take a paternity test. It doesn't change anything. She's mine."

"We should have a test to be certain. We need to be certain."

"I am certain." The pain in his eyes, the vulnerability on his face cuts through me, lays my soul wide open. I step up to him and put my hand on his heart.

"I want her to be yours more than anything in my entire life. But if she's not, if someone else is the father, that person needs to know."

"No, Ella. No." Grief rips across his face, and more tears pour down my cheeks. I want to make this better for him, want to take his pain but I don't know how.

"Just think about it," I say trying to get the words out past a raw throat. "If she's someone else's daughter, and I don't think she is, then she'll have twice the amount of love."

He hugs his little girl tighter. "I can't lose her. I can't."

My heart explodes with the love I have for this good man, and I'm beyond thankful that we found our way back to each other. Landon is a true hero, a man of integrity, a man who stands up for what he believes in, and never shirks responsibility. A man who loves with all his heart, and I can't believe I'm in his orbit, and a recipient of all that goodness. A part of him cares for my sister too, of that I'm sure and he most definitely loves his child.

"You won't lose her," Ivy assures him. "You'll always be in her life, as a dad or an uncle."

A big hiccupping sob catches in my throat. I turn to my sister, and pull her back into my arms. "Thank you," I say, the weight on my shoulders eases as she accepts my love for Landon and his for me.

"Thank you for not hating me, Ella." We hug and cry and Mom and Dad just cling to one another. After a long moment, Landon breaks the quiet.

"I don't know about you guys, but I need coffee, and presents and lots and lots of snuggles with my daughter."

We all laugh at that, the air in the room lighter as we sniff and wipe our noses. "I'll help you," I say as Landon hands his daughter back to Ivy. We step away, and in the kitchen, he turns to me, and our eyes meet and lock. No words need to be said, so instead we hold one another for a long moment, and I revel in his strong heart pounding against my chest as I go up on my toes and kiss him.

"Merry Christmas." I smile. "I'm pretty sure this is the best Christmas I've ever had."

He gives me a mischievous wink. "Not yet."

I eye him. "What are you up to?"

"Let's get the coffee, get back in there and find out."

"Landon, what have you done?"

He whistles innocently as he grabs the milk from the fridge, and I put the mugs filled with coffee onto a tray. In the living room, Ivy, Mom and Dad are playing with Piper, and my heart misses a beat as they all smile up at me. I glance at the glistening tree, the little white flashing lights, and that's when I notice a present nestled in the branches.

"It's for you," Landon says, stepping up behind me, his hands on my arms, rubbing up and down to keep me warm.

Ivy stands, picks up the present and hands it to me. "This was a joint effort," she says, and I glance back at Landon.

"Is this what all those private texts were about?"

"Maybe," he says and I shake my head at my foolish insecurities, thinking this man might be leaving.

Present in hand, I drop down onto the sofa, and I glance at Mom and Dad who are smiling. "Thank you," I say to them, and Mom takes Ivy's hand and pulls her down next to them. With every set of eyes in the room staring at me, including Piper's, I rip into the package. A loud laugh bubbles up from the depths of my throat when I set eyes on the gift.

"I can't believe this," I say, through a sob. "You guys got me a Furby."

"You don't like it?" Landon asks, worry in his voice.

"I love it." More tears fall. "How did you know?"

"I've never forgotten about the lipstick, Ella," Ivy says quietly. "That was so sweet of you." She glances down, a look of sadness on her face when she adds, "You saved all that money to buy me lipstick, when all you wanted was a Furby. I should have been a better sister. I should have gotten it for you."

"Well, you just did," I say, joy filling my heart with love. "It means more to me now then it would have back then anyway. I love it. Thank you, Ivy." I put my hand on Landon's lap. "Thank you, Landon," I say, understanding how hard it must have been for him to find this gift, and that's the reason for the secrecy at the mall. "This is perfect." In fact, everything is perfect. My whole family is here, Ivy is doing better, and no matter what, Piper will always be a big part of Landon's life, because this man will one day be my husband.

"One more thing," Landon says, and drops down to one knee in front of me.

I gasp and glance at Ivy. She's accepted our love, but will this hurt her. She smiles and nods, like she was aware this was going to happen, and I can only imagine Landon talked to her about this, to make sure she was okay with it.

"I love you, Ella."

"I love you, too."

"Will you marry me?"

"Yes," I say as tears pour down my face.

He wipes them away, and I glance at my Mom and Dad, my sister and my niece. "This is the best Christmas ever."

"It's just the start of many," Landon says, and I believe him. Everything and everyone I hold close is in this room, and I know Landon isn't going anywhere, except to my bed, where I plan to show him exactly what he means to me. As I look into his dark eyes, I know in my heart Landon isn't the man I want to grow old with, he's the man I want to stay young with and I plan to do just that.

Landon

One Year Later:

I scoop Piper up from her crib, and sneak downstairs. The rest of the family is asleep in the old homestead, but Piper and I want to get the tree lit and put a few more things in the stockings before everyone wakes up. Turns out Piper was my daughter after all, and the best gift that has ever been given to me. Honestly, I cried for a whole week, but don't tell anyone. I mean, I'm a bad-ass footballer and don't want to have to cash in my man card.

Over the last year, Ivy has been getting better and better and found a really great guy of her own, one she loves, and one who loves both her and Piper. Our co-parenting has been going great, as we both have Piper's best interests at heart.

"Aren't the lights pretty," I say to Piper as she smiles up at me. My heart misses a beat as I take in her eyes. I don't think I could be any happier than I am right now. Ella's career is going great, and she even got a promotion and I always tease that she's one step closer to working with Spielberg. Me, well, I've been playing football, and in my spare time, not that I have a lot of it, I've been working on that screenplay. Ella's been helping and she thinks it has real potential. I'm so glad I kept with the English classes, and my beautiful wife was my tutor. We married over the summer, and my parents and sisters were elated to see us so happy. Both Ivy and Peyton stood up with Ella, and Ella and her sister have grown so much closer over the year. It fills my heart with happiness and love. I truly am the luckiest man on the planet.

"What are you two doing up?"

I turn to find my gorgeous wife standing in the doorway, smiling at us. "We wanted to make sure the lights were on when everyone got up."

"You know," Her smile is warm and soft as she looks at me. "You're like a child when it comes to Christmas."

"Wonderful things happen at Christmas, you know that."

"You're right, they do," she says, and holds her hands out for Piper. I love how much they love each other, and how much my own family loves my girl and my wife. We'll be flying to Texas later in the week to have a second Christmas with them. No way were they going to let me get away with Christmas in California two years in a row.

"Come here, chicken nugget," Ella says, and I hand her over. She drops down onto the sofa.

"Why are you really up?" I ask. She's been so tired lately, going to bed early and sleeping in, I hadn't expected to see her for hours.

"Well," she says, a grin on her face. "I was hoping to slip something into your stocking before you got up." She stifles a yawn. "But I should have known you'd be up before me."

I sit on the floor in front of her and take Piper's little hand into mine. "You don't have to put anything in my stocking. I have everything I need right here."

"Oh, okay then. But it was something that you don't have, and I thought you'd like it, but if you don't want—"

"I want." I laugh. I really am like a kid at Christmas time.

She laughs with me. "Close your eyes, Landon."

I do as she says.

"Hold out your hand."

I hold my hand out flat and she places something on my palm. "Can I open my eyes now?"

"I suppose."

I open my eyes and stare at the plastic stick sitting on my palm, a pink plus sign on it. It's early, and my brain isn't up to speed, so at first I don't realize what I'm holding. I glance up at Ella, and the second I see the spark in her eyes, and the smile on her face, the pieces of the puzzle come together. Ella has been tired because she's pregnant and carrying our child. How could I not have figured this out?

"Ella..." I can hardly talk, as my heart hammers and tears fill my eyes.

"You're going to be a dad again," she says, her chin quivering as emotions overtake her too.

"Ella," I say again and pull her into my arms. "I can't believe this."

"Believe it, Dad."

"Dad," Piper says, and we laugh.

I kiss her cheek. "That's right, little one. I'm going to be a dad again, and you're going to be a big sister."

"She's going to be the best sister," Ella says.

"With a mom like you guiding her, she's going to be the best at everything."

She smiles at the compliment. "The best things really do happen at Christmas."

She's right they do, but with Ella and Piper and our families, every day is Christmas for me. It might have taken us time to get here, but we eventually got to where we needed to be. Life might not always be fair and we have to fight battles, but eventually we're all where we're supposed to be, and I wouldn't change the past. It made us who we are today, taught us about trust, values, and love.

I look at my beautiful, pregnant wife and my child. "I have everything I need right here, and then some."

"Merry Christmas, Landon."

I touch her stomach, the love I have for my wife, my daughter and my unborn child bubbling over inside me. "How about this," I tease. "Next game, if I get a touchdown, I get to have my way with you."

"Why would I bargain with you? What could possibly be in it for me?"

I flash her a smile. "If I don't get a touchdown, you get to have your way with me."

She smiles and puts her hands on my cheeks. "Sounds fair."

I press my lips to hers. "Sounds like either way, I'm the winner."

"So am I, Landon. So am I."

AFTERWORD

Thank You!

Thank you so much for reading **Fair Play**, book one in my End Zone series. I hope you enjoyed the story as much as I loved writing it. Please read on for an excerpt of **Enemy Down, available June 2021**.

Interested in leaving a review? Please do! Reviews help readers connect with books that work for them. I appreciate all reviews, whether positive or negative.

Happy Reading,

Cathryn

"Hot, right?"

I glance to my left, to lane number four as fellow track star—and my very best friend—Kaitlyn Collins catches up to me. I lift my face to the sky, to take in the late afternoon sun. It might be early fall, but it's always hot in Southern California this time of year. I swipe beads of moisture from my forehead and concentrate on my pacing and breathing. Our big meet is next week, and I have to take first in my category or...well, I can't think of the consequences.

"The sun is going down. It should cool off soon enough," I say, but before I get a chance to turn my focus back to my own lane, I catch her mischievous grin, and the wagging of her eyebrows.

"You know that's not what I'm talking about."

"Then what are you talking about?" I ask, instantly regretting the words spilling from my mouth. Stupid. Stupid. Stupid. Honestly, I'd have to be a total idiot not to know she's talking about the football team, and their...oh, how does she describe them in their tight pants: sexy, hot football butts. If you ask me, they all look like overstuffed sausages ready to burst wide open. I never did have a taste for sausages, well except those flat breakfast sandwiches ones from my favorite fast-food restaurant.

"You don't want to tap dat ass," she teases. I take a deep, fueling breath and focus straight ahead, putting an end to this conversation. I am not discussing butts with her, or any kind of sausage. But will she let it alone? Hell no, this is Kaitlyn we're talking about. She might want to work her way through the entire football team—bed every Falcon—but she can leave me out of it. I have more important things to think about than tapping any man's ass, and is that even a thing?

"What about Christian?"

"What about him?" I grumble.

Her grin widens and yeah, I get it. She just caught me staring at the quarterback as he called out the last play. I'd give just about anything to run track somewhere else, but no, Kingston had to efficiently build the track around the foot-ball field, forcing me to stare at cocky Christian Moore like it's my damn job. Well, okay when it comes right down to it, I don't *have* to stare. I don't even want to stare. I hate that guy with the power of a thousand burning suns, and honestly, that might not even be enough sun to accurately describe the extent of my loathing.

Then why the hell are you staring, Maize?

Isn't that the question of the century. But there is one thing I know. It has nothing to do with his butt in those pants. Well, almost nothing, and maybe everything.

"Christian is looking even harder this year, don't you think?" She lifts her arm and flexes her impressive bicep.

I put on my best bored expression. "I wouldn't know."

I pick up my pace hoping to leave my bestie behind, but she's not having any of that. I might be the school's top middle-distance runner, but she's the top long-distance girl, and there isn't a hurdle she can't jump. My stupid gaze slides to Christian again.

Speaking of jumping.

Come on, Maize!

Kaitlyn kicks out those long athletic legs of hers and catches up easily. Not that I really thought I could lose her. We're both attending Kingston College on sport scholarships. Most students here are on their parents' dime, but we're star athletes from the wrong side of the tracks. We met at Sweetwater high, an uber rich high school in So Cal. We both had to take three different busses to get there each morning, since it was outside our school districts. That's where I met Christian too. God, just thinking about him makes me want to hurl. The guy single handedly ruined my life in senior year.

I cast Kaitlyn a glance, and as if being pulled by some greater force, my gaze once again slides to Christian, only to find his eyes locked on me—like he could feel me staring, feel me thinking about him. Holy Shit. I tear my gaze away fast, and suck in air.

"We still on for the mall later?" I ask, trying not to sound winded. I could run for hours without losing my breath, but apparently, all it takes is one direct look from Christian to steal the air from my lungs.

Get it together, girl.

Her pace slows, as she finishes her run. "Yeah, but I can't be long. I have a group project meeting later."

I toss my words over my shoulders. "Okay, I have one lap left. After I shower, I'll meet you out front."

She nods and wanders off the track as I keep running. I pick up the pace, wanting to feel the burn in my legs—expel images of Christian from my brain. My lungs expand, and I enjoy the rush of endorphins racing through my body. Nothing, and I mean nothing—sex included—feels as good as running. Not that I've had a lot of sex. Hell, I'm practically a virgin. A few years back, my buddy Ryan—the boy next door back home—and I, decided we didn't want to be virgins when we went off to college. So, we did the logical thing, and had sex. It was awkward and fumbly, is that even a word, and it was sort of over before it ever began. I'm not even sure I climaxed. Yeah, pretty sure I didn't. I can barely get myself off with my own hand. Usually, I have to switch to battery operated which I hate to do in an old house with nothing but seaweed between the walls. I have four roommates, and I'd die of embarrassment if they ever heard.

Dear Mom, thanks for that strict Catholic upbringing and all the teachers who body shamed us. At Sweetwater, our uniforms were constantly assessed. I was told numerous times my skirt was too high. Um hello. Tall girl. Long legs. Capri's on other girls are like shorts on me.

I'm about to slow my pace, but the next thing I know, something big and hard hits me in the side of the head, and I lose all sense of balance. The direct hit, combined with my speed sends me flying forward, and the sound of bones popping, and skin ripping as I hit the ground hard, reverberate around me, and ring in my ears.

My jaw slams with an audible click as my face hits the track, and I skid. It takes forever for my body to stop moving and the world to stop spinning. When everything slows, I lay on the ground face down, too afraid to breathe...to move.

What the hell just happened?

"Are you okay?" I try to move, to check my limbs, but whoever is hovering over me puts his hands on my back to hold me down. "Don't move."

Move? I almost laugh, because I'm not sure I can move and that seriously freaks me out. I turn my head to the side, and that's when Christian puts his face right there, inches from mine.

"Maize, I'm so sorry."

What is he talking about?

"My football," he begins obviously reading the question in my eyes. "I don't know. I threw it, and Kyle missed it, and then you were right there, perfectly aligned for a hit. You weren't there a second ago. You must have picked up your pace."

"Oh, it's my fault is it?" I manage to get out.

His brow furrows, and he shakes his head. "No, that's not what I mean."

Voices echo in my brain as everyone comes running, and embarrassment floods me. I need to get up, to move, to run all the way to Canada, never to be heard from again. I move my hand, and once again Christian presses down, to stop me.

"Can you stop doing that," I say. "I'm fine. I don't feel anything."

His face twists. "Yeah, that's because of the adrenaline rush. Give it a second."

I swallow. Why do I get the feeling he knows something I don't? "Christian—"

"You're going to be okay," he says but the strain in his voice tells another story.

A burst of panic floods my body, and I lift my hand and touch my forehead to find an egg size lump. Okay, it's possible I have a concussion. The world spins and my stomach lurches from the movement. Great now I'm going to vomit in front of everyone. This ground might as well open up and swallow me whole.

"Here," he says, and slides his jersey under my head to cushion it from the ground. I sink into the soft material, heavy with the scent of soap and...Christian. Okay, I definitely have a concussion, because no way on the face of this earth would I be reveling in the stupid aroma of his shirt.

Damn him!

A siren sounds and I go to shake my head no. All I need to do is get up, throw a little dirt on my wounds, and I'll be okay. I give a very unladylike snort. That's what my Mom used to say to me when I was little and hurt myself. Throw a little dirt on it. Mom and me, we were a team. Just the two of us against the world. We did things on our own terms, and asked for nothing. Yeah, we worked for everything, or we went without.

"Maize, please," Christian says, the heavy worry in his voice stilling me. He drops to the ground, and lays on his side, his eyes locked on mine. Blue. My God, he has the most gorgeous blue eyes in the universe. I couldn't see them that night we were locked in the closet though, playing seven minutes in heaven. I wanted so badly to fit in with the 'popular' girls at Sweetwater. When Chelsea Haverstock invited me to her party, I was thrilled. Of course, I had no idea it would ruin my reputation, and leave me friendless, except for Kaitlyn. She had no desire to be a popular girl. She knew mean when she saw it. Now I see it everywhere.

"I think your ankle is broken," he says his voice low, like it will somehow soften the blow.

"No, it's not." I suck in a fast breath, determined to get up, but his big hand continues to push me down again and why the hell do I like that so much? What is wrong with me? I hate his face. I hate his touch, and I most definitely hate the way he's pinning me down, and making me wonder what it would be like if he were on top of me.

"The paramedics are almost here. Let's wait and see what they say."

"I'm not waiting for anything." Nope, I'm getting up, finishing my run, and meeting Kaitlyn for a fast trip to the mall for new laces. If I wait, they might tell me what I refuse to admit. If I refuse to admit it, then I won't be off the team, my scholarship won't be stripped from me, and I won't have to go back home, having made nothing of myself. I have big dreams for God's sake. I want to be a lawyer, want to right all the wrongs, and help people.

His fingers splay on my back, teasing all my nerve endings, until pleasure mingles with pain. I'm familiar with the sensations from running, and I have to admit, my body craves that rush. The next thing I know I'm being checked out by two men, and nearly blinded by a flashlight. Everyone is moving, fussing about, and my head starts to pound so hard, nausea grips my stomach. If they would all just leave me alone, I'll be fine. The two paramedics move me, and shift me to a gurney. I briefly close my eyes, wishing I was an ostrich and could shove my head in the sand. I might be an athlete, but I don't love being the center of attention, and right now, every member of Kingston's football team is staring at me—so are their girlfriends, and all the cheerleaders.

It takes great effort to go up onto my elbows, to check out my body, and a sound that seems to scare everyone around me crawls out of my throat when I glance at my foot, which is twisted in an unnatural way.

"No..." I whisper. "No, no, no."

"Maize," Christian says, and I turn to him as tears burn behind my eyes. "It's going to be okay." He puts his hand on my shoulder.

I swallow against the pain in my throat. Christian is a rich kid, born with a silver spoon in his mouth. He has no idea that his wayward football just put an end to my scholarship. How the hell am I going to pay for next terms tuition?

"You have no idea what you're talking about," I shoot back, and he withdraws his big hand from my shoulder, worry and guilt all over his face. "You ruined high school for me, and..." a humorless laugh crawls out of my throat. "And now, not only have you ruined my senior year of college, but you might have ruined my future too." He rears back like I just slapped him. His mouth opens and closes, like my words have shocked him but he knows what he did that day in the closet, what he's done now. I hold my skinned hand up to stop him. "Just go." He inches back, and I square my shoulders to pull myself together. No way, no how am I going down like this. I'm a fighter. A survivor. A girl who can stand on her own two feet —well, at the moment, on one good foot. As long as I can stand, I'll do whatever it takes—anything—to stay in college.

Well, just about anything...

ALSO BY CATHRYN FOX

Blue Bay Crew

Demolished

Leveled

Hammered

Single Dad

Single Dad Next Door

Single Dad on Tap

Single Dad Burning Up

Players on Ice

The Playmaker

The Stick Handler

The Body Checker

The Hard Hitter

The Risk Taker

The Wing Man

The Puck Charmer

The Troublemaker

The Rule Breaker

In the Line of Duty

His Obsession Next Door

His Strings to Pull

His Trouble in Talulah

His Taste of Temptation

His Moment to Steal

His Best Friend's Girl

His Reason to Stay

Confessions

Confessions of a Bad Boy Professor

Confessions of a Bad Boy Officer

Confessions of a Bad Boy Fighter

Confessions of a Bad Boy Doctor

Confessions of a Bad Boy Gamer

Confessions of a Bad Boy Millionaire

Confessions of a Bad Boy Santa

Confessions of a Bad Boy CEO

Hands On

Hands On

Body Contact

Full Exposure

Dossier

Private Reserve

House Rules

Under Pressure

Big Catch

Brazilian Fantasy

Improper Proposal

Boys of Beachville

Good at Being Bad

Igniting the Bad Boy

Bad Girl Therapy

Stone Cliff Series:

Crashing Down

Wasted Summer

Love Lessons

Wrapped Up

Eternal Pleasure Series

Instinctive

Impulsive

Indulgent

Sun Stroked Series

Seaside Seduction

Deep Desire

Private Pleasure

Captured and Claimed Series:

Yours to Take

Yours to Teach

Yours to Keep

Firefighter Heat Series

Fever

Siren

Flash Fire

Playing For Keeps Series

Slow Ride

Wild Ride

Sweet Ride

Breaking the Rules:

Hold Me Down Hard

Pin Me Up Proper

Tie Me Down Tight

Stand Alone Title:

Hands on with the CEO

Torn Between Two Brothers

Holiday Spirit

Unleashed

Knocking on Demon's Door

Web of Desire

ABOUT CATHRYN

New York Times and *USA today* Bestselling author, Cathryn is a wife, mom, sister, daughter, and friend. She loves dogs, sunny weather, anything chocolate (she never says no to a brownie) pizza and red wine. She has two teenagers who keep her busy with their never ending activities, and a husband who is convinced he can turn her into a mixed martial arts fan. Cathryn can never find balance in her life, is always trying to find time to go to the gym, can never keep up with emails, Facebook or Twitter and tries to write page-turning books that her readers will love.

Connect with Cathryn:
Newsletter https://app.mailerlite.com/webforms/
landing/c1f8n1
Twitter: https://twitter.com/writercatfox
Facebook: https://www.facebook.com/
AuthorCathrynFox?ref=hl
Blog: http://cathrynfox.com/blog/
Goodreads: https://www.goodreads.com/author/show/
91799.Cathryn_Fox

Pinterest http://www.pinterest.com/catkalen/